Through the Waters and the Wild

by Greg Fields

ISBN 978-1-64663-208-4

REVIEW COPY: This is an advanced printing subject to corrections and revisions.

Published by

köehlerbooks™

3705 Shore Drive
Virginia Beach, VA 23455
800-435-4811
www.koehlerbooks.com

THROUGH THE

WATERS

AND THE

WILD

A Novel

GREG FIELDS

VIRGINIA BEACH
CAPE CHARLES

For you, of course.
Always and forever, for you

Lay your sleeping head, my love,
Human on my faithless arm;
Time and fever burn away
Individual beauty from
Thoughtful children, and the grave
Proves the child ephemeral:
But in my arms till break of day
Let the living creature lie,
Mortal, guilty, but to me
The entirely beautiful.

—W. H. Auden, *Lullaby*

Come away, O human child!
To the waters and the wild
With a faery, hand in hand,
For the world's more full of
Weeping than you can understand

—William Butler Yeats, *The Stolen Child*

From Liam Finnegan's Letter to His Grandson, Conor

As a boy in Ireland, I heard tales told by firesides, across the tables of family and friends, and in the pubs of Dungarvan. We are a people that preserves its soul through our shared stories. In that tradition, I write to you now.

When last we were together, you asked me if I was content. I confess that this is something I had not given thought. Contentment has always seemed a wispy thing that we might chase without ever knowing precisely its shape or form.

But your question spurred me to regard this life as it approaches its end.

My age is neither reward nor punishment. It merely is, a condition no different than when I was five or fifteen or forty. Time is nothing but a vehicle. We count its value by what we carry within it.

I desire no longer the things I have lost. My body does not bend as it did. It needs more sleep and less food. I can no longer leap, nor can I dance nor hold a lady in my arms. I miss these things, but I no longer desire them with the fevers that once compelled me. I have been fortunate enough to know each of these pleasures in my time and to have known them in high quality. That is sufficient for me now.

People have come and gone throughout my life. Few remain, although in one form or another all are still with me, daily and in very real ways. Some still present themselves. I welcome their company when they offer it, but I do not expect it. I am grateful for whatever time, whatever attention or thought, their own lives permit them to spend on mine.

When I was a younger man, moving through a strange land, having nothing about me but my wits, my character, and my integrity, I did not think as such. I was hungry, seeing myself starving for want of something I could not define. I sought it constantly, sought it at every turn, searched every face I met for hints of it, looked everywhere I could conceive. I lost time trying to slake this unquenchable thirst, trying to satisfy an endlessly burning hunger. But in the end I knew precisely what I had been after all along. It is the folly of the young, part of their particular curse, to be so unaware, to be blind as well as hungry. To be in exile from themselves and not know they are away.

CHAPTER I

What are the roots that clutch, what branches grow
Out of this stony rubbish? Son of man,
You cannot say, or guess, for you know only
A heap of broken images, where the sun beats,
And the dead tree gives no shelter, the cricket no relief,
And the dry stone no sound of water.

—T.S. Eliot, *The Waste Land*

The late summer day welled up at its rise like a great, giant bird, wings spanning the horizon from end to end, allowing no breath of air to penetrate. As it did, Conor Finnegan woke as always. He showered, rode the train to work. Nothing new there. He blocked out the distinction of the day, wrestled with himself to make it seem commonplace, any other Thursday. The hours of work were an insulation.

Long ago, Conor had mastered the skill of creating the illusion of dedication. Those around him, those he answered to, thought him a utile employee, someone who could be relied upon for solid if not unspectacular work, someone who cared for the nature of what he did as much as anyone could expect. They did not need to know how he really felt. They need not know that he performed well below his capabilities, and that he did so by choice. Thirty-eight-year-old Conor felt secure in his job. He knew it provided everything he needed . . . except a challenge. He could go through his days mindlessly, expending minimal effort, showing minimal creativity. And at the end of each day, he could go home.

Days came and went this way. Conor did not stride through his profession as much as he sneaked through it, trying to draw as little attention to himself and his labors as he could. Long ago, he had abandoned any notion that what he did composed any part of what he was.

Today had been no different. At day's end, he could scarcely remember how he had spent his working hours, just what he had accomplished. The insulation had ceased. He had to go home now. He had to face that against which he had no insulation.

Conor left his office only slightly later than normal, walked slowly out the door, and headed down Independence Avenue. He walked past the Smithsonian, past the various buildings of the National Gallery of Art, past the monuments. The sun shone low, orange and hot. Waves of heat wafted up from the pavement around him. Tourists and natives sought to cool themselves with ice bought from immigrant vendors or bottles of soda. As during most of the summer, everyone tried to keep their movements to a minimum. Few Frisbees flew across the green lawns. Few bicycles pedaled down the wide streets.

Conor peeled off his jacket and hung it over his shoulder as he walked. He carried a briefcase, but he almost never opened it away from the office. This was his security blanket, another grasping effort to portray a role. He carried it only because he felt he should.

In due course, he turned up Fifteenth Street, and in two blocks he came to the Old Ebbitt Grill. He hesitated, but he had come to love the feel of this classic place. It was an authentic piece of the city, a throwback to the nineteenth century. He loved the rich paneling and the heavy, hanging chandeliers. He loved the staff's quick wit, period uniforms, and unflagging efficiency. Most of all, he loved the anonymity with which he could sit alone, allow himself to be absorbed with nothing at all or everything at once, and know that he would be undisturbed. Tonight, of all nights, he sought distraction, even knowing it would be no distraction at all. He opened the heavy door, walked in, and took a seat at the half-empty bar.

"Good evening, sir."

The bartender was predictably unctuous, a gaunt man in his early fifties, smiling on cue but lacking real warmth. A Washington bartender. On more serene evenings, Conor would wonder what it was that kept a man a bartender for so many years. Was that an aspiration in itself? Had this man, so comfortable in his duties, so deft with the potions of the grain, the potions of social numbness, reached his ultimate plateau? What, in God's name, could the rewards possibly be?

"Good evening. Scotch on the rocks with a twist. Johnny Walker Black." With the order of Walker Black instead of Red, Conor took his first step to commemorate what must come from the flow of the evening. This would not be typical. It was, now at last, foolish to try to deceive himself any longer. This evening was not typical, could not be. Because that was so, all governances could be put aside. Let the evening come out as it would. He would be more spectator than author.

The bar contained no surprises. Around him sat the usual contingent of government workers, mostly young, a near equal mix between male and female. At one corner table, two older men chatted. Conor thought they looked familiar, but he had come across so many faces during his years on the Hill that they had long since lost their distinction. He knew the type. They were senior bureaucrats, no doubt, perhaps civil service but just as likely to be legislative assistants—dressed conservatively, jackets across the backs of their chairs, enough lines on their faces to be "wizened" or "charactered" but not so many as to give any evidence of decline. They spoke intently to each other, completely oblivious to anyone else at the old grill.

To Conor's left, two young, attractive women came to take the two stools adjacent. He noticed their presence before he even saw them. Their cologne pierced his nostrils like two small stilettos, a sharp mingling of florals and oils. In the split second it took his brain to register the source of the scent, he turned to see the women, laughing between themselves. In another time, they would have engaged his interest beyond their perfume, and he would have entered a different mode. He would have become another Conor Finnegan, cultivatedly charming, boyishly shy yet exuding a gentle confidence, a sly predator thrilled as much by the hunt as by the conquest.

Almost ironic that he should find himself presented with such a situation on this particular night, he thought. Silly, really. It had been years since such skills had been necessary. Now, it turned out that he may well be in need of them again. Just not tonight. Tonight, he wanted to drink, that was all, and to do so broodingly.

The scotch arrived without comment, the bartender delivering it politely before turning his attention to the two newcomers next to him. The color of the drink pleased Conor. It was a rich gold, not the watered down light amber of scotch served weakly, with too much water. The first sip palpably warmed his gullet, a shaft of heat moving toward his stomach. It complemented the heat around him, the heat of the day, the heat of these past weeks. The heat of days now gone. The fire he had felt since waking, the fire that had welled within him for the past several days—not heat at all. Shame, that was it. A burning incarnation as much a part of him now as the synapses that carried the notion to his psyche.

Conor took a second sip, then another. He let the sounds swirl around and through him without allowing them to penetrate. He became at once a silent observer, an invisible bystander.

For several minutes, he sat on his stool. He drew a single finger blindly around the rim of his glass. He stared down at the circle it made on the bar, eyes numb to the image. The pattern of his thought absorbed only color and shape—the woody brown of the bar, the burgundy of the padding against it, the gold of the scotch that sat in his glass. The bar was a rectangle, the glass an uneven cylinder, the other patrons indefinable, colorless shapes. He occasionally felt their press on either side, but they took no mind of him, nor he of them. The night had begun to creep toward him, and he hated the thought of it.

His scotch disappeared by notches.

The bartender returned to make a perfunctory effort at conversation, an assumed part of his job but one he clearly approached with something less than enthusiasm. "A fine way to close a hot day, sir. Can I get you another?"

"My friend, the day for me has been only prelude. What really counts comes tonight. And by all means, bring me another. Please."

"That could be either wonderful or quite frightening." The words did not come from the bartender, who, with a nod of acknowledgment, had turned to his bottles to refill the order. Conor swiveled his head slowly to his left to find one of the ladies smiling, her head cocked slightly, her sharp blue eyes gazing at him in . . . what? Bemusement? Expectation? His own form of cultivated charm thrown back at him? The liquor, and all the dead years, stunted his ability to read her.

Despite himself, he smiled in return. "Excuse me?"

" 'What really counts comes tonight.' An ominous statement you made. You either have a wonderful evening ahead of you or one that you want to hide from."

"I've never been good at hiding. Not that I haven't tried, mind you. I've tried very hard. I just never managed to succeed at it. I've always been uncovered in the end." Conor heard his own voice as if it were detached. It sounded heavier, more leaden than normal. The lilt of it was nowhere to be found.

"Have I uncovered you here? Have I found you out?" she teased. She was undeniably lovely, a slender blonde, hair falling past her shoulders. She wore a lightweight dark suit, probably linen, and smelled like a distant fantasy. Her voice teased him.

"Apparently you have, lass. I thought I'd be invisible in this place and have a few moments to collect myself before what promises to be a memorably rotten night. You seem to be well on the way to taking a bit of the edge off it."

"This is no place to be invisible. Especially someone who looks as if he could use a new friend. I'm Jill."

Conor turned around on his stool to face her more fully, allowing her to see how his light-brown hair and brown eyes accentuated a round, handsome face. "Conor," he said. "And thank you for noticing."

"To be honest, I've noticed you since I walked through the door. I'll bet you had no idea you were making any kind of an impression." Her voice continued to tease him.

"None at all, and it was the furthest thing from my mind. Didn't you come in with a friend?"

"Who had places to go. I thought I'd stay behind and take a chance intruding into the life of a handsome young professional."

A familiar resonance trilled somewhere deep within Conor, something long buried, alive more as instinct than conscious thought. But conscious thought elbowed its way past instinct. Conor quieted the resonance.

"I'm sorry, angel, but I fear I'd be terrible company tonight. The best thing I can do now is gain enough of a head to get through the evening. I should be on my way." He quickly took a deep drink from the glass before him, enough nearly to drain it. The liquor swam his length then floated back to the space behind his eyes.

Jill frowned, a girlish pout.

She's quite good at this, thought Conor.

"Damn," Jill said. "My luck continues to run cold. You've mentioned again how little you're looking forward to the rest of this night. What is it you're up to?"

"A redefinition, lass, and a painful one at that." Conor took a final swallow then placed the glass firmly back on the bar. "One I never thought I'd have to suffer. But, really, I shouldn't be surprised at all. It's remarkably consistent. I won't bore you with details."

He rose, slightly wobbly but aware enough to gain control of himself. "I hope to find you here again, love. It's my loss that I can't stay."

"As you wish." Jill's smile returned, and her eyes darted around the bar. When Conor stood, she looked back at him, taking in his tall, strong, and supple form. "I come here often enough, usually at the end of the day. I hope to find you again, too, mysterious stranger. Be well until then."

"Doubtful," said Conor, and he turned to walk out the door. As he opened it onto the sidewalk, a blast of late-day heat struck him fully and caused him to reel. The liquor had had the desired effect.

Conor walked up Fifteenth Street to the Metro station at Federal Triangle. Down the tunnel he rode on the narrow escalator. He gripped the railing firmly, aware now of the effects of the scotch, the effects of the heat. He felt woozy. He wanted to sit.

His time at the Old Ebbitt had diffused the end-of-the-day subway rush. The platform was uncrowded, and those who were there were out for the evening, not going home after a workday.

Some minutes after arriving on the platform, the train arrived, almost silent in its smooth approach. Conor expected no trouble finding a seat at this hour, and there was none. The car was two-thirds empty. The doors closed, and the train pushed forward almost imperceptibly. "No more delays," he told himself. "No more equivocations." He sat back and closed his eyes . . . and for a short time, his thoughts took him away to words his late grandfather Liam Finnegan had penned to him in a letter thirteen years ago . . . the words of an Irish bard.

> *The crack spreads the length of the rock in silent phases. And where does the crack begin? What force of nature or of man sends a minute shard, imperceptible and unfelt, into the solid rock, there to start the slightest of rifts? We do not know it when it occurs. Our senses continue oblivious until the crack itself grows too wide, too strident so that it can no longer be ignored.*

> *But then, when our numbed perceptions finally break free from the stultifying comforts, from the smothering assumptions, it is too late. The crack has taken an animus of its own, like a living being, a demon that silently, immutably, pushes the rock farther apart until it becomes no rock at all. We become helpless in the process, bystanders only, as the crack works its way along our spines. All we can do is petition whatever power that guides the animus to have mercy, to let the rock remain somehow whole. And in the dimly aired chambers that rearguard our delicate psyches, we hear the faint tinkling of laughter.*

> *We stand then among pebbles, or, if Time and Fate have been particularly virulent conspirators, we sink into sand.*

* * *

The escalator moved Conor almost silently back to the street. From there, he walked the few short blocks up Connecticut Avenue to Woodley Park, then down the familiar pathway to his condominium. An overweight black man wearing a dark maroon coat and sporting ridiculous white gloves greeted him. His face, smiling in a manner of practiced deference, betrayed nothing beneath the surface, showed not a spark of hidden knowledge, although Conor had never even bothered to doubt that in fact this man knew secrets others could scarcely imagine.

James knew the comings and goings of the building, the places where the hidden keys were kept, the assignations, the mistresses, the cross-dressers, the abusers of drugs, alcohol, spouses, girlfriends, boyfriends, and each other. He knew the license numbers of the cars that drove up late at night with their lights turned off. He knew where to find an otherwise invisible husband when an emergency phone call arrived, and he knew when an emergency phone call was in truth no emergency at all. He knew a thousand facts, large and small, significant and inconsequential, and he held it all in intractable confidence. He knew everyone's business and cared about no one's. He held his station, provided his service, and, in so doing, offered a security valuable far beyond the meager pay he drew.

He knew whether Maggie would still be here. Or, more likely, whether she would not.

"'Evenin', Mr. Finnegan."

"Good evening, James," replied Conor in scarcely more than a whisper. "As always, my friend, it's good to see you here."

James's face softened very slightly, but the voice did not alter beyond its ever-familiar, well-rehearsed tone. "And where else would I be on such a hot night?" James opened the wide glass door as he spoke. The air conditioning of the lobby struck Conor bluntly. He caught his breath as it hit him, another subtle blow.

"Anywhere else would bound to be cooler, James. If I were you, I'd want to be anywhere but here wearing that hot uniform and being nice to the likes of me." Conor walked quickly past him. He had never become accustomed to another human being waiting on him like this. He was perfectly capable of opening his own door.

"Mr. Finnegan, you know it's always my pleasure to see you good people here."

Conor did not reply. He merely waved as a parting gesture

then headed down the hallway. The walk, no more than fifty yards down a comfortable, carpeted, cool corridor, suspended itself as he took it. He absorbed minutiae by osmosis, unconsciously noting the weave of the fabric under his feet, the flow of the walls, a single fly that buzzed before him then disappeared behind his head as he passed it. No walk he had taken before had ever been like this. He floated through the familiar setting, apart from it, a disembodied wraith, the wail of a banshee weaving its way to the ear of the sufferer.

He had no idea how long it took him to reach his door. He may even have stopped midway to lean against a wall or take a few deep breaths for courage, although if he did so it was not the product of forethought. After some indefinable length, he stood before the solid wooden door. No more delays. There was nothing left to do. He took the key from his pocket, inserted it into the lock, heard the familiar clicking as he turned the knob, then walked into the place he had assumed would always be his own.

"Maggie?" he called in a voice too low to be heard at the far end of the condo. He took two steps through the entryway and turned the corner to the great room. "Maggie?" he called again, louder, more forcefully.

No answer. All he heard was the regular ticking of the old clock on the mantel. Maggie was not home.

Conor took a quick look around the great room. From there, he walked into the dining room. Nothing on the table. Then nothing in the kitchen. Upstairs to his study. Nothing there. Then at last to the master bedroom, green and quiet. Nothing there. No sign of her. And, more troubling, no note. Nothing left behind for him to read. No final statement. No plea. No reconsideration. No part of her there to touch him.

The effects of the scotch had not worn off, would not do so for quite some time. Conor felt at once numb and sore. His head took on a vague ache emanating from some deep recess. It pushed its way from the base of his skull to the point between his eyes. A faint gloss of perspiration moistened his brow and upper lip. To his surprise, he noticed his right hand tremble, a tiny shaking he could not control. He wondered how long his hand had been spasmodic.

Conor sat on the edge of the bed to compose himself. There would be no need to rush. No, his entrance, and the silence that greeted it, told him that. Maggie was not here and would not come back until very late, if at all. Then she would not find him. That was her wish. As with almost all her wishes, it would come true for her.

Lights from the street seeped in between the window blinds and created a slanted pattern on the far wall. Conor sat without moving and watched the lines wave on the flat surface, watched them rise and swirl when a car drove by, watched them deepen and soften in turn. He sat there for a long time. The sweat thickened along his now throbbing forehead. A tiny line of it dripped down his cheek near the corner of his eye. He heard the blood pulse through his skull, felt the mysterious trembling in his hand, listened to the ticking of the old clock downstairs, clearly audible even in this distant room. Conor sat, numb and shocked, to face a reckoning he had never envisioned. Another failure. This time it was more graphic, less transitory. This time it tore at the very core of his soul. There would be not even the pretense of recovery.

* * *

Conor met Margaret Kelly eleven years before, when he was twenty-seven. He had been a confident but reserved minority aide to the Congressional Joint Committee on the Library. She had been a graduate student at Georgetown working on a master's degree in government. She had requested a tour of the office, some cursory facts of its operation, an overview of where this peculiar committee fit into the workings of a complex body ostensibly concerned with far more weighty issues than how the Library of Congress catalogued its holdings.

She had set the appointment with Stacy, the scheduling secretary and receptionist, who had promptly forgotten to mark it down on the master calendar and therefore neglected to arrange a junior staffer to walk Margaret through the office. Margaret had shown up there on a Thursday morning, exactly at ten. Stacy had greeted her professionally, asked if she could hang up her coat, offered her a seat in the lobby and a cup of coffee, then retreated into the back offices to search frantically for someone, anyone, who could provide an impromptu tour and treat it as if he had been expecting the privilege of doing so.

The first two desks, the area where the junior staff sat, had been empty. That day, Stacy spun her way further back into the suite and found Conor eating a doughnut and flipping through the *Post*.

"Conor, I've got a huge favor to ask."

Conor looked up, swallowed what was in his mouth, and leaned forward. "If I can help, Stace, let me know."

"Some grad student from Georgetown is in the lobby and wants to speak with someone about what we do."

"Is this a surprise?"

"Yes. Well, I mean no. It shouldn't be. I forgot to mark it down. Now I'm stuck. I'd be happy to do it myself, but I don't know anything."

"Right. You just sit up front, look good, and answer every inquiry that comes in off the street. I can see where you've been sheltered from the nuts and bolts. Christ, Stacy, you know more about this place than anyone."

"Conor, come on. She wants to speak with a real staffer. You can be charming and informative for a little while, can't you?"

Conor genuinely liked Stacy. She was young, one of the callow, eager faces that appeared on the Hill yearly and took any job that was offered, even if it was well below her competency. In this case, simple Stacy had found the proper niche. He rose to put on his suit coat.

"At least tell me she's cute."

"I can't tell you that, Conor. I'm sorry," she whined. "She looks like a typical grad student."

"Intelligent and oversexed?"

"Mousy and spoiled."

"Damn." Conor picked up his portfolio and a summary of the staff's operational plan for the year. "Well, lass, you're fortunate that I have nothing on my calendar for the morning. Show me to the mouse."

Stacy led him to the outer lobby where Margaret Kelly sat waiting. He approached her warmly with his hand outstretched. "Good morning. My name's Conor Finnegan. I'm the minority legislative assistant—an impressive title, but in truth it means very little."

"Margaret Kelly, Mr. Finnegan." She offered a hand, which Conor shook gently. Her touch was cold. Stacy was right. Margaret Kelly was definitely not cute. But to Conor's eye, she had the potential to be pretty. Her hair rounded her face, falling below her collar in an almost bowl-like pattern. It was thick and brown, surprisingly well maintained in contrast to the rest of her. She wore a plain beige skirt and a dark blue sweater that showed more than average wear. The woman's face seemed pleasant enough if not noteworthy, what he could see of it behind her huge glasses.

It was the glasses that first caught his eye. They were large and thick, a pair of goggles, really, that dominated the curves of her face. She had little color—no blush to her cheeks, no color on her lips, no shading around her eyes, or so it seemed. Her lips formed a nervous line. In doing so, they accentuated the distinctive cleft in her chin.

"I understand you're looking to see the committee's workings from the inside, so to speak," Conor said.

"I'm writing a paper for a graduate seminar on the legislative process. I chose this committee as my model. Whatever you can tell me, I'd greatly appreciate it."

"An interesting choice. Most people are scarcely aware that we even exist."

"I thought I'd have less competition in doing my research. Most of the students in the seminar gravitated to the more visible committees. Judiciary, Ways and Means, Armed Services—they'll all get worked over. I took a chance that no one else would select the Joint Committee on the Library."

"I'd wager that you took no chance at all. We're as close to invisible as the Hill can offer," Conor replied, his cultivated charm now on display, hiding the painful realization that his statement was in fact very true. "What can I show you?"

"Tell me how you're put together. Tell me what happens on a typical day, who you see, your lines of communication, the types of issues you deal with, any legislative initiatives. I'd be interested in all of that."

Conor began a monologue he had delivered before—the committee composition, how it came to be that way, majority and minority representation. He produced from his portfolio a summary of that term's pending legislation and its likely disposition. Usually, his audience was a busload of elementary schoolchildren or perhaps a senior citizens club taking a tour. He could not remember the last time he was called upon to give an individual presentation. Despite the fact that this was all extremely familiar and more than a little dull, he found himself enjoying it.

Margaret and Conor walked back through the office suite as he spoke, stopping in the middle of the cramped quarters long enough to give the impression of clutter, of too many people thrust together into too little space. The effect was minimal, though. No one seemed to be around, and those who milled about were hardly dynamic. Two of the younger staffers chatted at one desk. Another aide read the *New York Times*, oblivious to the fact that a guest was present. Conor resented the slow pace of this office. He had never considered himself as anything less than dynamic, less than the center of an eddy that he himself helped create. This committee worked in slow motion. It frustrated him on a daily basis and made him restless.

At Conor's own area he offered Margaret a chair then sat back behind the disheveled desk. Piles of paper occupied each corner. A trilevel inbox carried more papers—forms, memos, reports, summaries—than it could comfortably hold. On the wall behind him hung his college diploma and several topical cartoons. Although his space was hardly well organized, Conor knew precisely where anything of value could be found. Most items that had passed the point of being useful he kept piled around him anyway. It was all an illusion of busyness, an image of productivity that belied the true substance of what he did.

While Conor spoke, Margaret took notes. Now, she sat opposite him, her face not deviating from her notebook, where she wrote steadily even though the core of his talk had long since passed. After her initial nervous greeting, she had remained expressionless.

"Even though this could hardly be categorized as one of the Hill's glamorous committees, its work is essential. In fact, it stems from a profound historical precedent that constitutes one of the hallmarks of the American system of public administration. The Library of Congress is a unique institution, and, at its best, serves as the repository for our nation's collective published and unpublished chronicles. It's unlike anything else currently in operation anywhere in the world. That takes a certain level of oversight. Summarily, that's what we do here."

Margaret looked up to ask, "So, management and personnel decisions must first be approved by this body?"

"They all begin here, in fact. Major personnel appointments come through us, policy alterations, new constructions, things like that. This is Congress's oldest continuing joint committee. No one realizes it, but the committee was established in 1802, and it's been functional ever since. Its operations are solely in the public domain, so what we do here has a significance few other committees can claim." Conor paused. He recognized how little of this he truly believed. "What else can I tell you, Miss Kelly?"

"Maggie."

"Excuse me?"

"My friends call me Maggie. I can't be comfortable with 'Miss Kelly.' "

"Then Maggie it is. Can I ask why you choose to call yourself that? It seems that 'Peggy' is a more logical derivative of 'Margaret.' "

"There are a million Margarets calling themselves Peg or Peggy. But there are very few Maggies, especially these days. I wanted to be distinct." She grinned. Here, at last, signs of a personality began to emerge.

"And so you are. What brought you to Georgetown?"

"It's one of the best, isn't it? I had been an undergraduate at St. Mary's outside Baltimore. Government seemed like a solid field for graduate work, particularly here."

"What do you hope to do with it when you're done?"

"Teach, I suppose. I really haven't given it much thought."

"No desire to apply it then? I mean, in a more pragmatic sense. You don't want to get into government itself?"

"Oh God, no. To be honest, it fascinates me only as a model of human behavior. I think if I ever had to work at it, day to day, over and over again, I'd be horribly bored. Plus, there are so many people I'd rather not deal with. But as a laboratory of action and reaction, it's extremely gratifying. And, as a good Irish-Catholic girl, I grew up around an old-school family fascinated with the Kennedys. Studying government seemed a logical extension of all that."

"I can see part of what you mean. We're a hugely flawed

system, Maggie, and sometimes being entrenched within it means you necessarily have to absorb the flaws."

"How long have you been with the committee?"

"Two years. A bit more, actually. I was with a Senate staff before coming here, so I've been on the Hill for about five years total, ever since I graduated from college. Right now, it seems like the only thing I'm suited to do."

"So, if this work is so tedious and the system itself is so flawed, where do you take your satisfactions?"

"From the people who come through this office. From their curiosity and from their charm. Maggie, this may seem a bit bold, but I've got to ask—do you think you might like to have dinner with me Saturday night?"

So it had begun, this confounding dance between partners hearing the same music, interpreting it quite differently, and never touching.

As Conor considered this exchange now, years later sitting on a cold bed in an empty condominium, he was not able to identify the impulses that had risen up within him at that moment so long ago, the hidden currents of thought or emotion that had told a corner of his psyche that this woman might indeed be unique, that somewhere in his reactive subconscious a part of him had seen her as possibly attractive, interesting, sheltered, tranquil, and ultimately desirable. He looked back at this meeting, saw the person he was as he followed it through, and shook his head at his response. He would spend the hours that fell to him unexpectedly reflecting on the pathway that brought him here, the anguish over his mistakes, the countless errors in judgment, the shared blames and those that were singular. He would find himself truly amazed at the patterns of thought that coalesced into aspirations and the words that those aspirations created.

But retrospection provides neither true perspective nor does it give the slightest measure of comfort.

* * *

The condominium sat in silence except for the ticking clock. Conor stayed on the bed, his eyes staring without tremor to a single point on the far wall. He projected himself in a thin laserlike line to the point, through it, and beyond to the vacant blackness that must be its essence. The point was reality, a black hole that sucked in his consciousness and let nothing come back out. He had no idea how long he sat there transfixed.

After a time, he stood slowly, his limbs suddenly aching. He walked across the wide bedroom to the master closet in the wall adjacent to the bathroom. There, he picked up a suitcase packed very late the previous night, another night when Maggie was not here. It did not contain everything he would need, nor everything he owned, but it contained enough to make the suitcase heavy. He carried it back down the hallway, out the front door, and down the corridor to the elevator connecting to the parking garage underneath. After he arrived to the garage and placed the suitcase into the back seat of his car, he rode the elevator back up and reentered what had passed for his home.

It would have been easier, he knew, just to climb behind the wheel of his car and drive off. Yet syllogistic thought no longer applied. Conor stood in his entryway and regarded the three hooks aligned next to the door. They held all manner of outerwear—the coats of winter, the sweaters of spring and autumn. In the corner nearest the door, a few dried pine needles, no more than four or five, had tucked themselves out of the reach of brooms or vacuums, a remnant of a Christmas tree from some undefined year.

Slowly, he walked back into the living room. It seemed stark now. Maggie had put away the two paintings that had hung over the couch. They had bought them on a winter trip to Aruba. Conor had taken a love to the native painting there, the broad sweeps of color, the primitive line brought forward with simple brushwork. He had purchased these two works directly from the artist whose studio was also his shop in a small house in the Aruban countryside, the arid *cunucu* Conor still recalled clearly. The paintings were nowhere to be found. He couldn't fault Maggie for hiding them; it was just as well.

He moved deliberately through the wide room. In a far corner sat the old magazine rack, a spiky, metallic thing that had no aesthetic value whatsoever and little practical use except that it held Maggie's pretentious subscriptions, magazines she ordered not to read but to show proof of her self-proclaimed singular mix of intellect and social conscience. It was filled with *Harper's*, the *Atlantic*, the *New Yorker*, *Architectural Digest*, *Newsweek*. None had been more than thumbed through.

As Conor walked to the equally empty dining room, he brushed against the couch. That, too, had proven to be an irritant. Some time ago, at the end of a long week Conor had spent in Pittsburgh setting up two days of absolutely meaningless hearings, he had returned home to find this piece of uncommon ugliness—blue with a checked pattern, high-backed, and uncomfortable—sitting in a corner of the great room.

"What the hell is that?" Conor had said as soon as he walked through the door.

"Our new couch. I bought it earlier this week. They delivered it today."

"Jesus, Maggie, you could have at least told me."

"I did tell you. I said last week that we needed a couch."

"We need a lot of things. That's a little different than saying 'Gosh, Conor, I think I'm going to buy a couch this week.' "

"I thought you understood that I wanted to buy one right now."

"You might have consulted me, that's all I'm saying. Can I ask what we paid for this with?"

"Your bonus check."

Conor's eyes had glossed red when Maggie told him this. Bonuses for midlevel staff on inconsequential House committees were rare. By this point, Conor had moved on from the Joint Committee on the Library and was employed by the House Committee on Natural Resources. He had been awarded a $1,000 bonus mainly on the basis of having survived there for a few years with most of his sanity intact. He had deposited the money into their savings account. Its use had not yet been determined, but it had felt marvelously validating sitting there. Then it had been unilaterally squandered on a hideous piece of questionable value. The ensuing argument lasted the rest of that evening until Conor crawled angrily into bed next to a silent Maggie, who had determined that enough had been said on the matter. He slept fitfully until waking early the next morning, a Saturday, and slipping out to spend hours alone at the office, with nowhere else to go. The day had not been unique.

Now, he moved through the dining room into the kitchen, sterile and cold. While Maggie demanded order and neatness in all rooms, she was obsessed with it in the kitchen. Not a single stray crumb littered the countertops; no unwashed dishes sat in the sink. Shortly after their marriage, meals with Maggie became sprints rather than distance runs. She would prepare something quick, usually prepackaged, hurriedly eat it at the kitchen table, then clear the dishes immediately, sometimes before Conor was even finished eating. Plates, glasses, and silverware were washed at once, the table wiped clean and left wet. Everything in Maggie's kitchen had its place. She allowed nothing to disturb the order there, even at the expense of her own balance. Conor recalled too many occasions when she would accost him, eyes wide and voice pitched, over a plate left on the counter or a trail of a spoon still carrying the remnants of a dish of ice cream. Of all the rooms in the condominium, this room was hers.

Conor walked back up down the hall. He peeked his head into the study, really a third bedroom that they had converted. Although they styled it as both of theirs, in truth it was Maggie's almost exclusively. The books there, mostly government and history monographs, occupied three multilevel bookshelves. No artwork hung on the walls; no paintings, no photographs, nothing of any color. The single window looked out onto the park behind the complex, the closest they had to any view. Maggie would spend afternoons there, sometimes whole days, reading, sporadically writing, going through the motions of research without really producing anything. During the periods of greatest tension, she would retreat into this barren room, close the door, and collect herself while Conor brooded in the great room.

From the study, Conor turned down the hallway to the spare room, a space rarely used. Aside from the regular visits of Maggie's family, they almost never had guests. Conor's parents had visited once for five days. It had been their first trip to the city, and Conor had shown them the usual tourist stops, had whirled them all through the District, suburban Maryland, and the glorious green slopes of Virginia. He had done so alone. Maggie had found a series of excuses to avoid going out with them, instead staying behind to do "research," to read, or simply to rest from some ill-defined malady. When his parents at last left, Maggie's tense demeanor had softened at once. She reclaimed her home from these strange interlopers, relieved that they were gone.

But when Maggie's family members visited frequently, coming in waves singularly or by pairs, Maggie was with them, it seemed, every second. Shortly after moving in, her parents had come for ten days to "help them get settled." Mostly, though, Maggie and her mother had spent those days walking around Georgetown or Foggy Bottom, nosing through specialty shops, having lunch, or gazing at Rock Creek. Her father, a nervous, agitated man of little social grace, had remained in the condominium, reading or watching television. The city intimidated him. From what Conor could glean, the man had long viewed Washington as a morass of minority-induced crime, a place not safe for families of traditional values and certainly no place for his fair daughter. He made fewer visits than did Maggie's mother, who often would drive down to spend the night.

The rest of Maggie's large family—her married sister, who lived in Baltimore, and four brothers— dropped by with some regularity as well. Maggie characterized her family as "close-knit." Conor saw them as borderline incestuous. None of them, Maggie included, ever seemed to have any friends with whom they had not grown up, who they had not known for two decades, who had not been part of the fabric of their childhood. In lieu of normal social relationships, they had come to rely exclusively upon one other. Conor would forever be an outsider.

He walked the few steps from the spare room to the master bedroom. He did not go in. Instead, he stood in the doorway, trying to take note of all he had collected to make certain he was leaving nothing of immediate importance behind. The room evoked such a swirl of recollections that the net result was the color white—an amalgam of all colors, all reactions, spun together so tightly and so quickly as to be devoid of any character of its own. Satisfied that he had put together all he would need, he turned back to the stairs and walked back down to the great room.

He paused in the entryway, trying to find some definable emotion, struggling to name what it was that coursed through him. The circumstances of his life from this point forward would be forever changed, that he knew. He stood there befuddled, knowing that in some way his final perceptions might someday become valuable. Conor closed his eyes and sought to conjure some recognizable conclusion. Nothing came to him. At length, he opened the door, stepped through it into the empty corridor, and locked it behind him.

He met not a soul on the short walk through the hallway to the elevator leading down to the garage. The rhythmic stepping of his shoes on the concrete garage floor was the only sound to be heard. Almost all the spaces were occupied; nearly everyone was home, or so it seemed. Conor saw his car again where it should be, where he had parked it these past years. He would make certain that he retained the car. He loved this machine, the first real car he had owned. It was a late-model Honda Accord, a stylish mix, in his mind, of power and grace.

He noted his suitcase in the back seat. He unlocked the door, climbed behind the wheel, and started the engine. The day had been long enough to fill a week. The powerful whir of the Honda provided some nameless comfort. He put it into reverse, backed out of his space, turned the wheel, and drove to the garage exit. Very slowly, the doors opened automatically as he approached. He had always hated these doors. He always had to wait for them, and Conor, as a rule, disliked waiting for anything. That was one character trait that would have to change, or so he told himself. Especially now.

He eased the car onto Woodley Park Terrace, into the indifferent night, into the cityscape that blinked impersonally, that still breathed with the heat. The garage doors closed with a clank behind him. He noticed that the slight hand trembling that had plagued him earlier that evening had disappeared. He noticed, too, that the effects of the scotch had worn off. He would face the short remainder of this night completely sober.

The light at Connecticut Avenue showed green when he got to the intersection. He signaled his turn and moved the car with its confused cargo around the corner. Already, the condo started to fade behind him. Even so, he knew beyond a doubt that, while this scene might fade, it would never, ever disappear.

CHAPTER II

By then I knew that everything good and bad left an emptiness when it stopped. But if it was bad, the emptiness filled up by itself. If it was good you could only fill it by finding something better.

—Ernest Hemingway, *A Moveable Feast*

Explosions had knocked Conor's orbitals off course. Over the years, there had been several at various intervals. He had been fortunate enough to recognize most of them, but some were subtle, less explosive than quivering subterranean tremors that eventually shook their way to the surface and created gentle, almost imperceptible cracks that, over time and pressure, would widen.

Not all were violent, and not all the fissures they created were destructive. Some, in fact, had caused deviations that had saved him from stagnation. He had never been one to embrace a path of least resistance. Conor had always relished his challenges, had grown up believing that he could surmount anything in his path and, because of this, had never backed away from what others would term as difficult, naïve, or even foolish.

As a young man, he had had a successful athletic career and had been offered scholarships to play college basketball. That particular pinnacle achieved, he had rejected them all to spend his time pursuing other, newer dares. He had always been able to make friends, to establish himself quietly yet definitively as a leader, someone who could and should be followed. His charm, character, vision, and sincerity cloaked an impetuous worldview that assumed no errors of judgment or interpretation. People reacted well to him. For his part, he truly loved being around others, absorbing their stories, learning their fiber, measuring the depth and breadth of their hearts. He came to assume that the world around him was a benign, predictable space that, by dint of his special quality, would bend to his wishes while allowing his unique character room to give what it could.

At twenty-two, he had been able to draw a path from his college graduation to his grave, each step a logical, identifiable element in his progression. Ahead would lie the glorious embrace of a woman he loved, a career arc that was not ostentatious but would allow him to exert a positive influence on a society eager for redemption, a reasonable amount of material comfort, spiritual certitude, and an evolving understanding of the complexities he knew must exist but he did not currently grasp. It was all so clear.

So, there grew a veneer of hubris, an invitation to the Fates to take a swing at the one who saw himself so favored, so aloof from the exquisite agony that constitutes a shared humanity. The explosions, once so gentle and corrective, begun in earnest, changed almost at once from surprise and opportunity to violence and loss.

After three years, by age twenty-five he had lost a professional position he had treasured, his first position in Washington, as a Senate staffer, brought down by his own stubborn adherence to a profound naiveté that had convinced him that he alone knew how the system should work; deep friendships that he had assumed would carry him the course of his life, brought down simply by time and distance and the inevitable evolving agendas that force temporary parallel lives to splay; the counsel and friendship of his parents, whom he had left on the West Coast; his first love, a woman who had devastated his heart; and a thousand moments of brilliance or insight or joy, fueled by sunsets, sunrises, reflections of the day, the tingling, excited anticipation of what comes next. He carried these scars, as must everyone who emerges into the world unformed and callow.

These tremors had forced Conor to redefine himself and his role. Among the materials sent skyward by the worst of these explosions had been the cloak of his special character. He had forced himself to conclude that he was no more blessed than most. At his worst moments, he believed that he was in fact poorly favored, cursed with the realization of his own mediocrity after the exhilaration of such lofty expectations.

All those years ago, at age twenty-five, his despair had led him to drive from Washington to Chicago, the home of his paternal grandfather, Liam. He had needed to absorb the wisdom of this man whose quiet strengths had been a beacon, the legendary tower block of his youth. From his earliest memory of the stories his father had told him of his Grandda Liam's immigration from Ireland and determined obsession to build something different, something better than anything he might ever have attained had he stayed behind, Conor had revered the old man. How much of the stories were myth, he could not tell nor did it matter. His grandfather had carved his own pathway against huge odds and constant obstacles, and near the end of it all, he had emanated the grace of gratification.

When Conor had visited him, Grandda Liam was holding on in a crumbling walkup brownstone across the street from Wrigley Field. Things around him had begun to undergo gentrification, but the old man's building hadn't yet been sold out from under him. He lived in a middle flat both above and below neighbors whose space he had shared for decades.

Over the entire course of their lives, Conor and his grandfather had spent no more than two or three weeks in each other's company—a few days on a vacation, a stopover on a college visit, nothing extended. But Conor believed that his grandfather knew him better than he did himself. At that particular stage of his life, however, such perceptions presented no challenge. Having come apart piece by piece, his professional and personal lives equally crumbled, the sense of self he had cultivated and protected since he was a young boy had proven illusory by the torrents and currents of simply trying to make his way in a world that cared not a fig how special he might be. He had not adapted, had not compromised. He had not listened nor heard the clear clarion signals that demanded interpretation and response.

Liam Finnegan had correctly perceived his grandson's dejection as the threads of a young life that had begun to unwind. Conor had said nothing of his troubles, nothing of lost loves or lost potential, but they had perched on his shoulder like evil gremlins—gremlins his Grandda Liam recognized from his own tortured youth. So, on that visit, Liam Finnegan, seeking to help his grandson navigate the cold, hard realities of adulthood, told Conor the prescriptive story of his life. Some weeks later, he followed his story up with a letter to Conor that tied up some loose ends.

Over the years, it was a story that Conor's mind would turn over and over as he considered solutions to his own work and personal predicaments, and year after year, it helped him come to new conclusions.

But the one thing he came away with immediately after that visit with his grandfather, which would turn out to be the last time he saw the great man, was that it was not enough, would never be enough, to consider himself gifted or compassionate or brilliant, that his ideals and aspirations were worthless without the courage to navigate through harsh, relentless, and uncaring currents with agility, dexterity, and compromise.

It would take a long time, however, for Conor to reflect that lesson in his actions.

* * *

At the end of another common day, Conor shut his briefcase and made his way out of the Rayburn Building, to the Capitol South Metro stop. Two years had passed since he'd arrived at his condo to find Maggie missing, and in that time, they had divorced. Now, at the end of his commute, lay a simple one-bedroom apartment in a complex within walking distance of the Clarendon Metro stop. The place had been built exclusively for convenience of location. It had no real amenities outside of a fitness center that had too little equipment and too much odor. His apartment was basic, laid out unimaginatively, incorporating neither creativity nor flair. Conor had done nothing to broaden its appeal. He had hung a few pictures on the wall, including a pastel drawn for him years ago. That piece, he recognized, was special. The rest of it, though, existed solely to occupy space and to throw a dash of color against the off-white walls.

This evening, on his way up to his apartment, he stopped at the flank of mailboxes to collect his mail. He found in his box a credit card statement showing the monthly amount owed for a vacation he and Maggie had taken more than four years before. Usually, there was nothing of any import in his box, mostly sales flyers and solicitations. When something of consequence did come his way, it was most often negative, like this latest statement.

The divorce had left Conor financially frail. He had spent money on many vacations with Maggie, usually the safe, unadventurous sort at luxury resorts. Despite their lack of either excitement or relaxation, those trips had been wildly expensive.

He would have preferred keeping things simpler, staying close to the ground in guest houses and taking their meals in the simple eateries where the local people gathered, but Maggie would have none of it. She had only consented to travel if their trips would be insulated from any prevalent indigenous influences. She had wanted to feel safe, always, and the strange sights, aromas, and languages encountered outside such sheltered compounds had made her nervous. The resort at which they had spent a week in Barbados may well have been in Cleveland for all the exposure they'd had to Caribbean exotica. Even the beach was tame.

In retrospect, Conor saw those trips now—Barbados, Mexico, Japan—as desperate escapes, not from the pressures and contours of their daily demands, but from each other. The stagnation of their life together had crept upon them incrementally. Each knew the other to be discontent, although they spent too little time examining the whys. They did not talk, did not explore, did not feel for each other. Conor knew no way to penetrate in any lasting way the cold, defensive exterior behind which Maggie had crouched in judgment and fear. After a while, he had abandoned the effort.

When Conor had first raised the possibility of divorce, Maggie had been righteously indignant and professed huge levels of hurt and grief, but inwardly she believed it to be confirmation of the dissolute, impure nature she had observed for years. Conor, once in her eyes an uncomplicated practitioner of a higher path, had become just another man.

The divorce did not come easy, however. Each fought the hard realities of their perceived failure. Neither had believed that they could be capable of such a mistake. They wrapped themselves in denial and negation, acting out their frustrations harshly with each other even while they sought to convince themselves that they were still life partners.

But Conor forced the issue and so became to Maggie not just a fallen ideal but Satan personified. She had battled to squeeze every concession she could during the negotiations, characterizing him as a failed husband, emotionally distant, and irresponsible. She had fantasized about finding some evidence of adultery to brand him further and extract more flesh, but her best efforts on that front failed. Her attorney tried to counsel her away from her vindictiveness. Maggie, though, considered herself abandoned, rejected, tainted by the sins of another. Meanwhile, Conor was financially battered, putting up less of a fight than he should have simply to get it all out of the way.

As a final gesture of triumph, Maggie had gone straight from the courthouse, where it was determined that Conor would assume all credit card debt, and had withdrawn the limit of $10,000 from each of the five cards they had held together before Conor could cancel them.

Why, then, had it come to such a hard conclusion? Since the divorce, Conor had alternately tried to recover from this most graphic explosion and spent a lot of time reflecting on why that destructive fuse had come to be lit.

He was the first of his family to divorce, something that his Irish-Catholic forebears would have found abhorrent and an irreversible ticket to hell. What they could not have known, or would not have acknowledged, was that hell took its own forms in this realm. Conor's soul had been willing to take its chances.

Tonight in his bachelor pad, with this latest credit card bill in hand, Conor's mind drifted to a conversation he had had with an old friend several days after his divorce had been finalized. He had traveled to New Jersey to see Dr. Dan Rosselli, his Rutgers roommate and his first roommate when he arrived in Washington. He had been anxious to see his friend and eager for his great humor and perspective. The first among Conor's college friends to marry, Dan had also been the first to divorce.

"So, doctor," Conor had said to Dan, "what do you prescribe for post-partum depression of the matrimonial sort?"

On this particular evening, they sat at a table in an upscale pub near the Jersey Shore. Dan was treating. The plastic surgeon was doing quite well and was always ready to show it.

Dan flashed his Cheshire cat grin. "Another woman, Conor. There's nothing another woman won't cure. Besides, you didn't love Maggie. Anyone could see that."

"I don't know, Dan. Maybe I did. I know for a while it was all pretty comfortable."

"Bullshit, Conor. Don't mistake tranquility for comfort. She was stable. She was stagnant. She was 'comfortable.' Christ, you probably could have predicted every move she'd make from morning to night. And she probably never thought an original thought for as long as you knew her. No man can put up with that for very long. Especially you. You need to be challenged. I'll bet the sex sucked, too."

Conor grinned. "What sex? We had a bit of a problem with that."

"No doubt. She was all smiles at the wedding, as I recall, probably because she was thinking she had given her last blowjob. And she was landing a handsome young provider with a well-defined career path that would allow her to do what she wanted for the rest of her life—grow fat and never have a care, or so she thought. Don't deny it, Conor. I had one like that myself."

"One who put you through med school. That had to make the settlement hurt a bit."

"Hell, it was a small enough price to pay for my freedom."

Many years ago, when he was still a young man, Dan had fallen in love. He had done so not of the heart, but of the head. He had reached the stage where he thought it proper to be married, so he had found a young lady to fit the purpose. After a time, he had convinced himself that he was in love. It was all a tidy, logical solution to what was, if not a problem, then at least a situation that might breed awkwardness.

"Look, Conor," Dan continued, "I know how weighed down you were, even though you'd deny it. I was weighed down that way, too. It got to the point where I couldn't breathe. I couldn't hold a thought or say a word without her criticizing it. She took and took and took and gave away so little of herself. Ellen was no different than Maggie."

"Ah, but Ellen wasn't a conservative Catholic. Divorce is the work of the devil, you know. I'm now identified as one of the Legion of the Damned."

"Well then, you're in good company. Christ, how many lives get screwed up because we shove our humanity into a closet so that we can conform to someone else's fucked-up notions? That's all that is. When the Church starts to condemn the priests who bugger their altar boys then maybe I'll take their sexual and social proscriptions seriously. Until then, it's all a bunch of hypocrisy, rooted in power. But forgive me, Father Finnegan."

"You're absolved, Danny Boy. But she buys into all that stuff, so as an added bonus to all this, I became Beelzebub."

"Screw it, Conor. You've got to forget all that crap. You made a mistake, that's all. The same one I made. In the end, it's not as if you lost anything of value—some time, some money, a bit of your heart. But you've got plenty of all that in reserve. It's time to get on with it."

"You know, Dan, I think I was more in love with the notion of being in love than with the woman herself. I had convinced myself that I needed to be in love, that that was the thing to do at that particular point. A woman, a marriage . . . all part of the formula. That's really pretty sick when you think of it."

"All your life, or at least as long as I've known you, you've worked really hard to do the right thing. But what's the right thing, Conor? You can spend your whole life listening to your parents, and your teachers, and the Church, and your friends, and everyone's going to have an idea of what's right and what's wrong. But if you spend all your time listening to others, you'll never have enough time to listen to yourself."

Dan continued, "I would have thought you might have handled something like this a bit better, especially after you beat yourself up over Glynnis. You were a mess after that. But you got over it well enough. There's a lesson in that."

"Some recovery, Dan. I went ahead and made an even worse mistake with a poor substitute. That's all Maggie was, you know—a substitute for Glynnis. Stable, safe, with none of the passion, none of the adventure. It was time for a marriage, or so I inferred, and she was there for it. Big mistake. And despite what you might think, I never got over Glynnis." Conor looked off to the far end of the bar, toward a green veiled light that shone over the dark entryway.

"You never get over your first love, Conor. None of us ever do. But that's no reason to compound the pain by doing something foolish, which you clearly did. You run the risk of compounding it all even further if you don't put these things into context. Christ, you've got decades ahead of you. Look forward, brother, and snap out of it."

Conor drank more and sat back to look across at Dan. "I know you're right, big guy. It just takes some time, you know. It hurts a bit."

Dan looked from the table toward the bar, where two blondes in dark, low-cut dresses were drinking by themselves. One looked back toward Dan, who imagined he caught a glimpse of a shy invitation. "You know what would really hurt, Conor?" he said. "Letting this evening end without at least trying to talk to those two goddesses over there. If we're really lucky, I'll do you the great favor of getting you laid tonight. I promise, that will make you forget everything, at least for a little while. Leave it to Doctor Dan."

He did not wait for Conor's reply. Dan rose from the table and, in full charm, approached the two at the bar. Within a few minutes, the three of them were heading for the table where Conor sat alone. Dan ordered four drinks over his shoulder, and the night went on.

* * *

Despite the beauty sitting across the table from him that night in Jersey, Conor could not relinquish the thought of Glynnis Mear. As if she were sitting before him, he saw her long soft-brown hair, parted in the middle, framing her heart-shaped face. Her delicate features and her eyes, large and brown, tapered just enough at the edges to give them a hint of almonds, spoke to him still, and he envisioned her slender form passing before him.

He recalled the independence that had oozed off her, a young girl who had fled Boston for Philadelphia the year after cancer had claimed her father. Glynnis had been the first child to leave home, leaving behind two brothers and a sister. College had provided an escape from a family that, although she loved its members dearly, had appeared misshapen and grotesque without the man at the head of it. Her mother, a licensed nurse at Mass General, had kept things together with her customary strength and grace, but it could never be the same.

Conor and Glynnis had met by accident, a serendipitous meeting between two college students at the Philadelphia Museum of Art on a Saturday morning that became an obsession that neither of them could control. But eventually, Conor's passion for her and everything he did exhausted her even as it made her soar, as it showed her visions of her own self that she had never realized.

What Conor had not understood was that those visions were not her. They were not Glynnis Mear. While with Conor, she came to see herself as an illusion in her lover's eyes, an illusion that, if she followed it, would cause her to abandon the essence of the girl she really was.

CHAPTER III

*We are able to find everything in our memory, which is like
a dispensary or a chemical laboratory in which chance steers
our hand sometimes to a soothing drug and sometimes to a
dangerous poison.*

—Marcel Proust, *Remembrance of Things Past*

From Liam's letter to his grandson, Conor:

> *Behind the heart lie scars that do not heal.*
>
> *Pierced by arrows that fly in gentle arcs on wispy shafts,
> soft tissues rend and bleed, then, in primal self-preservation,
> close around the wounds, harden, and persevere. We call it
> healing, but it is not healing at all. The wounds lie deep,
> obscured by acts of will that force them into corners and compel
> their silence, although they do not fade. They do not heal.*
>
> *No one shall be immune from this. We each carry the
> scars that do not heal, that lie behind the heart.*
>
> *First loves, lost loves, the death of innocence, places
> brought to dust, passion grown cold, or comfort devoured
> in flame. Friendship betrayed, family lost, the cutting glance*

*of one who is now a stranger. A mirror's reflection that speaks
with too much honesty. A final ride, then darkness that,
like heartache, does not fade. Glory lost, youth consumed, a
heart made useless. We carry these scars, and more we cannot
name, and behind the heart they do not heal.*

Conor carried his scars in customary silence, honoring their
presence while denying them voice, even to himself. He dwelt on
what was lost in his own way. He could not forget what had gone—
what he had been—and how he had felt during those glorious days
of youth, and power, and unbounded, infinite, limitless potential.
He could not forget those precious feelings that come only once,
and when gone, cannot be reclaimed.

Before his marriage, before his career, before his friends had
grown to become the brothers he never had, before his body
had become strong and tall, before he had been born into this
life itself, a devotion he could never reclaim had justified Conor,
had defined the special air he would breathe, had delineated
all that his character was, could be, or could ever become. Now
gone, into dust, his old devotion haunted him in its silent ways
every day. He could not forget, and in the remembrance came
the harkening of every feeling, sensation, and conclusion that
had marked his days during the wondrous period when his world
was vibrant, limitless, and centered completely on another soul
whose very existence made his own worthwhile. He could never
forget this, these rare days, and what they had given him, the
conclusions to which they had driven him, now gone. He could
never forget, could never purge from his memory, those days of
youth and infallibility, and the deep, bottomless wellsprings of
two blended souls.

Even now, as a divorcé, Conor's every step echoed to him the
image of Glynnis Mear. Although he had not seen her in more
than fifteen years, she remained as present to him as breath.

Tucked into a far corner, away from all sight, lay the cherished recollections of what they had been to each other, the shared heartbeat that time and distance and circumstance had softened to a whimper but could not totally destroy.

Behind the heart lie scars that do not heal.

"Excuse me," he said. She turned. Conor extended the notebook. "You left this behind you upstairs."

She smiled and took it from him. Her voice came out low, with a hint of mischief. "I was wondering how long it would take you . . ."

So it had begun, never to finish in spirit, if not in fact. Later that same day, the day they met, Glynnis had told Conor, "I think you've got heartbreak written all over you. Not past, but future. You're bound to get hurt terribly somewhere along the way. You're young, and you're trusting, and you've got a conscience. Burdensome traits, those are. The primary ingredients for pain."

She had, of course, been correct. Conor had not considered that Glynnis herself would be the inadvertent author of the worst part of the inevitable heartbreak. But before the heartbreak had come moments of sublimity, the vulnerabilities that derive from hearts and minds lying in naked exposure, the discovery of one's own emotional depths.

It had been worth it, Conor knew. He had always believed that the exhilaration of Glynnis had merited the despair that followed. Their fleeting, too brief time together had shown him things he had never seen since and never really expected to find again.

When Glynnis had visited her family in Boston one summer, Conor had written her there. Because Glynnis went to school in Philadelphia and he went to school in Jersey, they spent most days apart, but here she was in new, more distant territory . . . and Conor was surprised at how lonely he found himself. This new circumstance had disturbed him, and the first night Glynnis was home in Boston, he had sat at his desk at Rutgers with a glass

of wine and delved as deeply as he could into this new matrix
of emotion, obligation, and distance. He wrote his soul, with
spiritual blood on every page, and concluded with perhaps the
truest words he had ever penned.

> *"I will leave you now, my lady, to your mysterious family
> and the Boston summer. I will leave you, with your long
> hair that smells of flowers, with your fair skin, and with
> your secretive eyes that see all sides of me. I will leave you in
> word, but never in thought. I am with you there, in prim
> and tidy Boston, although you cannot know it. I shall always
> be with you. I shall haunt you, in body and in thought, all
> the days of your life, and you will haunt me. Love itself is
> haunting, and we cannot do without it."*

How incredibly fortunate he had been to abandon all parts
of himself—intellectual, emotional, physical, and spiritual—
to another breathlessly beautiful soul who had reciprocated
thoroughly. Once abandoned to each other, for several years they
explored their youth together, spiraling outward in concurrent
circles until the force of their own characters had shattered the
delicate balance, shaken loose the drop of dew dangling from the
rose petal, and splashed it away beyond their grasp.

All these years after first meeting, what remained was the
scent of the rose, forever embedded, forever retained, as both
pleasure and torment.

Sometimes even now, on the loneliest nights, Conor's torment
played itself out against his will and despite all intent. On such
nights, he delved into the abyss of a troubled mind.

*Is it right, then, that years later, I still talk to you, even though
I cannot see you and do not know where you are? Is it right that
I still share with you my thoughts? Has it become instinct to turn
to you, to lean again, as I did so long ago, on your wisdom, and*

how that wisdom transfers its compassion to the likes of me? Is it right, then, that on dark nights, or rainy days, or snowy evenings, I hold conversations with you, soliloquies really, with no expectation of response but with every confidence that you remain the best path for me to work away my uncertainties?

For you were always certain when you were with me. You were always sure and peaceful, calm, poised, elegant, and always aware. You were always so, until those days near the end when you were not, and I saw it and knew that I held no power to reverse that sad drift. And in those days, I felt myself fade perceptibly, become less visible, less present in your eyes, and so in the world itself. I ceased to matter when I did not matter to you. I vanished from the place where I had been . . . where we had been. Although I fought against it, in truth I did not know what to do. I did not know what you wanted or needed, only that I no longer seemed to be able to provide it. You went away, as softly as you came. No explosions, no final confrontations, no drama, other than what transpired within us, reserved only for our private viewing. Gone to other lovers, to other lives, to other times and places.

I fantasize about your reactions to these new things. I try to visualize how your subtleties would be met by others who do not know them or perhaps have no use for subtlety. I try to conjure your face in new situations, in new cities, or walking on the beach with someone else. I fancy you in winter, put off as ever by the cold, which you abhorred, but to me breathless as snowflakes flecked your cheeks and clung to your coat, your colors reddened by the chill and so made sharper, more vibrant, your almond eyes blinking through the graying light. I see you in summer, the Eastern heat and humidity pressing your temples, legs bare and your long hair pulled back into a tail to allow air for your shoulders and swanlike neck. I visualize how other men would react to the quiet, composed portrait you paint, what would flare inside them and how they would approach you, and what you would do in return. I torment myself by imagining your touch on their bodies, and, worse, their touch on your heart. I see you writing them the same letters you wrote me, saying to them the same words that burned into me and have not left me since, looking at them with the same sad eyes that I could never leave.

But I cannot know any of these things, of course. I can only imagine and in the imagining continue to hold on to at least a small, fanciful part of you, an open scab that I continually delve into.

* * *

In late summer, the perpetual heat that drumbeats each day breaks, if only for a day or two. The morning breaks fresh, and the afternoon warms without baking. Then a softness permeates the end of the day as the sun diminishes, its shadows painting colors that hint of the coming autumn, the coming chills, and, in so doing, compels recognition of the cycles that we cannot escape.

Saturday morning, mid-September, light gently rising to overcome a sleep-tossed night, Conor rose to the day's coolness, his obligations less burdened than his thoughts. Nothing before him today; everything, it seemed, behind him.

Over breakfast and the *Washington Post*, he reviewed his options. Although no deep friendships had developed over his now eighteen years here, he still had people he could call for a game of tennis or a few drinks at a bar. But it was too early in the day to feel if any of that would be right.

Washington always threw its cultural doors wide open on the weekends, and so a day in the city sniffing around the museums or walking the Mall might do. Even in late summer, there were always tourists from all over the world, a fascinating accent to the exhibits themselves. If, as Conor believed, each face told a story and every soul had merit, then what stories might lie behind these curious strangers from India or Japan or Brazil or Nigeria? Often, he would intuit their excitement, especially if they were with children, and with it confirm that there were indeed things at his fingertips worth prizing and little of it housed in formal exhibits. He loved the museums for what they showed him, for how they made him feel, and for the way they impelled this recognition. The stately National Gallery of Art, the Corcoran, the Museums of American History and Natural History . . . any could do when he felt as he did, that an atmosphere and the people who walked within it trumped whatever was on display.

With that thought in mind, on this crisp Saturday morning, Conor decided to visit a museum . . . except it would not be one in Washington. He would instead head up north.

As Conor turned his car out of the garage of his apartment building, the gaseous closed air gave way to the fresh, sharp bite of late morning and sunlight flooded his vision. On one of the trees across the way, near the park where he sometimes went for a run, an army of starlings perched and chirped, swaths of black against the budding green.

Two days ago, it had rained heavily, two inches of sloppy, heavy wetness that had almost shut down the city for the day. Storms had rolled through one after the other. After they had subsided, the air had hung heavier than before, humidity as thick as cotton, and standing water had turned every sidewalk and road into a splashway. There was no magic in rainfall anymore. As he grew up in Southern California, where rainfall was a rare event, Conor had looked forward to the storms that came perhaps once a year, the gentle, fleeting showers that washed out almost as soon as they had begun, the feel of cool falling water on his skin, throwing his head back to open his mouth to catch and drink fresh rainwater, and the strange slapping sounds his shoes made on wet pavement. No more of that. Rainfall was to be endured. This last storm bred resentment with its inconvenience.

But now, only vestiges of the storm remained, and the sidewalks and streets were, for the most part, dry. The sun rose, the day unfolded, and underneath the leaden spirits engendered by humidity, heat, and storms through a dreary workweek there bloomed a small rose of spirit.

Conor drove along the Beltway, skirting the District and into Maryland. He drove to the music he played, his mind otherwise empty. He breathed the sharp air through windows he left open by two inches. Driving and breathing.

He took Exit 33 to I-95 North, as he had done countless times and for various reasons. He knew this road. He knew its curves, congestions, trucks, and odors. He knew the way Baltimore would rise as a bump in the distance then become distinguishable by its familiar buildings, by Camden Yards and the harbor. He knew the off-ramp for the Harbor Tunnel and the road that led to Fort McHenry. He knew the BWI Airport exit. He knew the feeling of release once he had passed the city, where the lanes narrowed and emerged on the northern side into a freer, more open, greener space.

He passed through Maryland, through Delaware, stopped for a tasteless lunch, sipped hot coffee, and kept driving. When he crossed into New Jersey, he considered veering to the New Jersey Turnpike for the drive to Exit 9. He had done this so many times, ending in New Brunswick and Rutgers. So many years later, the college still called him back, the place where he had learned more about himself than any course could teach, where he had forged friendships closer than brotherhood, where his future had appeared limitless and glorious and bold. He relished his return visits when he had time to walk the campus leisurely, feel the familiar sidewalks and smell again the river's aromas mixing with those of the food trucks, hear the life force of the College Avenue campus, listen again to voices younger than his own in casual conversation, and imagine that he was twenty years old, a bright, confident stranger in a land growing less strange by the hour.

Twenty years old, twenty years ago. The casual pulses of day to day accumulate into the press and flow of time, imperceptible in the moment, but as inviolable as life itself. Flesh once soft and strong sags at first in hints and whispers; voices vibrant and melodic start to tremble, start to rasp; the lightness of movement becomes just slightly heavy, then heavier, until we find ourselves slowed; thoughts once fresh grow banal and tiring. Always the mistakes right before us, or right behind, confront us with our failures, which cannot be denied, and which make the burning, tawdry years harsher still. For we see what we have lost, in body, in mind, and in spirit, and we see how we have lost it.

We see what we have squandered—youth, promise, and the vast, boundless potential of spring mornings, taken away through the drip by drip of passing days, filled with our errors. Errors of judgment, errors of commission, errors of omission. Errors of callousness and of not knowing who we really are or what we have the chance to be. Errors of hubris. Errors of assumption and presumption. Errors of blindness, where we do not see the souls of those around us because to do so requires an effort we choose to withhold. The accumulation of these errors places us where we are, not where we were meant to go those twenty years ago, when every morning breathed adoration and every sunset celebrated the blood that flowed gloriously within our veins. Twenty years passed, and everything false now, derailed by our own hands, compromised by the shortcomings so well hidden, self-delusions preserved like precious metal.

Summer's days shorten in September, teasing a subtle hint of the coolness around October's corner. Across the Ben Franklin Bridge, into the city, and through the narrow, old streets, still jammed on a late Saturday, people breathed the week's end, and the summer's end, and the end of sorrows promised by a fresh early evening. In the midst of this scene, Conor drove a familiar path to the Ben Franklin Parkway, then down to the park, and past the Franklin Institute—Philadelphia, he mused, had too few heroes, and Ben was overworked. Although the landscape had changed, with new buildings, glass and chrome, the streets ran the same way, in the same directions. Conor knew his way.

He parked his car in Fairmount Park, then up the broad steps to the Art Museum he went. He paid his contribution then wandered the ground floor, which held no galleries. Up the stairway to the second floor, American art on his left and the Europeans to his right. The Europeans had always drawn him, especially the Impressionists. Especially Degas. It was a painting by Degas, *After the Bath*, that had lured him here two decades ago, that had changed his life. He ambled slowly down the hallways, through the galleries, and found Degas's gentle bather still displayed in Gallery 165.

Before the painting, he stood silently, studying its lines and shadings as he had done before, absorbing, if he could, the feel of the moment Degas had surreptitiously captured. Degas was all light and shadow and suggestion when he had painted this study, one of so many he had completed of young women in their baths. During this period, Degas had drawn few hard lines but let light play with color and form to allow the viewer to see the most appropriate incarnation of his or her own expectations.

But Conor's study this late afternoon bypassed Degas, bypassed this painting and those that hung near it. He knew this painting. After all these years, he still remembered all he cared to about the painter and what he had sought to do. It was not the beauty of the work that had compelled him here, but its meaning, which lay in a far different corner than Degas had ever intended.

Across from the painting, in the middle of the gallery, there still sat a low-slung wooden bench, simple and with no backing. Conor turned from the painting to the bench, stood over it, and sought the spot where, twenty years ago, Glynnis Mear had left her notebook and walked away. On that bright, early spring morning, Conor and Glynnis had been two birds in a mating dance. Conor had taken his chance then, grabbed the notebook, and followed her down the steps into a future glowing more gloriously by the second.

Here it had been, where it began to play out. Still here, all of it. Degas, the bather, the bench, the same soft lighting, the same air. Nothing had changed in this place except those who walked through it.

At five, the museum set to close. Conor had arrived late but saw what he needed to see. Down those same steps where he had chased her . . . noting the feel of them, the sound of his shoes on stone . . . here, it had been. Then, out the front door to look down the Parkway, an arrow into Center City, green from the summer on both sides. Conor stood for several minutes.

A few hundred yards on the left stood the Rodin Museum. After Conor had returned Glynnis her notebook, after the first few minutes of introductory banter, after he had first looked into her eyes and smelled the ever-present scent of lilacs she carried with her, they had gone to the Rodin. Conor had known little of the artist, nor did he particularly care to. But that morning in spring, he and Glynnis had walked through the Frenchman's museum before finding a place for lunch. Rodin forever after became an icon.

Conor walked down the Parkway once again, past the Rodin, with the day's life of the park dismantling. Any buskers had left, street vendors had closed and gone, and children finished their games on the grass while their parents tried to edge them away. Walking still, to Logan Circle, with its fountain still spraying, and the benches where he and Glynnis would sit sometimes on the afternoons when he had picked her up before taking her back to New Brunswick for the weekend. Just beyond, the great green dome of the Cathedral Basilica of Saints Peter and Paul, where they had once or twice gone to Mass when he had brought her back. And beyond that dome, the city itself, now changed, with new buildings, higher than before, sleek and upward. When he had come to Philadelphia in the years before, William Penn's hat on the top of his statue on city hall had been the highest point in the city. No more. Billy Penn had shrunken in stature, outdone by a modern era that had little use for outmoded traditions.

So long ago, this city had called to him, enchanted him with the special magic that lay within it. Glynnis had been here, so Conor had wanted to know every step, stone, street, and byway of the city where she rose, studied, laughed, and slept. Easy to romanticize it all at the time. Easy now. It did not matter that Philadelphia housed as much confusion and complexity and corruption and crime as any other major conglomeration of man's impulses. It did not matter that millions of strangers made their way equally through these same streets, each with his or her own agenda and cares and curses. It did not matter that fires raged or that young people gunned each other down or children cried with hunger or fathers ran off with their mistresses.

None of that mattered. Glynnis had been here, in this city, so this city surpassed all others. It drew Conor to its character, those many years ago. Tonight, twenty years on, it still did.

Slowly, he walked back up the Parkway to where he had left his car. The sun drew low, and light played across the buildings in sharpened blazes of red and orange, enhanced it seemed by the chilled air that embedded itself into Conor's chilled heart. Occasional cars growled past, and the first stirrings of a Saturday night began to rouse. People had things to do and places they wanted to be, people they wanted to be with.

He found his car, unlocked it, and climbed inside into a womblike warmth. He backed it away then drove one last circuit around the art museum before heading up the Parkway. He would catch 95 after recrossing the Ben Franklin Bridge and creeping back through Camden's squalid rot. By the time he passed through Maryland and found the Beltway, the sun had long vanished, and another day's measure had faded into lost meaning.

* * *

Back in his apartment in DC that night, Conor awoke to the dance of distant thought . . .

Exiled. Disconnected. Separation of the here and now from anything else. From anyone else. The deep, empty, spatial void from the self to . . . where? To what? Who is out there? The immense loneliness of it all. Thoughts unformed, and, if formed, unspoken. No place to take those thoughts, and no one who cares enough to hear them. Speaking to myself, and the words, the reactions, the incipient and flitting passions die there behind my eyes, not worth the voice to give them life. It's become a way of life, or rather a way of death—a way of intellectual and emotional death.

I remember nights coming home to Maggie, back when I thought it all mattered. I had never thought two people in such close proximity could be so isolated, so cold and alone. Home, then, at the end of a day, and not a single question about how it went, about how I was, about how she was. We pursued separate conversations. "We need to close the windows tonight. It's getting too cold to keep them open." "Is my best shirt in the laundry? I'll need it for a meeting on Monday." "There are ants in the upstairs bathroom." Separate strands that never met, never twisted together into something binding.

And after a day spent on different sides of a wide gulf, there came the isolation of the night. We shared a bed but rarely shared a touch. We did not speak as we drifted off on our separate islands; there was no pillow talk. In the morning, one would rise without a word and go into the bathroom to start the preparations for a grand repeat. Nothing changed. Days and nights without rhythm other than a somber, monotonous, silent throbbing beat. I was numb to it all. She had grown old too soon, and I let it happen until I could not let it happen anymore. Until it became obvious even to my blind eye that this could not continue, that passionate, complex humans were not meant to live as mummies interred within their own shuttered psyches.

Glynnis spoiled me. I know that now. Even when I rhapsodize about first loves and how the excitement and discovery of something so fresh and new could never possibly be replicated, I realize that, despite the logical and inevitable conclusion that I would never find the like again, that is what I pursued. I was bound to fail. Maggie came to me as a safe harbor, but I traveled with my own deep-sea mines. Detonation was unavoidable.

Still, my frame of reference was fixed. Glynnis brought beauty, intrigue, and a daily unfolding of some new layer within myself, layers I could not have known existed were it not for her touch, and her soft words, and her constant, or so I thought, faith in me. For a time, we lived for each other, the completion of two half-drawn circles. Instead of hesitation, she instilled commitment. I would dive into anything, no matter how impenetrable, knowing that what lay ahead would be worth the effort, if for no other reason than to share it all with her as I went along. She was muse, inspiration, conscience, and provocateur.

I remember telling her, "The senator wants me to shelve the nursing home aspect, Glyn, and move to more general housing issues. But I can't abandon what I've seen. I just can't do that."

"Conor, you have to. He's your boss, and he calls the shots, right or wrong. Besides, my love, there's nothing you can't do. Everything you pursue, you do well. Do this well, and make me proud."

"You're not already proud?"

"I'd be prouder if you were more flexible. The world isn't

always going to play your game. You're going to have to play someone else's game, too, from time to time. Besides, you're still going to do great things for people who need great things done for them."

I could tell her anything, and she would listen, not with docility, condescension, or indulgence, but with insight and compassion. She would challenge, prod, and question. She would praise, celebrate, and grow excited sometimes by things I thought were too simple or commonplace to merit excitement. She saw things I never could; she heard me in ways no one else ever has. I came to assume that any woman could do those things.

Then she was gone. There came Maggie, and she's gone, too, although I account it scant loss except for the investment of time and money I'll never reclaim. Gone as well is every other woman with whom I shared a conversation, or a drink, or a kiss, or a night of shallow pleasure. I discovered a new order of things.

We do not connect easily, none of us, and perhaps I am so flawed that I can no longer connect at all. I live now in disconnection, isolation, and silence, my life a whisper rather than a shout or an exultation. I wrestle to subdue a depression that tells me daily that I cannot recover what's been lost and that what I have in hand will always appear shabby and tired. Alone now in the ways that matter most and exiled from what I sought so hard those years ago. Exiled and apart, carried to the waters and the wild.

CHAPTER IV

He feels the truth: the thing that has left his life has left irrevocably; no search would recover it. No flight would reach it. It was here, beneath the town, in these smells and these voices, forever behind him.

—John Updike, *Rabbit Run*

I remember the last time we made love, the night and how it unfolded. How we felt, there amid the tension, amid the despair and the blanket of impending loss. I think about that night often, especially now, when I've moved on to make my mistakes, the thousand usual, common mistakes we all make, the cost of growing up and growing out. But there were other mistakes, too, the kind you can't take back or undo. The kind that leave deep, jagged cuts beneath the skin. Yes, I think about that night often. I think about it now.

You had come down on the Friday train, and I met you at Union Station, as I always did. We went out to dinner at a little bistro near Dupont Circle, a place a colleague on the Hill had told me about, where the lights were low enough to be romantic and the clatter and din was low enough for conversation. We sat *at a corner table and ordered wine, then escargot. We talked, although I can't recall precisely what we discussed. No doubt it was the usual pattern that dominated our last days. No doubt I told you about work and asked about your week. No doubt I asked if you really had to leave the next afternoon, couldn't you stay through Sunday like you used to do? No doubt you grew defensive, or exasperated, or glum, then responded with your quiet voice that stayed low throughout the remainder of the meal. No doubt.*

After dinner, I drove back across the Roosevelt Bridge to the apartment I shared with Dan. It was a small two-bedroom cell in a nondescript building off Bailey's Crossroads in Arlington, completely lacking character and just like a hundred other places in a bedroom community, but I was damn proud of it. We had furnished it with pieces his parents had given us, mixed with a few things we bought for ourselves—matching kitchenware, bookshelves, a good television, and a living room set. We could afford it. We weren't scavengers anymore, stealing cutlery from the university dining room like we'd done in the past, and we made that apartment comfortable. We made it ours.

When you and I arrived there, Dan was gone. He had traveled home to New Jersey for the weekend, as he did every month or so. I walked up the stairs carrying your bag, which was smaller now, an overnight case really. No more suitcases. I set the bag down, unlocked the door, and you stepped in. A few moments later, you walked into the bathroom. When you emerged, I was seated on the couch, minus the tie I had worn all day and the shoes that had pinched my feet.

You sat next to me, and we talked. I don't recall what we said or how we said it. This was always the time when you were most relaxed, after the initial joust over my resentment and your defensive parry, after the silence of the rapprochement. You were less guarded during these times, and the talk flowed more freely, slightly less afraid of triggering a hidden landmine or losing your footing on a rocky slope.

After an hour or so of gentle conversation, we rose. Perhaps we kissed then as we stood in front of the couch and recognized that despite the frustration and the separation and the impending loss, we still loved each other, that something indelible had been cast against every threat and assault, strong enough to survive, but not strong enough to sustain. We knew this, and it made us sad. There was nothing we could do.

My bedroom was small, but it was clean and well ordered. Unlike most single men, I made the bed every day. I put my clothes away, hung up my suits, and made sure that the things I wore that needed washing were in a laundry hamper. Because you were coming, I had sprayed the bedspread with a lavender mist that left a subtle lingering floral scent in complement to your own pervasive perfume of lilacs. I wanted the simple act of stepping into this room to be like stepping into another realm, delightful to all the senses, safe from threat or conflict, apart from the passage of time and the demands of space.

You went into the bathroom to undress and put on what you would wear to bed. This night, you emerged wearing something understated, a white sleeveless gown that was not sheer but still showed the hint of your glorious body. I was in my shorts, and I lay in the bed, under the covers, watching you. I never tired of that. I loved watching you, in even the simplest of movements. I could have sat transfixed watching you pour a glass of milk or written a poem celebrating your washing of the dishes. Even the smallest movement told me something, and I didn't want to miss a flick of your wrist or your tiniest step.

Some nights toward the end, we would not make love. Often, this was because of the sore feelings that stemmed from the hurt of your quick comings and goings, from the day-to-day ache of not having you with me when I thought you should be, and of *how poorly I expressed myself. Confusion deepened the pain, and I flailed about looking for a toehold on the surety I craved. We both flailed, and when we did we both hit soft targets. On those nights, we would climb into bed and claim our separate sides. A quick and perfunctory kiss, then back to back we would pretend to go to sleep as the night grew colder and the clock counted off the minutes until your departure, with nothing gained and the twin treasures of time and affection drawn down to nothing. I learned to stop forcing the issue. Sometimes it was hard, sometimes impossible. But I tried. I didn't want to argue or badger or seek to impose guilt.*

This night, the last night, we nestled in bed together, and I breathed deeply the flowing fall of your hair, entwined with the whisper of lilacs. I held your slender shoulders tightly, marveling at their perfect petite form, then I moved my hands down your back to feel the ridge of your spine and ended at the firm rise below it. I was moved sexually. Who would not be in the arms of this woman? What type of man could hold Glynnis Mear in such a way and not feel passion or want to delve into her beauty with all his might? And here I was with you against me, holding on to me as well. Despite all the fears and foreboding, I was in my own paradise. I was still in the midst of my deepest fantasy. Nothing I have seen since has ever come close to this.

We moved into each other in the familiar ways, beginning with deep kisses and then caressing the parts we each wanted caressed. When we first began, you would moan in pleasure and wonderment at what we were about. Your moans aroused me further, and we progressed with much heat. But there was no moaning tonight, just deep breathing and kisses, which we each meant, and gentility, and tenderness, and great care. I entered you as you lay beneath me, and your breath quickened as your hips rose rhythmically to meet me in the regular way.

Your hands ran the length of my back. We did not speak, as we often did, nor did we whisper each other's name. We made love in the most basic way. Your pace became more rapid as you neared your climax, and I responded similarly. I always tried to make sure that you climaxed, and I knew the signs. To this day, I don't think you ever faked anything, but that might just be the rationalization of a bruised male ego. You never really know.

When we finished, I raised myself above you on my elbows and looked at you deeply. You looked back up and smiled then lifted your head just enough to kiss my chin. I said nothing. At such moments in the past, I would whisper my love for you, my gratitude that you were in my life, relying on hyperbole and contrived imagery to convince you that what I said was real. It was. I meant every word, and I would have said them this night if I thought they would play to a receptive audience. But I knew better. Such words would only have been awkward.

As I rolled off you to my own side of the bed, you held my hand then made your only reference to what we had just done. "That was fun, Conor. Thank you."

I had never considered our lovemaking "fun," although that was certainly one of its best attributes. To me, it had been an expression of the most deeply centered emotion I could feel, a manifestation of the meaning I sought to ascribe to why I was on this planet. It was an act of giving, an act of engagement and commitment, an act of devotion. An act of worship. And yes, it was "fun," but it went far, far beyond that. You had meant to be kind, I knew. I also knew that what you said told me all that I needed to know about what would come next.

We slept the night through, and the following afternoon, we climbed back into my car and drove the short way to Union Station. After arriving, we sat in the hard plastic seats to wait the final few minutes before the boarding of your train. After the boarding announcement, we kissed, also for the last time,

and you turned to walk into the crowd that massed toward the
boarding gate. Then you were gone.

Despite my calls, despite going to the train station on a few
Friday nights when you would have been due to arrive, looking
everywhere for you, I never saw or heard from you again.

* * *

On the Monday after his trip to Philadelphia, Conor showered and donned his usual business uniform of a pressed shirt and light summer suit. Work loomed, as it always did, and he made his way into the city on a crowded, jostling Metro train then walked the few blocks up the Hill to his office in the Rayburn Building, where he greeted colleagues, put down his briefcase, started his computer, and plowed through the day's responsibilities in his role as a staffer on the Foreign Affairs Committee.

After all of his years of professional fits and starts, this plum assignment had landed in his lap just as his marriage was ending. He appreciated it that much more when he considered his prior career trajectory, or rather his career downfall, flailing around from one monotonous and nonproductive assignment to the other, from serving the junior senator from California, to working on the Joint Committee on the Library, to his last job, as a staffer on the House Committee on Natural Resources, the post he held while he was still with Maggie.

But a change in his future had become set in motion a few months after his divorce proceedings had begun. At that time, he met with his own congressional representative regarding a piece of pending wetlands legislation. Northern Virginia had little in the way of bogs or marshes, but a proposed bill would have raised the legal cap on effluents entering downriver, which Conor knew would back up to Alexandria and Arlington with the Potomac's tidal flow. The minority position had needed an ally in its futile effort to block this thing, and Conor had reckoned that his congressman might provide that voice.

He had met the representative two or three times previously at receptions or lunches. The occasion of meeting to discuss the wetlands was their first extended conversation, and Conor found the man insightful, honest, and pleasant. They spoke for an hour about the impact of the bill and what it might mean to those living along the river just below the District. Conor's research and the strategy of opposition for which he was being recruited had impressed the congressman.

In the end, the congressman had agreed to come on board. "I'll sign a statement in opposition to the bill if you draft it for me. But frankly, Conor, this thing is going to pass. It's possible that we can get it tabled to the next session, or if it's brought forward, it might be slightly watered down. That's the best we can hope for. We can't stop it at this level. Still, I'll sign the letter and do what I can."

"Thank you, sir," Conor replied that day. "I'll have something to your assistant by the end of the week. Thanks for your time." He got up to leave.

"Got a second more?" Conor sat back down. "Listen, you know I'm the ranking minority member of the Foreign Affairs Committee. What you don't know is that our lead minority administrative director just got pirated by USAID to manage a multibillion-dollar vaccination program in Sub-Saharan Africa. Actually, 'pirated' is probably the wrong word." The congressman paused. "The pay in my office isn't what you'd expect and the work is long and hard. John willingly jumped, and who can blame him? Anyway, I like the work you've done here. You've been on the Hill for a while, and you've got good experience. Plus, you're a constituent. You're a logical candidate for me to push forward, if you're interested."

Conor gathered his thoughts. He was genuinely stunned. Foreign Affairs was near the top of the House's food chain. Lord, it had to be more stimulating than what he had been doing in recent years. "I think I'd be interested in learning more, Congressman."

"Good. Send me your resume. Send it directly to my personal email." He scribbled the address on his card and handed it to Conor. "No guarantees. There'll be other candidates. But I'm happy to push you forward."

Three weeks later, Conor interviewed with four of the minority members and two of the majority, including the chair. A week later, the offer was made. The congressman was right—the pay was less than he would have thought, but it was a definite increase for him. He would be free of Natural Resources and the flotsam of a broken career. Maybe there was something to hang on to here. Maybe there was something to be excited about.

Two weeks later, he packed up his things and moved down the street to the Rayburn Building, where his new office was equally crammed, although it was larger and had a working door that he could close. He would have three junior staffers to manage in addition to his own duties. If he needed it, he would have administrative support in the form of one of the Hill's typically beautiful, ambitious assistants. This was a step up in every way.

Now, more than a year later, at age forty, he had some standing with the committee, a reputation for solid, meticulous work that remained fresh. To his own surprise, he had found a new fervor despite his lingering depression over his personal life. Conor had come to embrace the mandates of foreign engagement, not for the cold and utilitarian reasons that guided the country's foreign policy, but for the humanistic applications of the work. His research had opened up a window he had not regarded before. He had come to see the developing world not as political entities whose affections needed to be manipulated and ultimately controlled but as sovereign bodies filled with individuals striving to create security, purpose, and, at the worst, survival from debris and chaos. He had come to see a commonality.

Part of his duties included traveling as staff support on overseas junkets. For one who had never been outside the boundaries of his homeland, each trip was a revelation and a chance to explore something new, some unconsidered aspect of how people get along. Instead of hovering in and around the luxury hotels where he and the delegation were housed, Conor spent his spare time trying to delve behind the obvious. The new lands, with their new peoples and their new desperations, intoxicated him and drove his curiosity to the point of mania.

* * *

Several weeks after his impromptu drive to Philadelphia, Conor found himself preparing to travel to Rwanda. Years after the end of the genocide there, his committee was developing a position on national reconstruction, with potential ramifications for foreign assistance allocations. While Congress, along with every other governmental branch, including State, willingly turned its back on Rwanda as the horrors unfolded, an opportunity to deepen a portal within East-Central Africa had pushed the country up the priority scale. The committee could help them rebuild, help them reconcile with one another, and they would go back to loving the US. All that was needed was a comprehensive policy statement crafted around a dollar sign. So to Rwanda they would go, the committee chair, the ranking minority member, Conor, and another staffer.

In advancing the trip, Conor had immersed himself in the history of the country, the roots of the genocide, how it eventually was resolved, and the major players. He had made calls at all hours of the day to the US Consulate, Rwandan government officials, security personnel, and regional prefectures to coordinate the three days they would be in-country. But he had also called those who had been there as reporters or observers and who had seen the genocide unfold. He had spoken with anyone he could who might be able to shed some light on what he would find there, below the official, well-escorted government pathways they would walk. He wanted to see the ground beneath his feet.

Now, the flight itself went through Amsterdam, stopped for a few hours and a quick noncommittal press conference with the Dutch and English media, then proceeded to Nairobi. In Kenya, they changed planes for the quick jaunt to Kigali, and it was there that Conor began to feel uncomfortable because of his skin. There were no white faces in the Nairobi airport except for his traveling party. He noted the security forces with large batons and larger guns, unsmiling and watchful, and he felt his skin glow ghostly.

"Hey, Tim," Conor whispered to Tim Soderholm, the majority counsel, "do you think we stand out much here?"

"A bunch of well-dressed white guys?" he responded. "Nah, we fit right in."

"Makes me think about what it must be like to be a black man back home—a clear minority surrounded by something you'll never be able to absorb."

"Careful, Conor," said Tim. "The liberal in you is coming out. I thought you were as cynical as the rest of us."

"I am, Tim. But, Jesus, how can you ignore being so overwhelmingly in the minority."

"Not my issue, Conor. We're just here to do a job."

Then the flight to Rwanda, lifting off from a runway bordered by squat windblown trees and rising over Nairobi National Park, where, looking out the window, Conor made out a pack of, what—wildebeests?—grazing on a sloping plain. After a while, Mount Kilimanjaro rose to the left, a stark contrast to the flatness below. As the plane crossed out of Rwanda, the land began to undulate and small hills broke the flatness, then across Lake Victoria and over the thick green rises of the Land of a Thousand Hills. As the plane descended, Conor looked down on simple villages linked by dirt roads, with huts and small houses, most of which appeared empty. In those few moments, over the lake where dead bodies had drifted from Rwanda's rivers, and seeing the untilled lands of slaughtered families, Conor's academic grasp of the genocide translated to a different level. This was real, all of it.

When they landed, a delegation from the consulate met them and escorted them to the Hotel des Milles Collines, the best and only accommodation worthy of dignitaries. Still, Conor's room was simple cinderblock with a large window that opened onto the courtyard. There was no air conditioning, but the desk had provided a mosquito net so that he could sleep with the window open if he wanted. On his way down to breakfast the next morning, he noticed bullet holes in the soft block.

After breakfast, the four Americans traveled with the consulate delegation to a refugee camp in Byumba, an hour's drive north of Kigali. They saw people driving their cattle along the roadside, carrying goods to and from the markets in each small village or walking their children to school. Some just sat on boulders to watch the scattered traffic, to pass the scattered day. The road rose dramatically into the northern hills. Conor noted that, amazingly, even this terraced land was cultivated. Some farms seemed to rise almost vertically up the slopes.

In turning through one of the road's final curves, the camp came into view at once in front of and above them. It spread like a blotch. Almost 15,000 refugees lived here, most of them for years. They had nowhere else to go. They occupied blue and green tents that spread down the sides of the camp in all directions, marked off by flimsy fencing to differentiate it from the farmlands in use farther down the hill. Inside the fencing, the camp's inhabitants moved between the tents, into the open areas, in every direction through this forced community. A juxtaposition of squalor against the quiet, green landscape, the entire scene reeked to Conor of desperation.

After the American delegation disembarked from its vehicle, a contingent of local officials greeted them with plastic smiles that hinted at suspicion and distrust. For over an hour, the officials gave them a glimpse of food distribution and medical care facilities, which bored Conor to no end. Of course, the refugees were fed, and of course, there were nurses to tend to the sick or give the occasional immunization. This was, after all, what the government's investment in refugee resettlement was paying for. Conor felt no need to capture the details.

In one of the medical tents, he whispered to Tim, "You want to get out of here? I feel like taking a walk."

Tim nodded then motioned to the committee chair that he and Conor were heading outside. The chairman nodded back in acknowledgment, and the two quietly slipped out of the back of the tent to walk through mud, a consequence of rain from the night before, to an open area about fifty yards away.

Conor looked around him as he walked, his eyes taking a quick count. "Tim, do you notice anything about the people here?"

"Other than the fact that I'd hate to be them? God, look at this. These tents are tiny, and every other one has a hole in it."

"Yeah, but that's not what I mean. You realize there are almost no men here?"

"What did you expect? They're dead or off fighting someone else's war. You've seen the statistics, right? Six out of every seven refugees are either women or under the age of sixteen."

"But to see it is something different. Statistics don't have pulses."

There may not have been many men, but there were children everywhere, and as the two white men walked through the camp, they drew curious peeks from behind tent flaps or around corners. Some started to follow them, timidly at first and at some distance, but then Conor stopped, turned around, and through gestures asked if he could take their picture. One boy, probably eight or nine, came forward with a broad grin. He gave an exaggerated pose, flexing his tiny arm to show his muscle. Conor laughed out loud then took the picture, after which he pressed his hands together in thanks.

The two Americans walked on, but the ice had been broken. Around each corner, the crowd of children grew and they followed more closely. Conor alternated between sharing observations with Tim and turning back to the group, smiling and clapping. When he took out his camera again from his pocket, the children excitedly jumped in front of one another to be in the picture. Conor obliged them all and laughingly snapped and snapped and snapped. Any barriers had been annihilated.

The children clamored around them then, chattering and asking questions in French—What is your name? Where do you come from? Do you have any money? Conor knew little French, but he grabbed their hands and felt them reaching to his back and occasionally hugging him around the waist.

A group of boys broke off when they reached a flat field that had been cleared enough to accommodate a soccer game. One carried a makeshift ball made of rags and twine, but it was quite close in size to a regular ball. They gestured for the two men to join them.

"Come on, Tim. Let's run with the local talent.'

"You go ahead, Conor. I'm heading back. Be careful, huh? You don't know what these kids are about."

"Ah, Christ, Tim, they're kids. They want to have some fun with the funny looking white guys. Something a bit different in their lives, no?"

"Just be careful, Conor. Don't be too long."

Conor shook his head then ran with the boys to the field, and they began to kick the ball around. After a few minutes, they broke off into two roughly equal sides and started a game. Conor sloshed through the mud with them, running the length of the field and back as the game demanded, with a constant smile and much laughter. The boys were quick and fast, accustomed to playing on uneven muddy ground. Conor kept up with them, made some stops, made some passes, and had the ball taken off his foot more than once. For the first time in years, he felt as if he could run forever.

No one had scored yet when Conor broke away, conscious of the time. He gestured that he had to go, then pressed his hands together again in thanks. The boys stopped their game then, gathered around him, then one after another gave him a quick hug. Not one of them rose above his shoulders.

As Conor left the field, a crowd of children was standing by. Almost all of them were girls who had been watching the game. Watching the strange new player.

When he walked over to them, one little girl dressed in a green frock grabbed his hand. She was tiny, no more than five or six, and she didn't smile, even when Conor knelt before her and looked directly into her face. She said nothing and peered at him intently. As they began to walk, she clung fiercely to his hand. They walked back up into the camp that way, joined fast by their hands as the other children jostled around them, taking turns grabbing his other hand or patting his back.

At one point, they had to leap over a small drainage trench. Conor pried away his little girl's hand to make the jump, but before he could launch himself she had already hopped across. When he made his own jump, she immediately clasped his hand again before any of the other children could reach him. They walked on.

Conor stopped and squatted. Though he knew little French, he could fake the basics, and he asked her, *"Comment tu t'appelles?"* She stared hard at him and said nothing. *"Je m'appelle Conor,"* he said. *"Je suis Américain."* Again nothing. No response other than the intent stare, a furrowed forehead, and concentrated dark eyes. Other children pressed in on them until Conor squeezed his girl's hand then stood back up. They continued to walk that way, hand firmly in hand, until they reached the edge of the camp, where the delegation had gathered after completing its official tour.

The ranking minority congressman saw Conor approach. "Jesus, Conor, what did you do—roll around in the mud?"

Conor looked down and saw mud speckling the length of his slacks. His shirt was in disarray and had dirty handprints along the side and no doubt in back where the children had touched him. His shoes were two indistinguishable mudballs.

"I'm sorry, sir. I got caught up with some of the local young people."

The congressman chuckled. "It looks as if you've got a new friend."

Conor stopped and looked around him. Up the hill the camp flared outward to the edges of his sight, a sprawl of blue-green filth and despair. But there was a dignity there, too. From what he could see, the people here fought hard to keep alive their most precious lifelines—family, security, purpose, and peace. He regarded the mist that shrouded the top of the camp, considered the mud that shifted and slopped beneath his feet, breathed in the green of the surrounding hills, the faint whiff of unnamable flowers, recognized the immensity, the enormity of loss, and the resilience of the human character.

All around him now were smiling and laughing young faces, still chattering at him in words he could not understand, although he could make out these words: *"Votre chérie,"* they said, pointing at him holding the hand of his new friend—*"Your dear one."*

Still, his little girl clung fast to him. Tears filled his eyes. *Votre chérie.*

The congressmen and the consulate staff took their leave of the local officials. It was time to go. Conor squatted down once more and faced the small girl. "I have to go now," he said in English. There was no other way, but perhaps she could intuit what he was saying. Perhaps she could feel the unexpected heaviness in his heart.

"I have to go," he said again, and still she did not respond. "But I will remember you always, sweetheart. All the days of my life. Good luck, lass. *Bon chance*." Then he stood and turned toward the truck. She released his hand at last, then remained still while Conor walked away to climb into his vehicle, just a few feet away. The truck burped alive, and they prepared to head back down the muddy road out of the camp.

As they did so, Conor turned to look out the window to see his girl, still staring at him, her eyes tightly fixed, still intent, and two large tears running down either cheek.

In that moment, something was reborn in Conor. Amidst the despair and loss and lingering sense of death, a hole opened up within his heart, and a piece of him that had closed off cracked ajar. Suddenly, he saw his work as capable of moving beyond the bureaucratic, fallow context that had previously characterized his time on the Hill.

Conor could not undo his mistakes—the self-righteous smugness that had caused him to act independently when he first came to the Hill so many years ago to work with the senator, his certainty in what he was doing and why it needed to be done, his disregard for procedure and process. But he could learn from his mistakes. He knew enough now about how things really worked to temper the wild, youthful idealism that had nearly wrecked him and channel it into what was possible, however slight that might seem.

What mattered less now was the end result of his work, which was bound to be compromised, diluted, and weak, even if all the variables came together—relevance, multiparty interest, acceptance by a fickle electorate, budgetary realism, and a thousand other factors that worked to paralyze the legislative process and keep even a whiff of systems change completely moribund.

What mattered most was doing the right thing for the right reasons and in the right way. He would offend no one, nor would he sidestep authority or think himself wiser than his bosses. But he would be persistent in doing whatever he could to ensure that the forgotten corners of a complex foreign policy grid got at least some consideration. He would keep in mind the refugees, the displaced, and those clearly and impossibly outside the reach of any government-driven economic development. He would evaluate each assignment, each potential piece of legislation, each hearing for places where those marginalized voices might be heard, at least in a whisper. He would assess pending bills in part for what they might bring to those on the farthest end of the line. He would be a conscience—gentle, respectful, and collegial—but a conscience nonetheless. And, for the first time in memory, Conor saw that he was finding a purpose in the simple daily manifestations of what he believed, and who he really was.

Over the ensuing several weeks, the committee's minority positions subtly shifted away from an exclusive focus on policy implications to embrace at least a sliver of attention to development and humanitarian assistance. The representatives on his side of the aisle were receptive to what Conor offered, even if the sense of the full committee remained entrenched. Riders were attached to military appropriations bills requiring specific relief initiatives in targeted areas, and bills to expand embassy appropriations to include discretionary funds for community investment were regularly brought forward. They were introduced, referred to committee, amended, and in the end were either voted down or tabled indefinitely. To Conor, though, each bill, and the idea behind it, was a pinprick. He whispered to a tone-deaf collective conscience.

Through all this, thoughts of Glynnis haunted him still . . . and kept him going.

Through the years, I have waited for a sign, a hint of where you are, some shred of evidence that I still live on with you in some form. Each unexpected phone call might be you, and most days when I check the mail I fantasize that I see your writing addressing something to me.

I could track you down. It would really not be that difficult. There are few women your age named "Glynnis." If your surname was something common, a Smith or a Johnson, presuming you're not married or didn't change your name, I might have more of a challenge, but your last name is another distinctive thing about you.

I have no need to see you or even to speak with you. The thought of either paralyzes me. How can anyone reach back across twenty years and hope to find the same things waiting? The most likely product of seeing you now would be disappointment and a rekindling of the regret that now lies dormant in a far corner of a tender psyche. But to close the circle of it all a bit more tightly, I want to know where you are. Who you are.

* * *

Over the days and months that Conor wrestled with his professional aspirations and personal obsessions, thoughts of his grandfather visited him more frequently than they had in the past. The man who had been a beacon continued to provide light as Conor traveled down his new path. Conclusions Conor was reaching about how to conduct himself to help the refugees in Rwanda and people in other far reaches of the world hinged, in part, on lessons Grandda Liam had shared with him all those years ago when Conor had visited him that last time in Chicago. His grandfather's musings about love and how to recognize it, keep it, nurture it, and make it his own occupied a great part of his mind, too.

Day after day, as Conor made small progress here and there in his role on the Foreign Affairs Committee and no progress in his personal life, he pondered what his grandfather might do in similar circumstances. What tough decisions would Grandda

Liam make in a quest to make himself whole?

Liam Finnegan's life had been defined by finding his place in this world as well as by finding love. He had been the exemplar of courage and had made his way through a contorted, sometimes violent pathway to a place of contentment.

Conor had never had cause to do the same, but now it had become imperative that he do so—the urgency for taking such action had been thrust upon him against his will. He was at a critical juncture, on the verge of finally doing some good in his work with a level of measurable impact, yet the dregs of his personal past continued to weigh him down.

The lessons his grandfather had shared with him so long ago had shown Conor that to live in the present, he would have to look toward the future. While he understood this intellectually, he recognized that his heart was still struggling mightily with hopes and dreams about a woman he had last seen nearly two decades ago, that he was still reliving a time that had long passed into history.

Instinctively, Conor knew that to live fully in the now, to have his greatest chance at professional and personal success, he would do well to embody the spirit of his grandfather's life, to demonstrate that he had indeed not only truly heard what his grandfather had told him in that crumbling Chicago brownstone when he was in his twenties, but that he was now prepared to live the lesson, too.

One weekend night, after a particularly hard week overseas, back in his sparse apartment and with time on his hands, all these thoughts swirled through Conor's mind. They were underscored by the details of his grandfather's sweeping life story. It was a story about Liam Finnegan's fight for personal independence, so detailed, so vibrant, so engaging that Conor felt he could actually hear the great man's voice telling it again now . . .

CHAPTER V

We're like a magnet, dragged through the sand. We pick
up little bits of filings, tiny shards of metal without feeling
them on us. But in time they weigh us down. Their heaviness
accumulates until we no longer believe we can move at all.
But, Conor, we have to.

—Liam Finnegan

Dungarvan, County Waterford, Ireland, 1920

Mick Ryan wiped the pint glass with his bar towel and stood in silent regard of the scene around him. Saturday night, and scarcely anyplace else to go in that part of a sad island. Habit and boredom combined to fill Ryan's pub. The men came from farmsteads and fisherman's cottages. They came from the small shops in the village. They came to drink a bit, to swap stories, to share news, to smoke and, in some small manner, to remind themselves of their own reality, the stark fact that they were still drawing breath.

Mick, a lean, strong man, had learned with his trade the value of keeping quiet, of being a good listener and a better watcher. He did not aspire to own the best pub in the county. He simply wanted a successful one, a place where men could find comfort, good spirits, and companionship that was not contentious. That part of the county had no claim to pretentions. It was enough just to survive, to enjoy some degree of accomplishment.

From across the pub, a young man approached the bar. He was in his early twenties, of good feature without being traditionally handsome, dark hair and a face lined in reflection of more years than he had actually lived. His body showed the sinew of a workingman.

"Another one, Mick."

Mick took a new glass from under the bar and placed it under a spigot. He drew ale in a broad brown line along the edge of the glass. "That's another shilling for you then, Flaherty. I expect to see it in my hand before I see the hands of those who might claim it from me," Mick grumbled.

"You're a good man, Mick, and a trusting one. You know I've never stood you for my bill. I'll not start now."

Mick handed the glass over with a nod, and John Flaherty took it back to his table near the entryway. He sat alone there, eyeing the men drinking their ale or throwing their darts. The bar filled slowly with small groups of three or four.

In one such group, a brash young man, taller than the others, stronger, more handsome and self-assured, was holding forth with his mates. His name was Devon Coghlin, and if anyone could be thought to hold such effect, he set the tone for Mick Ryan's Pub. He gestured through his stories, arms flapping wildly, then lowered his voice at times almost conspiratorially only to raise it in a burst of throaty laughter at the story's end. His friends laughed with him and held on to his words as if they were their own.

After a time, Devon broke from his group, took another pint from Mick at the bar, then crossed to the table where a single man sat.

"Playing the hermit tonight, Johnny? Or are you putting on some sort of false airs?" he asked as he drew a chair opposite. His expression conveyed an easy familiarity.

"The evening's still young, Devon, and I've no need of undue company. I saw fit to wait until you freed yourself from your obligations. So, now that you're here with me, I'll cut through the preliminaries and move to the core. What news have you heard?"

"Not a word, Johnny. No news since last we spoke, and you know enough to take that as a good sign."

"No sign at all, Devon, and I take no comfort from such neutral words."

"You've less to worry about than you think, Johnny. Assure yourself of that. You've got to learn to take things as they come, then react accordingly. You can't anticipate the devil or those who work for him."

"It's not you they'll hang, dammit," John hissed through a tight mouth. "It's not your throat that will be stretched."

"Johnny, your own worry is the worst sort of giveaway. Do you not think they'll notice your nerves? Calm yourself, lad. There's scant they can do."

John Flaherty took a long draught of his ale. He sat back and sighed, looking across at the other, his eyes locked onto the younger man's bemused expression. "That's much easier for you to say, Devon, than it is for me."

"I've heard nothing, Johnny, and you know that I would if there was aught to be heard. The truth is, they've no clue as to where to look or whom to speak with. And, to tell you further, there's not a great deal of concern. Even the Brits don't care much about what happens to the Black and Tans." Devon was referring to the fighters of the Royal Irish Constabulary, recruited by the British from the ranks of the unemployed, the unemployable, and the prisons to squash the movement for Irish independence from British rule. As a paramilitary group, the Black and Tans were ungoverned by the rules and conventions of warfare. They imposed their own form of justice on staunch members of the Irish resistance—the "Fenians," of which both John Flaherty and Devon Coghlin counted themselves as members—and on suspected conspirators and anyone to whom they took a disfavor.

"Do you suspect that there are informers?"

"Not a one, Johnny, though not for lack of trying. The Brits have worked their way through the younger boys looking for a weak link. Last week, they hauled in Tommy O'Dwyer and tried to work him over. I've kept an eye on Tommy since, but he's a good lad. He told them nothing, of that I'm sure. He'd sooner spit in the face of his own mother than turn around to the Crown. They're whistling after the wind, Johnny, and hoping to catch a break. That's all they can do."

Devon stood and clasped John's shoulder in a powerful hand. "You're to calm your fears, Johnny. What's done is done, and there's no escaping it, for better or worse. We all live with the consequences. I, for one, pray that one of those consequences is a free land. But what comes to you, and what comes to all of us, we cannot avoid. Whatever happens, face it like a man. And be proud of what you've done. Don't cower, and for God's sake, don't quiver like a rabbit beside a snare."

"You'll tell me if I have reason to run?"

"If you have reason to run, then running will do you no good, but, yes, if I hear word that carries your name, I'll let you know. A good evening to you, John Flaherty." The younger man turned away from the table and rejoined his friends across the pub.

* * *

On a headland two miles away, a young man sat on the wet ground. The late afternoon sky glowered darkly, showing neither light nor break. No rain fell, or perhaps it did slightly and intermittently. The young man did not notice. The moist soil subsumed him. It seeped into him from below, ran up his spine, and chilled his core. If in fact rain fell upon him from above, it would have scant effect.

Before him the Irish Sea spread like grey gauze. The water was the color of tattered wool, worn through by years of wear. Its grey reflected the grey of the sky so that the two became indistinguishable. Horizon and sky were one, water above to water below, partners in a somber single-step dance. Waves ripped into the shoreline below the bluff. Rock there broke the inward sweep of the water, as it had all day, as it had for years, as it had since the first day of morning. Ever the waves swept in to punish the rocky shore, and the shore resolutely accepted the blows in a perpetual droning rhythm. It was an Irish shore.

The young man watched the sea, heard the thumping of the waves, felt the moist soil bleed through him from the headland. Springtime in Ireland, cold and wet. Grey, always so grey. Where was the rebirth that springtime promised? Where was the renaissance of the land and with it the renaissance of man's spirit? Where was the hope that the good sisters had promised a young boy as a natural emanation of an Irish spring? Could he see it in the sky above? Could he see it across the relentless waves? Where were the birds' songs and the blossoms that drew them out?

Was it only this, then, to be young, in Ireland, in the springtime?

How could life rise from dead soil? No amount of rain, no sun, no light, could cause a new shoot to break through the ground if there was no seed there to begin with.

The young man sat for an indeterminate time, watching nothing. The sky darkened with the day's end. He felt the rain then for the first time, lightly at first, little more than a mist, but then gaining in intensity, as steady and as relentless as the waves below. He wore a thick jacket that he pulled closely around him. With the day's waning light, he realized that he was indeed chilled—the benediction of Ireland's springtime.

He rose at last, stretched legs taut from being too long compressed, then turned his back to the indifferent sea. He could abide this headland and its lifeless view no longer. He sought warmth of some sort, but he could not begin to know where to find it. There were so few alternatives, so few places to seek it.

The young man trod back down the slope toward the village, his boots sinking into the muck with each step. He had no idea, no conscious thought, of where those steps might take him.

* * *

Maire Coghlin rose from her bath taking care not to lose balance or footing against the wet. The air, cold in contrast to the warm water, swept across her and made her shudder. Small bumps rose along her flesh. She reached for the towel on the adjacent stand and started to dry herself.

Maire loved her bath. She relished the pure physicality of it, the sensuality that stimulated each nerve end. She looked forward to the repetition of the ritual. She knew the scent of the soap that caressed her and left a soft film on the water's surface. She knew the feel of the water itself as it flowed along and through every crevice. She knew the sound of the water lapping against the side of the tub as she moved. She knew how droplets condensed along her neck, across her cheeks, and along her forehead, there pinning strands of her reddish-brown hair in silky ropes. She knew it all, savored each detail, and took it to be one of the finest comforts a woman of her station could expect.

Maire was regarded by the young men of the area as a rare prize, one of the most beautiful young women to be seen in that, or any other, county. Her skin was fair and white, sometimes in bright sunlight showing a translucence that was almost mystical. Her hair framed her face, accentuating her green eyes and full lips. As it hung down her back, one could not help but notice the delicacy of her figure. She had the full attributes of a woman, and she carried herself with such subtlety, such confident elegance, that few of the young men in that area did not carry her image deep within them.

The youngest of James and Aisling Coghlin's three children, she was the only daughter. A simple farmer squeezing a livelihood out of overworked family lands, James Coghlin knew the value of well-reared children. Her brothers, two and three years older, were strong, well regarded, and likable. As she grew, they buffered her from the sharp accents a childhood in that part of the country could provide. They were her protectors, her intercessors, her agents and brokers.

At home, Maire had tended to her mother's lessons in domesticity. She had done so dutifully but without enthusiasm. Even so, Aisling Coghlin had come to rely increasingly upon her levelheaded daughter to help her with the mundane drudgery of a typical week. At a young age, Maire had been sent to the town market on Saturdays to pick up items to supplement what the Coghlin farm produced on its own—a few eggs, some vegetables, perhaps a piece of beef or pork. Always, Maire would bring home the right goods in the proper quantities purchased at a reasonable price. But it was on those journeys into town that she had also experienced new aspects of the world that she could not regard on the Coghlin farm—commerce, what passed for the arts, music on the street corners or sometimes rolling out of the pubs, new sensations, new sights that spoke of broader avenues.

That is how, at age seventeen, Maire came to work at Brendan Phelan's millinery store, the county's finest store for ladies. On many a Saturday, she had admired the millinery shop's array of dresses, hats, scarves and silks, fashion that customers would travel from all parts of the county, and sometimes from a county or two over, to buy. On one of those Saturdays, Brendan Phelan himself had approached her outside on the sidewalk as she eyed a rich, dark-green dress on display. That day, he had plied her with compliments about her good taste and her family, calling her father "stalwart," the Coghlins "upright," and her brothers "the best among us, fine lads." Then Phelan, who was nearing sixty and slowing down, had offered her the job.

James and Aisling Coghlin knew their daughter was not like other girls, that she would not be content with farm life. She had a spark, an imagination, a spirit that was scarcely contained at home. They agreed to let her work for Phelan, and shortly after her eighteenth birthday, they let her move into town, where she took a room above the store. She was living apart, young by most standards, but purely capable of setting her own course. Most girls in the county regarded her with huge amounts of envy.

In that room now, Maire sat before her bureau and brushed her long hair after her bath. Droplets flew off the end of the brush as she pulled it through in even, firm strokes. The robe warmed her against the chilled air, as did the motion of the brushing, and a subtle blush rose to her cheeks. The moments after a slow bath could be almost as satisfying as the bath itself.

Suddenly, she heard footsteps on the stairs leading to her door, and then a knock, not sharp or aggressive but tentative, a rapping with the backs of the knuckles. She rose, pulled the robe close around her, then moved to the door. Before she got there, she heard a voice, scarcely above a whisper. "Maire, are you in? Maire?"

She unlocked the door, took the hand of the young man on the other side, and pulled him in. "Liam, you're soaking. Where have you been to get so wet?"

He answered by sweeping her into his arms and kissing her deeply.

They embraced for several minutes, lips together and arms locked around each other. Maire felt the chill of the young man's body revive her own. She nestled even more tightly against him to ward off the cold.

"God, Maire," he said, breaking away from her mouth. "You'd warm the fish themselves that swim along the coldest currents. You're a wonder."

"And you're chilled to the core, Liam."

Maire released herself from Liam's embrace, moved to her pantry, and pulled down a bottle of whiskey. She pulled forth two glasses and filled each halfway. The young man watched her as she walked the short distance across the room. She felt his gaze along her barely hidden form.

As she returned, he kissed her again, lingering at her mouth for several seconds, then took one of the glasses from her hand. "To winning the battles of an Irish springtime," he said as he lifted the glass to his lips.

Maire sipped her whiskey. "Some things are beyond hope, Liam. But what battles do you wish to win? What battles are you fighting today? New ones, are they? I hope so. Your anguish can be a bit tiresome."

He crossed to the far corner and dropped himself into a chair.

"You've been at the headlands again tonight, I'll wager," said Maire. "Where else would you have gotten so soaked and muddy?"

Liam laughed. "You read me too well, Miss Coghlin. It seemed the only place with any appeal tonight, besides being here, of course, but it was too early in the evening for that."

"So, you stayed out there through the rain because you had to wait for me to be ready for you. I think not. Don't play the martyr for me, Liam. It's all over your face, this romantic agonizing. You know, you've become something of a standing joke. 'So, Maire, does young Liam speak to you these days? He says nothing to us. Just walks by and gives us a grunt or two. Can't imagine what's on his mind. Does he grunt with you, too, Maire?' "

Liam looked at Maire and smirked. "I had no idea I was such a curiosity."

"What could you expect?" She moved next to his chair and

leaned over him against the arm. Her breasts fell forward against the thin robe, one brushing his shoulder. Her hair, mostly dry now, fell against his cheek. "You go about your work and speak to no one. You walk through town and speak to no one. You don't even go into the pubs anymore, not like you did. People notice such changes, Liam, and they wonder."

"I don't give a tinker's damn."

Maire leaned forward so that her breath rushed warmly against his eyes. "Then," she whispered as she kissed his forehead, "do you give a tinker's damn about your lovely young lady?"

Liam's arm reached around Maire and pulled her down into his lap. Again, they kissed deeply for several minutes. Liam felt his passion rise like a flame to banish the chill. His arms ran the length of Maire's back, played with her hair, felt the weight of it, the texture, the softness. He placed one hand behind her neck to hold her in place against his mouth, an indulgence, a relief for which no penance would be required.

Maire broke away then took a longer drink of her whiskey. Liam did the same.

She brought up the headlands again. "A fine use of your time, looking at a dead sea in the rain, mists blowing down your shirt, mud oozing into your boots."

"As opposed to what, lass? Sitting in Ryan's to stare at a pint or two or three, swapping stories and boasts with louts who give no thought to the coming day or the day after that? Trying to win a meaningless game of darts? Would that be time better spent?"

"It might, Liam, if it gave you pleasure. You cannot wall yourself off from your mates, from those you grew up with. You can't go on brooding or pouting or pitying yourself, or whatever the hell it is you're doing. I swear, there are times I cannot see you."

Liam felt a flash momentarily spark but quelled it. He looked up at Maire almost shyly. "There are times, Maire, when I cannot see myself—most times, if the truth be known. And you must know that the only pleasure I truly seek is with you. You comfort me in ways I cannot describe."

"You describe them very well, it seems to me," she said. "And you impart as much pleasure as you receive."

He reached for her again, this time making no gesture to fight his passion. "There are no meanings to be found tonight, lass," he whispered. "There are no answers in this world beyond Liam and Maire together, giving and receiving, playing the immortal games as best we can."

Maire rose. She untied the string holding her robe, let it fall off her shoulders, then reached down for the hand of her young man. Rising then in her grasp, he followed her into the next room.

Neither had had a previous lover, but each knew intuitively how love should be made.

CHAPTER VI

By a hearth fire still necessary even though winter had given its final shudder months ago, Maire sat quietly in one corner of what passed for her family's drawing room. A Sunday night in late May, she had taken dinner with the rest of the Coghlins. Afterward, finding no ready excuse to allow her to leave the old home and reenter her own world, she had retired to the largest room of the house. Her mother had characteristically waved her out of the kitchen when she had offered to help with the cleaning. Aisling Coghlin never stood on false or pretentious courtesies. Now that Maire had secured her own place, she was regarded as a guest, not to be burdened with what had been expected of her for so many years after the week's premier meal. Maire did not object to this new status. Indeed, even before she had moved away, she had come increasingly to regard herself as belonging elsewhere. Accordingly, this night with nowhere else calling to her immediately, she had accompanied her father and brothers to the large family room.

The room itself was enough to be considered comfortable without being cluttered or ostentatious. Indeed, the Coghlins had scant means to be extreme in either decor or lifestyle. Still, they took pride in the cleanliness and taste of their home. This room remained quietly underspoken, a handful of family photographs hanging on the walls, a fireplace whose mantel held a clock and two plates, two thick wooden chairs, and two deep chairs lined with fabric. In two of the corners sat vases with wildflowers picked a few days before by Aisling Coghlin on her way back from market.

Maire looked absently out the window to the fields that surrounded the Coghlin home. The Coghlins worked these fields, had done so for generations. They sloped away for several acres, large enough to be a notable property in that part of the island, large enough to secure a livelihood that rose above that of most of the families who worked the land, yet not so large that any future promise of ease or comfort presented itself. These lands themselves, reasoned Marie, were comfort enough. Their simple beauty whispered a peacefulness that, once ingested, was not easily lost.

In just looking across the fields—verdant, more fertile than they had cause to expect, dotted with trees that grew irregularly along the land—Maire could perceive a harmony too readily dispelled by lesser concerns. These fields, the lands around them, the steady and gentle slope down through the village proper and on to the sea, were the Ireland she knew. She saw the timeless glories of these timeless lands, the unforced union of their components that created the landscape against which she had played out the length of her life, the breadth of her experiences. It was more than a setting. It was more than a home. These lands were the physical manifestation of the internal landscape of Maire Coghlin. If she looked at them and gathered a peacefulness in the process, it mirrored only the peace that she expected for herself, the elusive harmonies that summoned her girlish imaginings.

For as long as she could recall, the lands here had whispered to her. They caressed her with unspoken, assumed familiarity. When, as a very young girl, she would walk through these fields, she noticed every type of grass, every sprig of flower, and she catalogued the knowledge without knowing precisely why. She noted the slant of light at day's end, the nameless colors engineered by an autumn sunrise, the salty sweep of the rushing air as it blew in from the sea. Her knowledge never changed. As a young woman, she knew intimately every crevice of this land, every aroma it could generate, every sound its birds or animals could create. Maire relished the comfort of this knowledge. She knew this part of the island in instinctive ways that no one else could divine, or so she believed.

This kinship, as inviolable as breath, was a foremost reason Maire shared Sunday dinners with her family. She looked forward to sitting quietly and gazing across the selfsame fields she had known as a girl, would know forever. She looked forward to watching the sun lower along a familiar horizon, to seeing the colors come to her eyes in defiance of any description man or woman might pen. The views, and the emotions they conjured, reaffirmed her. So, each Sunday she was able, she came back to the Coghlin house to share dinner, to share the knowing words of her family, to share days vaporized by the mystical seepages of time—a homecoming, to be sure, but one more profound than even her own blood could know.

Maire sat in the corner and stole her glances while her father walked to the standing cupboard near the fireplace.

"Brandy, lads? It strikes me as a special night, and there's nothing finer to top off one of your mother's meals."

Devon, the elder of the two brothers, regarded his father warmly. His eyes never failed to hold their glint. "Brandy, Da! It's not Christmas, is it? Or Easter perhaps? You're as spare with the brandy as the king with his pardons."

"Not at all, Dev. But it's not a thing to be passed around like the bogwater that you claim to be beer." He pulled forth three tumblers from the cupboard, followed by a large bottle of brandy, a rich burgundy through the glass that held it. "It's a man's way of finishing off a meal, lads. And let's never forget that the Coghlins are men above all else." He poured three generous portions, handed one to Devon, then stepped across the room to hand a glass to his younger son, Will.

"'Twas a fine meal, Da," said Will, "and this makes it all the more so."

The three hoisted their glasses toward one another in a gesture of good cheer then sipped the liquid deliberately. The brandy's heat slid down their throats to full stomachs, to mingle with the meals there and help their definition.

"A fine meal, Da," repeated Devon. "We should be grateful that the Coghlins are such men as can eat as well as we do. There's corners of this land going hungry, we all know that, where the widows have scant food beyond their own wailings of grief. 'Tis precious difficult to find any nourishment there."

"Sad for a fact, Dev, but I see it as little concern for us beyond the sadness. We have no call to make more difficulties out of what seems to flow so naturally."

"You mean we have no business trying to correct the sins that have been visited upon them. Let's speak honestly, Da."

"I'll speak honestly, then, Dev. I see no need to wave a flag that's bound to be torn to tatters. You know how I feel about these troubles. They've plagued me since I was born, in one form or another, and I see them coming to no end. It was a damnable day when the Brits first appeared on our shores, on that you'll hear no quarrel. But it was a damnable day, too, that we ever took up arms against them, and now against one another. Sometimes, I think we're a nation of cattle-headed fools."

"That's the point, Da, as I see it. We're hardly a nation at all now, are we? Certainly nothing that commands any respect that I can see." Devon paused to take a broader sip of his brandy. "Don't you think it might be past time that we claimed for ourselves what others have had for centuries? I see little radical in that."

"A fine ideal, lad, but one we've been chasing for far too long, and we're no closer than we were when we started. I've seen the troubles take away many a good man, among the finest I've ever known. The Land League troubles when I was a lad . . . " A pallor of memory clouded Jim Coghlin's voice. He spoke deliberately, very softly. "At the start, I was a fine one for the talk. 'The glory of our land' and 'A free Ireland.' Up the Fenians, lad. And all around me were the strong, bright, quick young men I knew, of whom I was one, or so I thought. It all seemed so simple, as if our freedom was nothing more than a harmless oversight. We had asked for it nicely, but now we took to rattling some bones. That's all we thought we had to do.

"I say 'we,' but it was never really me," he continued. "It was never a battle I made. My friends talked the row, and I listened. I was taken with their fancies, I admit. I cheered them and mouthed the right words. But down deep I knew it couldn't be as easy as all that. It would have to take more than a few burnings, a few landlords cast out into the night air, to remind Britain that we had a few debts owed us.

"I had never fired a gun except at a rabbit or goose. I had never even exchanged violent words with another man. How was I to go about the business of freeing my homeland against the greatest empire in the world? I grew a bit older, and the fiery words began to sound hollow. We were shaking our fists at shadows.

"My good friend then, Gerald Byrne, used to run with me every day. I've told you about Gerald, I know that, but stay with me here. It was Gerald who had the fever more than any of us. He had the fire in him that the rest of us thought we had. And Gerald was a bold lad and a fine cut. When we were young, there wasn't a race in Dungarvan that he didn't win, nor a wrestling match, nor a contest of skill, nor a girl's heart, I'll wager. At the height of the troubles, Gerald was about burning down every landlord's house, claiming every piece of land in the name of the Irish people, and finding the constabulary to throw them into the sea. Of all of us, Gerald believed it was so simple, just a matter of doing it. The poor lad thought it was just another wrestling match."

Jim sipped his brandy and resumed. His sons and Maire sat quietly, respectful of the tale, respectful of the father who told it. Maire turned her gaze steadily out the window.

"It was at the height of it when Gerald tried to bring all of us together for a nighttime raid. 'Waterford's blow for freedom,' he called it. Across the fields where O'Donnell's place is now, there was a man living named Edwards who held title to these lands, whose family had held title since God knows when, probably since the days of Cromwell. I didn't know him. I probably wouldn't have recognized him if he had come up to me at market and punched me in the gob or offered me his sister for the night. He was a stranger, a faceless, nameless man who owned our land, that was all. He was a fair man, I thought. I never heard a word against him, not that I would have noticed, but it seemed that Mr. Edwards kept his lands well, tended to his tenants without undue stress, charged reasonable rents. We all seemed happy.

"But he was a landlord, a man not Irish who owned Irish land. Gerald told us we had to set him right, that we had to claim the land for ourselves, for our families, and for Ireland. We were fifteen. A fine age for freedom fighters, eh?

"The night of the raid, we gathered at the Byrne place, out

back near the animal pens. I carried my da's gun. I was one of the fortunate ones. Most of us, about twelve, I suppose, had nothing but sharp sticks, rocks, and a surly attitude. Gerald's plan was that we would take him by sheer numbers, call him out in the middle of the night, and demand that he renounce his lands for the people of Ireland. If he refused, we would beat him senseless then parade him into town in his nightshirt and turn him over to the Fenians. Gerald claimed he had a contact. We'd be heroes. I loved Gerald Byrne, boys. I believed in him, and I'd do anything he said. He'd never failed, and we all thought he never could.

"The night came, and we crept across the fields to the Edwards house. When we got near the house, we formed a group behind Gerald, then stood tall. No one had seen us, of course. There was no one about. There we were, twelve young lads, some armed, most offering nothing more daunting than a sneer, and Gerald stood at the head of us.

" 'Mr. Edwards,' he shouted. 'Come out, landlord, and face the people of Ireland.' "

Jim paused long enough to sip his brandy deeply, to turn his eyes out the window with Maire's, and to draw a deep breath.

"What happened when he came out?" asked Will very quietly.

The old man sighed. "He never came out, Will. We never saw him. To this day, I'd still not recognize him. Gerald stood there as proud and as defiant as could be. I recall his face quite well, young and bold, as always, but that night holding something different, something older and harder—not a sneer, not a scowl, just a fixed look of iron, immovable. Eternal."

Jim continued, "We heard a shot, and the next second, Gerald fell backward, a hole blown in his chest." Jim drank again from his tumbler. He turned his eyes back to the room, back to his sons.

"Edwards had taken his hunting rifle, opened a window, and pointed it at Gerald's heart. He didn't miss. Our rebellion ended right there. The courts, in the throes of a hysteric fear of uprising, dismissed Gerald's death as defensive, perfectly understandable given the times.

"So, we had seen death. Not just a common death, like you regard at a wake. You mouth the proper words of regret and comfort then take a pint or two in honor of the demised soul who 'lived a fine, full life and sleeps now at the foot of the Lord's bed.' No. We saw the death of the best of us, the death of someone we could not hope to be. We knew it had occurred with no more fuss than the swatting of a fly."

He drank again, throwing off the brandy altogether, then got to the point. "I'll have no part of your wars, Dev, nor the wars of any man. I've seen all I care to see of a free Ireland. My life, your lives, are as fine as we can make them, and they're not bad at that. I want no part of your wars, today, tomorrow, or evermore."

The room remained silent for an indefinable time. The clock ticked softly on the mantelpiece. Outside, as the sun lowered, the evening birds chirped to a burgeoning springtime.

At last, Devon spoke, scarcely above a whisper. "No one's asking you to fight a war, Da. You've fought your own wars all your life."

"And won them, Dev. At least I've won the ones that were most important to me. I doubt any other man would give them a care. But I don't much fancy losing a son to some foolishness that in the end will change nothing, except the lives of them that fight the battles. I know what you're about, Dev, and I'd ask you, from a father's heart, to let it go."

Devon shook his head. His face embraced his natural boyishness, his innate disarming manner. "Da, you're fretting over phantoms. I'm up to nothing that's not honorable."

Jim turned sharply to his son, his face a quick scowl. "That's my fear, Dev, that you think what you're about is honorable when really it's the notions of selfish men—selfish men seeking only to exchange the power of others for their own. You're naught more than the pawns they play with, son, like Gerald Byrne and a thousand like him. Can you imagine what this poor land might be if those souls had lived, had not been chopped down to die as empty fodder for a fruitless crop? Can you imagine what talents we sent into the ground that might have made a true change in this land and lands beyond?"

"It's not us who sent them to their graves, Da."

"It's as much us as if we pulled the triggers ourselves. We chased the folly of war, of rebellion against what cannot be repelled. We may as well have been rebelling against our own natures. We may as well have taken up arms against the rising of the moon itself for all the good it's ever done."

"Past failure need not point to future failure, Da. Men work at matters as long as they need to, that's all. Only a relentless man can best a relentless foe. Besides, good Father, this all misses the point."

"The point being?"

"That you have nothing to fear for the losing of your son. I'm up to nothing that creates a danger. I'm up to nothing that runs the risk of tainting my name, of that you can be certain. But you know my sympathies, Da, and they'll not be changing anytime soon."

"I know your sympathies, Dev, as well as I know your nature. Just know that whatever it is you're about, it's no game and cannot be treated as such. Lives are always at stake, and it's riskier still because one side views our lives as inconsequential. You'll have forever more consequence here in the midst of your family than out fighting the Brits."

Will spoke from his corner. "What makes you think Devon's tussling with the Brits, Da?" He smirked at his brother. "All I've seen him chase are the town's skirts."

"That much is true, Da," said Devon. "There are better matters to occupy my attentions than the Black and Tans."

"A man hears things, that's all. You're one to be noticed in this county, Dev. There are few like you here, and people tend to watch you, even when you can't know it. I always thought that that singularity was a blessing, but I fear it may turn out to be more a curse."

Devon walked across the room to his father and cupped the back of his neck with one hand. "Da, if people seek to watch what I do, they have precious little of their own lives to pursue. And if they do, they place themselves fully in danger of being bored half to death. I give you my word on it as your eldest son and as the son of your wife."

Jim looked upon his son, his perceptive soul only slightly eased. He clasped his shoulder, their eyes held each other for a few seconds, then the elder Coghlin turned back to the cupboard for the brandy bottle. "I'm afraid I poured off that fine drink too quickly. There's more here for anyone who needs it."

Devon followed him to the cupboard and refilled his nearly empty tumbler. He raised his glass to his father and clinked it against the elder man's glass. "To the strength of our family, Da. And not the forces of Britain, Ireland, nor God Himself might tear it apart."

From across the room, Will raised his own glass. "And to a free Ireland."

Jim fired a quick and angry glance across the way. "Lad, after what you've heard, you still persist in your insolence. Drink your toast to yourself if that's your sentiment."

"It is, Da. I've seen enough of both your worlds to know that Devon's speaking for the future. I'd rather take a gamble with integrity than play safely and not know my own heart."

Devon spoke before his father could reply. "Will, every time I think you're on the verge of manhood, you seem driven to convince me that you're still a boy. You've a good heart, brother, but you don't know how dangerously it might lead you. There's no romance in fighting, regardless of the cause. I pray that you might never have to make the choice between what you call 'integrity' and silence. I pray that these troubles now are coming to an end."

"With your own help for it, Dev," said Will. "Don't be defensive with me, brother. I have no knowledge of what you're about, but I know you too well to think that it's nothing. If nothing else, there's a chance to make some mischief. That alone should engage your interest. But, unlike our gentle father, I do not condemn you or think you should back away. Indeed, I think I may continue to admire you in the guise of the supplicating younger brother."

Devon smiled at Will's remarks, took a drink of his newly refilled glass, and gestured his brother away with the back of his hand. "You speak nonsense, young lad, and you do it just to get a rise from me. But I know the source, so it's easy for me to ignore your bleating. I've done that for most of my life and for all of yours."

"As you wish, Dev. There's no shame in waving your country's flag."

"My country has no flag, Will. I'm the prime minister, legislative chairman, and sole citizen of the Sovereign Land of Devon Coghlin. We're a righteous, poor country, lad, but we carry ourselves with pride and bow to no foreign potentate."

Will laughed. "And is there a queen in your country's future, Your Highness?"

"Not a queen, humble peasant, but rather a string of royal concubines, each one finer than the last. The country's affairs must be maintained as pleasantly as possible."

"If that's so," their father said, laughing, "then you're bound to fight wars far more vicious than the Great War just passed. There's nothing more violent than the temper of a scorned woman. Is that not right, Maire?"

Maire turned her gaze from the window to the discussion in the room. Her reverie had been only partial. She had followed the conversation among the men. In truth, she had heard parts of it before. Politics, the state of the nation, the guerrilla raids—all of it bored her. It had little bearing on the day-to-day rhythms of the existence she had so fortunately been able to craft for herself. She resented anything that might threaten it, that ran the potential of disruption.

"So I've heard say," she replied deliberately, but with her customary lilt, "but I've not had experience at being scorned. No man would dare."

At that moment, Aisling Coghlin entered the room with a platter carrying slices of a thick berry pudding, thereby ending all the back-and-forth. "Here's some filler for you all," she said. "The last course."

The evening passed quickly thereafter. At its end, Maire separated herself from her family and began the walk across the fields she loved to the quiet town that had become more her own than she would have imagined. For life itself had become more her own, more a function of the integral identity of Maire Coghlin than the world around her. That happy, unforeseen evolution made all talk of this pleasant day dissipate like the soft, salty wind that blew into her face as she walked home. It did not matter that her brother had boldly lied to his father, had tried to lead him to believe that he was innocent of the political workings that had grown up among the county's young men. It did not matter that she had been witness to his cultivated detachment. It did not matter that she had spent much of the day as a silent observer rather than a valued participant, more ornament than instrument.

It did not matter, any of it, any of the things that a more agitated mind might have read as troubling or insulting or deceptive. She walked through a land that she knew, *she knew*, would outlast whatever turmoil was visited upon it by whatever forces chose to assert whatever claims they created. It was all artificial. What mattered was the salt she breathed in, the glow of a dim horizon, the softness beneath her feet, the scent of growing things, the town she approached and whose streets she knew intimately. What mattered was the life she had created—independent, as fashionable as her circumstances permitted, as comfortable as she could contrive. That, above all else, would last. In that realization lay a pride she had never felt before, a validation she would not have been able to define verbally but which sustained her every day of her new, glorious, fulfilled life.

* * *

Earlier that same day, Liam, his father, and brother rose early enough to attend Mass, came home to drink strong coffee and eat a bracing breakfast, then headed out for their work. Across Maire's fields, in his own corner of Ireland, Liam swung his loy against the clotted and soggy dirt, breaking clumps into a soft muck. Spring brought the tilling time, as it had every year since the Finnegans had planted their first seeds uncounted centuries ago. The hovering wet gray of an Irish springtime let the soil hold the winter's moisture. It relinquished it reluctantly, but it left behind a soil fertile enough to predict a family's livelihood. So it had been for the most part—the Great Hunger had interrupted the cycles of fertility, as had a few lesser spasms of destitution over the centuries—for as long as County Waterford's collective memory could grasp.

Liam stood in the morning chill and swung the long-handled tool time and again, marking his progress along the row by meters. With each blow, the loy sent bits of mud into the air. Some of them flew far enough to splatter Liam in his face. Within the first hour of his work, his hands were caked with mud and specks of dirt pocked his chin, cheeks, and forehead. The mud initially felt soft, like some type of animal fur, but it took only a few seconds for the cold to penetrate his skin. The mud held the smell of the salt air. His nostrils flared with the irritation of it, sharper than usual.

His father, Michael, a man as furrowed as the fields he tilled, and his brother, Tomas, worked within sight of each other. Rather than split the work in such a way that they would be scattered across their holdings, each year they tilled, planted, and reaped in sections, the three of them sharing the same task in an area small enough so that the tedium could be broken through occasional conversation but more often through the mere knowledge that the others were just a glance away and working just as hard.

The death of their mother and wife from consumption two years prior had bonded the Finnegan men closely. She had ailed for three years before dying, becoming slightly less visible with each passing season until one April morning when Michael Finnegan awoke to hear her cough one last time. Eileen Finnegan passed into the earth to join her forebears as peacefully as her disease had allowed. Her funeral brought the parish together ritually, but with her interment she vanished from the consciousness of the Finnegans' neighbors. The Finnegan men, the latest in a strong line of survivors, shouldered this latest and not unexpected burden silently, then went back to the business of living as they instinctively defined it. The fields that supported them would not abide sorrow, nor joy, nor fatigue.

Liam paused in his swinging to let the muscles of his back and arms recover. He had found that he could accomplish more labor within a day if he rested frequently. He would stop his work, stand in the field, and look slowly all around, his arms at his sides almost reverberating with their exertions. He would draw several deep breaths, perhaps wipe a sweated forehead, take away some of the mud, then resume his work. Often, he would try to find a scene—something common and usually unnoticeable, like the line of a birch across the way or a squabble among wrens in their branches—and memorize it. He would try to recall it later in the day, a validation of his earlier work, a confirmation that his mind, what there could be of it in such tedium, was still alive and active.

During this pause, he set his gaze on his younger brother.

Tomas was three years younger, seventeen years of age, and notably stronger than his older sibling. Tomas had great power in his chest and arms. He showed well at the Waterford games, especially the lifting. His legs were solid and firm, no slack to them at all. He could not run as fast as others his age, but he could run longer than they could. He could run forever and not tire. Those magnificent legs could take him to the end of the island and back if he needed them to do so.

As Liam watched him, Tomas worked rhythmically, his loy swinging back and down in predictable measure. Even from several meters distance, Liam could see flecks of mud fly with each blow to the ground. Tomas's gaze never wavered, never left the patch of land directly in front of him. He worked there in a row, head down, shoulders bucking forward and back, his strong arms and back propelling his tool into the ancient ground. In watching his brother's steady, strenuous movement, Liam could not help but regard that he was watching every Finnegan who had ever worked the land.

The three of them worked through the day's light. It would take several more days to prepare even this modest parcel of land for the planting that had to follow almost at once. Finnegans had always extracted their lives from the land.

It was their father who called to them to put down their loys as the light faded. The sun had fallen below the horizon, and great shadows cast themselves across the fields. A sunny day might last longer and therefore allow them to be more productive. This Sunday had been cloudy from the start. Nightfall came early; it was time to quit.

"That's enough, boys," their father said. "At least it is for me."

"Right, Da," called back Tomas. He dragged his tool across the mud to make a wide mark so that he'd know where to resume the next day. He stood straight, seemingly for the first time all day, arched his back, and took two or three deep, tired breaths, after which he hoisted the loy onto his shoulder and began to walk back toward the small shed where all the tools were stored.

He walked past Liam, who stood there looking outward toward the dark horizon. Liam let the strange color of day's close play through his mind, burn itself into the back of his sight. He breathed the old wind with its hint of salt. He felt the cool rush of air against his skin, moist with perspiration, moist with exertion. He did not brusquely stop his work and head for his dinner; he never did so. He saw the end of the day as another in a series of small miracles.

Liam thought no deep thoughts about his religion. He knew what he knew, and that was sufficient. As had every generation of Finnegans, he had been raised in the Catholic faith. As a boy, he had embraced the mysteries with reverence and awe, appropriately seeing himself as an overwhelmed yet thoroughly loved part of God's universe. He memorized his prayers. In school, he would sometimes find himself reciting the Ave or Pater Noster without even realizing he was doing so until something called his attention back to the present. He loved the lyrical rhapsodies of the old prayers. He loved the sureties of his religion, and, as a boy, doubted none of them.

The priests he knew, in his parish and at his school, were generally stern, unsmiling men, but they exuded an aura of authority that superseded any other form that entered his life. They exuded something else, too, something less definable. Of all the men he had observed in his young life, it was the clerics, and the clerics alone, who displayed what the boy Liam could not know to be serenity, could not know to be a personal tranquility authored by a certainty of their position, of their acceptance, of their path in the world. He could not know that these slightly older men had determined that their lives would leave some form of mark after they had passed, or so they believed. He could not know that these most favored of men possessed elements foreign to the vast majority of Dungarvan men. It was not their education, their facility with a dead language, their certainty of doctrine, their capacity to dispense the sacraments. What Liam perceived in them was indefinable to his young mind, but it was definite: It was their remarkable sense of self.

As he grew older, Liam found his religion to be more flexible than these priests would have preferred. He could not tell when his skepticism toward the rigidities of his faith began to occur. Perhaps when he was ten and reasoned away his hunger on a fast day by saying to himself that God would not want his body, which, after all, was a temple, to suffer in such a way that his mind would be distracted and he would be unable to learn his lessons and acquire knowledge, which, after all, brought man closer to the Almighty. It made no sense when he looked at it that way, and so, panged with a sharp hunger late on the Feast of the Assumption, a holy day, he had tempted fate by sneaking into his mother's kitchen and devouring part of a dried shank of lamb. The day finished like every other holy day, and he rose the next morning with all his parts intact. His tongue had not burned away; his stomach had not changed to stone. It dawned on Liam that perhaps all these sacred proscriptions were more advisory than regulatory. From that point forward, he felt more open to the natural questioning of the world around him, a questioning that the priests would have told him vehemently was unnecessary and in some ways blasphemous.

Still, Liam believed in God, the Father Almighty, Maker of Heaven and Earth. He believed, too, in Jesus Christ, the Only Begotten Son of the Father. Through him all things were made. For us men and our salvation, He came down from Heaven. He believed, too, in the Holy Spirit, the Holy Catholic Church, the communion of saints, and the forgiveness of sins.

He believed in much more than this as well. Liam believed in the majesty of Irish sunsets. He believed in the laughter of a beautiful woman. He believed that to lie in her arms was to come as close as mortal man could come to lying in the arms of God Himself. He believed that men were inherently inclined to do good, and that it was only the bad influences of other men who allowed them to do otherwise. He believed that his poor land's predilections for rebellion and conflict only cursed it to more suffering. He believed that the political affairs of men amounted to little, that what mattered most were the internal affairs of men. He believed in the ideals of integrity, honesty, clarity, and hard work.

But mostly, Liam believed in himself.

Where this belief arose, why it existed at all, he could never begin to say. But he knew with every fiber of his being that he had the chance to be a remarkable man, perhaps, if he were lucky, as remarkable as the wondrously serene priests that walked through his boyhood. He knew that, if he kept his mind agile, if he kept himself open to the simple marvels of the world around him, he might have the chance to escape the tedium that surrounded him now, had surrounded him all his life. For if he was born to Ireland, if he was born to the relentlessly difficult life of a small farmer on its south coast, that singular fact must only be one factor in the compendium of who he was. *It must be only a portion.*

Liam thought no great thoughts. He allowed his conclusions to come to him instinctively, wordlessly. He knew what he felt, and he knew how these feelings translated into the way he should live. He would let the consequences of those instincts present themselves to him in due course.

So, at the end of a tiring, unremarkable day in late May, he took time enough to look away at the horizon. The act itself was instinctive; he could not have explained it. He merely knew in some hidden inner cavern that it was what he had to do right then.

"You comin', Liam?" shouted Tomas over his shoulder as he headed for the shed, preparing to end his workday.

"Right," he replied, too low to be heard. In the dimming light of a cool day, he bent over to pick up his loy. Despite the mud underneath him that suckled in his steps, Liam broke into a run to catch up to his younger brother.

* * *

Later, that night, after a simple dinner of bangers and eggs with thick dark bread, and after all three Finnegan men had attacked their daylong thirst with several huge glasses of water, Liam sat in his upstairs room with last week's newspaper. He had no idea what to do with himself. Despite his physical fatigue, his mind felt restless. Too few options presented themselves when he was in such a state. The thought of the pub bored him. He knew he was in no condition to see Maire, and they had not planned to be together that night anyway. His body told him that taking a walk through the empty night would quickly turn into an ordeal. After working in proximity to Tomas all day, he had little appetite to banter with his brother. Another sterile day, he thought, and really, what had he accomplished? He sat in his chair next to his bed and leafed through old news, not paying any attention to the words that flowed through him. Old news on an Irish night.

The hour drew late enough for Liam to think about going to bed and abandoning the day altogether. He rose from his chair and was turning down the lamp on the stand next to the bed when he heard a familiar voice from outside.

"Young fella," the voice of the man said from the lane adjacent to the house. He neared Tomas, who watched him with neither alarm nor suspicion from the family's porch. "You must be the youngest of the Finnegans. I've seen you about town, you know, but we've not had the chance to meet. I know your brother."

"Aye," replied Tomas. "I've seen you about as well. It's Liam you're looking for, I take it."

"It's a fine enough night for a walk, lad, and my purpose in taking it is not to disturb either you or Liam. My way just seemed to lead me here."

"Every way has to lead somewhere," said Tomas. "You'd do worse than finding your way here."

"Is your brother still about, lad? I'd not disturb him if he's already retired. I have no business with him other than a friendly word."

The familiar voice puzzled Liam. He almost never got visitors. It was not the way of the life they all led to call on one another. More likely, friends would wait to run into each other at Ryan's Pub or stop to share a few words after Mass or in the markets. Liam waited for Tomas's call, and, when he heard it, walked out his door and down the steps to the family room, where the voices had migrated.

Behind Tomas stood a familiar form, although Liam would have been hard-pressed to call him a friend. They knew each other from their days together at St. Brendan's. Afterward, they had run across each other at the pub. They had never been close, never really passed beyond the simple courtesies. Liam knew little about him other than that his life differed not at all from his own, as he could perceive it. They were of the same time and the same place, so therefore thrust together in the guise of friendship.

"Hello, John," said Liam. "It's an odd night for a walk, lad. May always brings a chill. Shall I bring you something warm?"

"No need for that, Liam, but I thank you for the thought. 'Tis good to see you. You've not been about much of late."

"Da, Tomas, this is one of my mates from town. John Flaherty, meet my family—my father, Michael, and my brother, Tomas." John extended his hand to Tomas, who shook it softly, then took the few steps to Michael's chair. The elder man, who had been reading the *Irish Times* by the fire, looked up at the newcomer with neither warmth nor welcome, some trigger having been tripped deep within him. He slowly lifted his hand for John to shake. After the younger man did so, Michael turned back to the fire and stared at it blindly.

"What brings you by, John? It's not a special occasion of any sorts, by my reckoning."

"It needs no occasion for an evening's walk, Liam. My path just seemed to take me here. I'm glad to have found you in."

"Where else would I be on a cold spring night, eh? And a Sunday at that?"

"I thought perhaps you might be with Maire. You know, you're the envy of the entire town, lad."

"For reasons I cannot imagine."

"Can we step onto the porch, Liam? I know it's a cold night, but I'd favor a few moments to catch up on things."

Tomas sat down in a far chair with the remnants of the newspaper that his father had finished. The older man continued to stare at the fire. Liam and John walked out the single door into the sitting area outside.

"This is not an idle conversation, John, is it? And this visit is no accident, I take it," said Liam once they were clear of the house.

"It's always good to see a friend, Liam, that's all."

"While I hold no ill thoughts of you, John, I'm hardly what you'd call a friend. We've shared a few pints, as I see it, and not gone much beyond that."

"True enough that we've had too little commerce between us, but that doesn't diminish the fact that we're of the same county and of the same town, that we're of the same age. Something in all that should be binding."

"What brings you here, John? This is not just to exchange pleasantries."

John turned to look away, his eyes lost for some moments beyond the darkened horizon. When at last he spoke, he did so very slowly. "No, Liam, it's more than pleasantries. It's a need for another voice. A need for a place where I don't have to be afraid."

"Go on."

"I've not known you well, Liam, but I know your reputation,

and I know what I've seen of it myself. You're a man of character. You don't give a tinker's damn for the matters that concern most people, and you're all the stronger for it. That's what I think. And I'll tell you this, lad—even those who think you odd know full well that you've a fine mind and a reputation for being as honest as any man who walks this sorry earth. Perhaps I'm here because of those simple impressions. Perhaps I've a desire to see for myself if they hold up. Or maybe it's just that I've no one else to talk to anymore."

"Why is that, John? You've been known to have no shortage of friends."

"Friends come in various shades these days, Liam. It's become a complicated time for all of us. Well, for most of us—certainly for the likes of me."

"We create our own complications, John. No man lacks the power to step outside them."

"Aye, but how many of us have the strength to use that power? Precious few. I'm not one of them, of that I'm sure. I've complicated myself a bit too much of late, and it's caused me a fair amount of disquiet."

"That I can see just by looking into your eyes, John. You've got a demon there eating away at you. A fierce one, too, I'd wager. But your business is your own, man. I wish you to release from it, whatever it is. I fear I can offer no more than good wishes, though."

John turned back to look Liam in the eye. "You have no idea how much those good wishes can mean to one in my state, Liam. It seems that the whole bloody world has naught for me but ill will these days. I've come to suspect everyone whose path I cross. I've come to fear them. I carry with me a guilt heavy enough to sink a vessel, man, and I've no one to tell it to. I have not a soul that can give me guidance or advice or just a sympathetic ear. I'm as alone as St. Jerome. Do you know what a fearsome feeling that is?"

"I've had no experience with such anguish, John. I have no way of knowing what plagues you. I don't care to know, John, of that you must be certain. But know that you have nothing to fear by being here, and I'll listen as long as you care to talk."

"When I walked through your gate, Liam, I had a notion to share my secrets with you just for the sake of being close with another human being, to tell myself that, despite it all, I'm still human myself. Do you know why, of all the souls in Waterford, I would come to you?"

"You've hinted at it, John, and I'm flattered by what you've said."

"It's not just that. I know that whatever I tell you here dies with you. You're an odd man, Liam, unlike every other of our mates. Where they'd go running through the countryside to share a secret, you'd keep your own counsel, even if it meant assuming some of the threats I've assumed. Of that I'm certain."

John paused, standing against the single board that served as a porch railing, and looked again into the distance. Liam stood quietly next to him. The visitor at last spoke once more. "I'll be on my way, Liam. I've disturbed enough of your night. I'd ask only that you think kindly of me in the days ahead, no matter what might come upon me."

"Do you find yourself truly in that much danger, then?"

"I do, Liam. I fear I do. But I've come to you simply as an unsettled soul, and I'd ask you to think of me as that and nothing more, as a man, with all his faults and failings—as a friend, perhaps, that you might have had and sometimes valued as much as he would have valued you. For that lost time, I'm truly sorry."

John stepped off the porch and back toward the lane that ran to the town itself. "You've given me a respite tonight, Liam, and I thank you for it."

Liam took two steps off the porch to follow John's retreat. "I haven't done a thing, John."

"I won't trouble you further, Liam. Please remember what I've said, and hold it in trust."

"You have my word."

Liam watched the man's back disappear into the night, then he turned back into his house. Tomas still sat in the far chair, reading parts of the newspaper. He looked up when Liam entered. "What was that about, then?" he asked.

"Nothing I can say, Tomas. I fear John has gone to run with the wrong crowd."

"Is that so troubling?"

"It is when you're forced to leave the substance of you to cower behind every tree and bush." With that, Liam walked up the stairs to an overdue bed.

CHAPTER VII

*The gates were closed, the sun was down, and there was no
beauty left but the gray beauty of steel that withstands all
time. Even the grief he could have borne was left behind
in the country of youth, of illusions, of the richness of life,
where his winter dreams had flourished.*

—F. Scott Fitzgerald,
"Winter Dreams" in *All the Sad Young Men*

Spring passed on the south coast of Ireland with its usual
reluctance. The days held short and wet, a perpetual gray
lingering as a fact of life. Cold winds blew in from the sea.
Men and women walked the inconsequential streets bundled in
scarves, caps, and heavy jackets. They shuffled to their purposes
without delay, pausing rarely for undue talk so that the cold would
not seep any deeper than necessary. Farmers plodded through
their tasks numbly, their hands gloved as much against the raw
winds as against their chores, but still, at day's end, they would
find their limbs without feeling, icy appendages into which they
would try to rub back sensation. In the evenings, they would sit
by their fires, speaking little, and listen to the winds break their
uninterrupted rush from America on the walls of their village.
Everywhere loomed the scent of salt.

Though it was late May, the cold lingered, dispersed only occasionally by a bright sky or a sun rising high enough to reassure the passing of the seasons. The ground by slow degrees became less sodden, the rains less constant. The wind began to relent. Whispers of an impending summer murmured into the collective soul of the county. Moods brightened with the sky; spirits warmed with the sun.

The Great Hunger had robbed the county of predictability. The processes of land, the rhythms of time and nature could no longer be taken for absolute granted. When the crops failed, years running, nature became invalidated. While infants and old men starved, while women in gnawed rags begged beside the lane for any crumb before abandoning hope to sit idly, wide-eyed and slack-jawed, to wait for a hopeless death, while the best young men of the land desperately sought passage away from it, all laws previously known were waived. The sun may as well have risen in the west, the rain might have fallen upward. It all made the same sense. The land rebelled, and rather than nourish its people, it killed them. Such scars did not vanish quickly.

And so, three-quarters of a century later, summer held no assurances. The disappearance of spring, while logical, could not be expected fully. The wet times held on longer than normal. People did not speak of it.

But when at last the symptoms of summer began to appear more regularly, the people of the south coast allowed the pleasures of the warming months to consume them. Farmers entered their fields without reluctance. Their women went about their chores more lightly. Couples in the town paired off in the traditional rituals of youth. They would find secluded spots between the thin woods and the fields to let the sun play along their bodies, to smell the wildflowers, and to experience the wonders of youthful discovery. Townspeople would walk along the highlands overlooking the sea, now less forbidding, less hostile, and watch the sun sink below the horizon while painting the sky indescribable colors. The spirit of rebirth, a clichéd reserve of springtime, breathed freely along the south coast only in summer. The recognition that the processes of the seasons had survived for one more year at least fed the collective exhilaration. Fate, which had been so capricious, so damning in past years, had not chosen this year to explode upon them. Their damnations, if they came, would arise from their own hands and not those of the natural world.

Into this unfolding summertime stepped Emmett Carmody, twelve years old, and his mates, three others of his form at St. Brendan's, all residents of the town whose fathers were among the handful of shopkeepers able to eke out a respectable livelihood from the county's limited clientele. The four boys had left St. Brendan's at the end of the school day. All day, they had squirmed in their seats under the unsympathetic watch of the brothers who taught them, a stern-faced, humorless lot.

When the interminable day had finally released them, when the brothers had at last signaled them to leave, Emmett and his friends had bolted from the schoolyard. Now, they walked swiftly down the single lane that led away from school toward the center of the town. About a hundred yards along the lane, the four of them looked at each other with broad and innocent grins, hopped off the pathway, and ran headlong across the field adjacent. Whose farm this was they had no concern. The land was friendly, the glorious late afternoon beckoned them. They had neither plan nor goal. All that mattered was movement through the day, warmly drenched, legs and arms free to propel them, lungs strong enough to drink in the soft, rare air.

Across the broad green field, the boys ran as a group, slapping out at one another, laughing mindlessly, without purpose or provocation, in the joyfulness of unburdened youth. A thicket lay at the far end of the field, a copse of trees no more than fifty yards wide. It bordered a shallow pond. They all knew the place.

As they ran, it became wordlessly apparent to all of them that, despite their lack of a consciously devised plan, they were headed for the thicket and the pond.

The lateness of the day did little to soften the sun, and by the time the four boys reached the covering of trees, all were wet with perspiration. It clung to their shirts and ran down their backs and sides in rivulets. Their hair pasted to their heads in wet strands. Emmett was the first to reach the trees, sprinting ahead to beat his mates to claim victory at what was never a contest. The others caught up, and they paused to catch their breaths. Each bent at the waist and took large gulps of air. The cool of the shading contrasted with the odd heat of the day. Their breathing in short order returned nearly to normal. All four felt marvelous.

"How high up do ya think I can get on that beech?" said Dermot Halloran, pointing to the tallest tree. He was a slight, angular boy with a reputation for twisting himself into places his friends could not get to, between the closed doors of a barn or under a low fence. He was also the best climber of the bunch. Dermot skirted up trees in ways most squirrels would envy.

"As high as ya want, Der," said Mike Finnerty, too heavyset to be a climber. Mike looked away from the tree toward the pond. "But ya'll go up the thing alone. I'm after a swim." He began to pull off his shirt and pants. The others, except Dermot, followed his lead and started to take off their things.

"I'll join you in a bit." Dermot eyed the tree then tested the grip on the lowest branch.

"Come on, Der," called Emmett. "The trees'll still be there when we're done. Come swim with us."

"Sweet Jesus," cried Tom Lynch. "That poor bastard thinks he's a bleedin' sprite. Leave him to his bleedin' branches," he said, and then he ran headlong to the pond.

The three of them splashed their way into the cool water while Dermot scampered up the tall beech. Seconds later, Dermot found a branch sturdy enough to support him as he indulged his love of heights. He wrapped his legs around the limb and leaned back against the trunk, perhaps twenty feet above the ground, high enough to see the pond beneath him.

Dermot put his head back and let the late afternoon breeze whisk his face. He heard the swishing of leaves as the wind gently moved through the coming evening. The sound blended with the liquid tinklings emanating from the pond, the splashing of the water, and the shouts of the boys playing in it.

He opened his eyes and let his gaze find the source of the pleasant sounds. The pond carried a gold-based hue, a mingling of late daylight on surface water undulated by the soft breeze. Around its banks, short, marshy plants sent green reflections into the water. Dermot imagined the numbers of small fish swimming below the surface, fish he could not name, did not know, but often caught only to let go of again on summer afternoons when he snuck away from his chores.

He looked out across the pond and saw his mates splash their way into the deeper water, the places where a boy's feet could touch the muck on the bottom while the water closed over his head. Growths of weed and water mosses lined the pond floor. Sometimes, they broke free to float near the surface, tendrils of brackish green bobbing ghostlike just below the waterline.

But today, in the dimming light, Dermot noticed something else below the water. He leaned his head forward through the branches and squinted. His friends had not yet seen it. The ill-defined thing lolled several meters ahead of them. It seemed large enough to imply an animal or perhaps a great fish.

Dermot called out, "Fellas . . . Hey, fellas!" But he knew he could not be heard through the splashing of the boys and the leaf-rustling breeze. His friends continued at their wet play, oblivious to whatever it was that was in front of them. Dermot surmised that they had gone out as far as they would go. If he wanted to see what that thing was, he would have to climb down and join them.

So he did. He scaled down the tree, making sure of his footholds before taking each step. When he reached the bottom, he ran toward the edge of the pond. He called to his mates again, but again they could not hear.

Dermot reached the shore then stripped off his clothes. Naked, he waded in. The cold of the water exploded along his legs to his hips. He paused long enough to let the sensation settle, to convince his lower torso that the cold would cease and that normal movement would again be possible. As his legs passed from frigidity and he felt blood once again palpably moving through them, he dove headlong into the pond. He swam briskly out to his mates, gulping breaths as he pulled himself along.

"Fellas," he panted when at last they were within earshot.

"Hey, it's Dermot!" yelled Tom. "Come down off your perch, then, boyo?" Tom shot a stream of water between his hands at the newcomer.

Dermot ignored the spray. "Fellas," he repeated, "there's something out here." He pointed to the center of the pond. The others turned their heads. The sun, very low now, glinted across the ruffled surface.

"Sure," said Mike. "Dermot's been seein' things from his perch. What is it, Der? A bleedin' sea monster?"

"Maybe it's just your fat arse reflectin' off the bottom," said Emmett.

"I'm tellin' ya," Dermot said with urgency. His curiosity had consumed him, tinged with a faint sense of adventure. He had not seen the likes of whatever it was that was floating near them. "I'm tellin' ya, there's something a little farther out there. Something big."

Emmett dove beneath the water and took a few strokes toward the center. As he did, he kept his eyes open. The murk thinned enough to show him the usual things he always saw underwater. But then he saw an indistinguishable form, five or six meters ahead. Whatever it was, Dermot was right: It was something large.

He broke the water and called back to his friends. "He's right," he said. "There's something out here."

The other boys swam out to Emmett. When they got close, he gestured to the area where the form hovered just below the surface. Even in the dim light, they all could see the darkness of a heavy mass.

"Let's take a look," Emmett repeated, and the boys splashed out slowly. An air of caution permeated them now, an air of discovery that, in their young and so far unsullied imaginations, always seemed to point to rare excitement.

Emmett reached the bobbing form, just before him now, and stuck out his hand tentatively. The form did not move. Carefully, he brought his leg under him, then, through the shadowy water, he kicked gently at the thing. Suddenly, a large air bubble coughed its way from it to the surface.

"What is it, Em?"

"We won't know until we get it onto shore. The damn thing's big. We'll all have to take a pull. Come around. Everybody grab a corner."

The boys dipped their arms below the surface, grabbed an edge of the form, and together struggled as they dragged it slowly through the water toward the shore. Breathing heavily, they slogged back up the slope with their pack in tow. About ten feet up the shore, they stopped to gather themselves. They could see the thing now, a large sack of brown cloth.

"What do you make of it?" asked Mike between pants.

"There's but one way to find out what the hell it is," said Emmett. He looked around and found an oblong stone with what could pass for a pointed end, then he picked up a corner of the sack and swept the stone quickly under the edge of it. The cloth gave way at once with a loud tearing. A pungent odor, stunningly rancid, like the bottom of a latrine, penetrated their nostrils.

All four turned away, coughing violently. When they regained themselves, they looked at one another without speaking. Emmett nodded toward the partially open sack. Wordlessly, he stepped back to it, holding his breath. He reinserted the edge of the stone and with a single thrust ripped the sack from top to bottom.

There staring back at the boys with eyes that did not see was the moldering form of a British soldier wearing his black and tan.

* * *

Summer ended for the boys before it began. With the discovery of the body, summer ended for the entire town. It became an act of faith merely to walk the streets, to risk being run in randomly by one of the British troops that swept down upon the county.

No one was caught by surprise. It was one of the tenets of warfare: Soldiers, hated by their very nature, disappeared. When they did so, retribution had to be swift and pervasive. It was nothing personal.

That the missing soldier was a Black and Tan lessened the impact, if that was possible. No mitigating factor could totally quell the blood-hunger of retaliation, but even the British themselves would admit that the Black and Tans were the dregs of the military—criminals, really, with official empowerment, and free to exercise their most brutal instincts against the troublesome Irish. It was hardly news when one of them turned up at the bottom of a pond or under a press of concrete blocks. It was not news at all when one of them was sniped from ambush or had his lorry blown up from underneath him. Still, it required a certain official reaction.

And so it came to the unfortunate county where the poor soul of a soldier had finished his days. His name was Terrence Bradbury. He had been raised of humble stock in Leeds, near the mills. He had run the streets as a boy, acquired any number of bad habits, had in fact a not-very-serious criminal record. The Black and Tans had given him an outlet for his aggressions, his incipient resentments, and veiled hatreds. His parents held a memorial service for their lost son back in Leeds. Most of the family attended.

Standard procedure called for the deployment of a huge body of Black and Tans for at least the next three or four weeks. Aside from the obvious display of force, they would serve a more insidious purpose. They would sweep the streets at all times of day, pick up young men who could be rebels, boldly approach young women who might have rebel sympathies, and block the paths of older people who might have sired them. They needed neither writ nor court order; their very presence was the law itself. They acted on whim, instinct, and fancy. Whoever struck them as potentially suspicious could be a target. If they had time on their hands, woe be it to whomever happened along, suspicious or not.

Dungarvan lapsed into a period of subtle, unqualified apprehension. Neighbors of longstanding passed each other with only cursory greetings and rarely a smile. No one dared give the appearance of community. Usually raucous young men stayed to themselves, going about their jobs as needed before retiring silently to their homes to spend evenings behind closed doors. Young women, normally given to the ritualistic pantomimes of romance, took pains to remain unobtrusive and unnoticed. The raids would come; everyone knew that. One just hoped that when they did, they would rip apart someone else's life.

It never balanced out. It never came close to being even. For every British soldier ambushed, maimed, or killed, a dozen countrymen were punished. For every British auto blown to bits, a score of homes would be torched. Beatings, theft, the occasional rape—all this as payment for the nationalistic dreams, the collective folly of a minority of men and women, mostly quite young, whose turn it was to step forward in a cause their elders knew to be aimless, a sad conclusion drawn from their own folly. Bystanders paid the same steep fare as the participants. It was far more random than it should have been.

It began with the four boys. Emmett, Dermot, Mike, and Tom were hauled before the local commander of the British detachment, together at first, and then singly. The questioning was harsh, direct, and relentless. "Where did you find the body? What time of day was it? Who else was around? Did you see anyone in the area? What were you doing in such a remote place? What did you expect to find there?" This went on for hours, the same questions over and over. The questions lacked the customary forceful punctuations only because the boys were too young. Rarely did the British pummel twelve-year-olds on mere suspicion. They would need something more tangible for that. It was clear even to them that these four lads were only the discoverers, not the perpetrators.

Once satisfied that their initial points of contact were innocent, the authorities expanded their investigation. At the same time, they discarded rules of civility and process. The entire county fell under their martial jurisdiction. The path to justice might prove circuitous; let the trip there be adventurous.

* * *

On a Saturday morning, Liam and Maire lay sleeping in Maire's room above the Phelan shop. Summertime daybreaks brought with them an array of colors, scents, and sensations that painted that part of the island with pastels at once brilliant and delicate. The early sun filtered through Maire's flimsy curtains to project veiled and mysterious shades along the far wall. The light blended orange, red, yellow, and lavender to create nameless hues, unidentifiable yet softly lovely.

The curtains themselves twitched inward with a slight breeze, which cooled the room and made the lovers' blankets necessary. The air smelled of salt, but mixed with it were the awakening scents of the weekend village—fresh bread and sweet rolls, flowers, and the burning of morning fires. Muted sounds lifted from the street and the occasional soft conversation if the participants conducted it near the shop.

Liam woke first but did not stir. He saw the patterns on the wall, the abstruse colors there, and regarded them as a child might watch the forms of clouds floating overhead on a summer afternoon. He felt the wisp of the breeze flow across his naked shoulders and along his face.

After several minutes, he turned just enough to watch the ends of Maire's sleeping, then he gently slid his arm around her shoulders enough so that his hand touched her long, rich hair. He stroked it silently, very softly not to rouse her, and looked at her quiet face. He saw the rising and falling of the blankets that covered her chest as she breathed with the steady pulse of sleep. Morning in Dungarvan.

Friday night had been theirs, as was nearly every Friday. They had spent the time simply. After his chores were finished, after he washed himself, changed into decent clothing, and splashed himself with the toilet water he kept hidden lest his father or brother accuse him of "girlishness," he had met Maire at Mick Ryan's. They had shared two or three pints, bantering with friends or acquaintances who happened by but directing themselves almost solely to each other. The week's end, and the celebrating of it, struck them both as rather arbitrary. For Liam, Saturday and Sunday did not negate his duties. The Finnegan land knew no calendar except the one driven by the inexorable patterns of nature—tilling, sowing, thinning, harvesting. He would be back in his fields today. Maire, too, always had to tend shop on the weekends. Saturdays were customarily Phelan's busiest day. And Sundays were marked for her family, at times as burdensome a responsibility as her position with Phelan. But Friday nights carried with them a sense of freedom, the release from immediate concern, and so held cause to revel in the ways allowed them.

On Friday, after the pints had worked their way into both of their blood, when the walls of Ryan's had begun ever so slightly to waver, they had headed down the street to Maire's room. Over wine, they had eaten a simple yet full meal that Maire had prepared that morning—a lamb, seasoned with local herbs, boiled leeks, and champ.

Liam had held his wineglass up to the candlelight to watch the red change tints with the play of the light. "Maire, you know I've never had a taste for the grape until I met you. It always seemed to hang on my tongue and turn bitter. But now, I seem to be getting a grasp on how it should go down. And, lass, it goes down well." He took a generous sip then looked up at his lover, returning with a refilled platter of lamb.

"In your humor you'd be willing to drink anything with a kick to it," she teased. "It would be cheaper for me to drain some heating oil from Mr. Phelan's burner and float a sprig of rosemary in it. You'd not know the difference."

"Not so, lass. I've come to appreciate the body of a good wine. And I know you'd never serve me something so bitter, at least not in a glass." He reached for the platter and placed three thick slices on his plate, then he grabbed a slab of fresh bread. He had come to love the mingling tastes of bread and wine, the texture of the bread as it absorbed the wine from the edges of his mouth.

"So you say, Liam, that I'm refining you?"

"You'd stand a better chance of training a pig to dance. But you've shown me things I never expected to see, and I'm richer for all that."

"I like the sounds of that, young Liam. Tell me what I've shown you that you'd not expected to see."

He gestured with his wineglass. "This, for one. I'm from a family of poor farmers who prize the pint and think of nothing else. You've shown me fine food prepared by loving hands. You've shown me summer breezes on a hilltop and let me see how they move your hair. You've shown me the walk of a breathlessly beautiful woman who doesn't know she's being watched.

"And," he continued, his voice softer, "you've shown me the secrets of your magnificent body. You've shared its curves and rises. You've let me see the passion burn in your cheeks. I have seen you with your eyes closed, your hair splayed across a pillow. I've seen you reach for me to pull me next to you. I've heard the patterns of your low moaning when I hold you. I've felt the warmth of your bed and the fire of your heart. And, darling lass, I've had no cause to expect such glories. I dared not dream of them. Yet now that I've known them, I'll not give them over. I'd not be Liam Finnegan without them. Without you."

She sat opposite him, and, while he spoke, met his gaze with her own. Her eyes did not move. Liam noted the flecks of color imparted them by the candle, how their green became diffused by points of gold and yellow. When he finished his words, Maire reached across the table, grabbed his hand, and brought it to her cheek.

"You have nothing to fear, Liam. You'll not be losing me, unless you cast me away, and you'll have those gifts as long as you want them."

"And such gifts they are," he whispered, then rose from his chair to walk around the table. There, standing behind her, he enfolded her in his arms, bent over her to breathe in the scent of her hair, to see the candlelight sparkle across its flow of auburn. After a time, he drew her up. She turned to face him, and their embrace deepened. There was no more food that evening, nor drink, nor soft conversation. The day, the week, their very lives once again had attained their fullness.

Now, this Saturday morning, after the night of ale, good wine, warm food, and warmer lovemaking, Liam gazed at his lover and let the day tiptoe into their room. He mouthed a silent Hail Mary while his mind retraced images from the night before. The streets outside answered with a garbled "Amen."

He rose as quietly as he could to not disturb Maire. The cold of the floor bit into his soles. After relieving himself in the adjacent bathroom, he splashed water on his face. Its cold balanced the floor's cold, and he felt at once warmer all over. Moisture caused his hair to cling to his forehead and the sides of his face. He returned to the bedroom to dress, slowly again so as to let Maire continue sleeping. Once dressed, he took the chair near the bed, waiting for her to rouse. His eyes alternated between her face, the wave of the curtains trailing into the room from the window, the curves of the room itself, and the patterns of new light that changed almost by the minute as they coursed across the small quarters.

After some time, Maire moaned softly with the first reaches of consciousness. She rolled to her side, her arm extended in search of her lover. Not finding him, she opened her eyes and looked at the vacant space. Liam sat in the chair, smiling. She was indeed the loveliest of women.

"I'm here, lass. You know I'd not leave you without tender words and a morning kiss."

"I want you to come back to our bed, Liam, and warm me proper."

Liam crossed the two steps to the bed and lay himself down next to her, above the coverings. He kissed her deeply on the mouth then let his lips kiss lightly her eyelids and forehead. "You make a tempting case, my darling." Her arms wrapped around his shoulders, and she pulled him to her. They caressed each other that way for several minutes. Liam felt the familiar stirrings of passion begin their path up his legs and to his core.

He took his mouth from hers and gently whispered, "Your temptations, Maire, are more than any man can withstand. But," he said, and he kissed the space below her ear, "you know I've a full day ahead of me to make amends for a night of pleasure."

"For one day, Liam, can you allow Tomas and your father their share of the work? I do long to spend the day with you. I'll tell Mr. Phelan I'm not well. We could make a lunch for the meadow." She reached her face up to his and playfully kissed him along his lips, his nose, his cheeks. "We could find a place for ourselves alone. We'd have the entire day for it, Liam. Just ourselves, the rabbits, and the sunshine."

"Their share of the work is no different than my own, Maire. I owe them that. And I'd wager that the rabbits and the sunshine might be waiting for us another day, very soon."

Maire straightened then pulled away enough to look Liam fully in the eye. "You *owe* them, you say? Owe them for what, Liam? You speak on end of how dreary your life is here, of how nothing about it will ever be due to change. You tell me you're sick of the drudgery. You know for yourself that you'll never be rich from anything you do here. Tell me, then, lad, what do you owe them that a day away with me might negate?"

Liam returned her look. He sighed, then spoke slowly. "They're family, Maire, and the lands are our own. You know you'd do no less."

Maire paused then softened against him in embrace. "I know that, Liam. You're a good man, my love, and I should respect you for that rather than try to seduce you away from what you are and what you should do. But I do so love being with you, and this day looms so precious."

Liam kissed her again deeply, several times, before replying, "There'll be days enough for us, Maire. Know in your heart that nothing could be more precious to me than seeing us pass this day together in the sunlight. But," he said, and he broke from her to stand up next to the bed, still holding her hand, "I have too much other to be about this day. I'll come back to you soon, though, lass."

"Come to me, my lover, any night. You'll find me here. Will you not have something to eat before you go dashing off?"

"Thank you, but it's time I eat Finnegan stores rather than live off your generosity. Besides, darlin', what food could a man desire after once feasting on the bounty of your love?" He looked down at her with a teasing smile.

She scoffed, "The words that come from you, man. Be on your way, then, if you'll not have me with you." She threw her pillow up at him. It bounced off his chest. He grabbed it then pounced back on her to wrestle it playfully over her face. Laughing, Maire cast the pillow away and kissed him again. Liam gathered himself with reluctance to head for the streets of Dungarvan and the lane that led to his father's farm.

* * *

Liam had just left the village proper, the morning sun well above the horizon, his step light in the freshness of the day, when he saw the lorry turn the corner ahead of him. Inside it sat three Black and Tans. He slowed his step, summoning some deep reserve to keep himself calm and nonchalant despite the rising apprehension that now palpably welled up through his throat.

To not appear guilty, he stepped to one side of the road. The vehicle slowed, the driver obviously eyeing a young Irishman, strong of body, on his own on a bright Saturday morning just outside the town. Liam saw him say a few words to the soldier sitting next to him. Then he saw the lorry stop fully. He continued walking slowly down the side of the road, looking straight ahead.

The three soldiers got out as a group, their carbines apparent and at the ready. From the corner of his eye, Liam noted the resentment in their demeanor, the disregard for their appearance that, despite official uniforms, still lent an air of disorder. Two of them smoked cigarettes as they watched him walk on. All of them stared hard at the lone figure, until one at last stepped into his path, his hand cradling the carbine, ostensibly at rest but, Liam immediately noted, pointed at his knees.

"Where're ya off to, Paddy?" The man's eyes were as dead as flint. His voice came forth in something barely above a hiss.

"I'm back to my farm, the Finnegan place about two miles down." He had no idea whether this bit of fact might be helpful. Perhaps these soldiers took note of the farms in the area. He doubted it.

"And if you're just a simple farmer, why the hell would you be in the village so early on a Saturday morning? Up to some mischief, are ya?"

"I was with my lass. I was with her all night." Liam saw the two soldiers behind the other trade glances. Each cradled his gun the same way. *I might be gunned down here*, Liam thought, *and no one would ever know*. An image of his father shot through his mind at once then just as quickly left.

"Ya look too young to me to have a lass worthy of an all-night fuck. Tell me, Paddy, was she good?" The two soldiers in the rear laughed coarsely.

"I'll dishonor neither her nor you by answering. I'd be grateful if you'd let me pass. If you need any confirmation of who am I or what I'm about, you can come with me to the farm and speak to my father."

"I'd rather be speaking to your woman, Paddy. I'd speak to your whore. Do ya think ya might arrange that for us, ya filthy piece of bogshite?"

Liam's throat tightened, but his gaze held firm. He said nothing as the soldier stepped up to him, his face nothing more than a sneer.

"I asked ya a question, ya fuckin' potato-eatin' ape. Where's your woman? I think we'd like to confirm your story with the dear young thing."

"She's too fine to be exposed to the likes of you."

At once, the world exploded into a bright white. Liam heard the bone of his jaw crack against the rifle butt that swung against it with as much force as the soldier could muster. He fell backward into the gravel that lined the side of the road. His mouth filled with blood.

He saw the soldier follow the path of his fall. The soldier stood next to him, looking down at him, his rifle now pointed fully at his head. The soldier swung his leg out of the fallen man's field of vision, then it reappeared in an instant and slammed into his ribs. The other two soldiers ran to the spot and stood on either side. Instinctively, Liam rolled to his side, his arms tucked between his legs. When he did so, one of the other two soldiers kicked him in his back. The heavy boot, the power behind it, caused his kidneys to scream. Liam stifled a cry. The third soldier placed his boot across Liam's forehead. He pressed down hard. The blood backed up into Liam's throat. He fought for breath through the agony that now claimed his ribs, his back, his jaw, his head. His heart.

"Tell me, Paddy," said the first soldier now, softly, precisely. "Now, tell me straight off—what's your mischief?"

Pain seared through Liam's lungs as he rasped, "In truth, I'm up to nothing. A farmer . . . the son of a farmer . . . no more."

Again, a boot exploded along his spine. The contours of his brain ebbed in upon themselves to coalesce as nothing more than a watery mass. He fought to retain consciousness.

"I'll ask ya once more, and I'll expect a true reply. What mischief, Paddy?"

Liam turned his face to the mud. He whispered into it, resigned, "It matters . . . not at all . . . what I tell you."

With those words, his senses were pounded into blackness.

* * *

Liam heard himself groan. The sound of it, a low and guttural exhale, reverberated off the stone walls to invade his ears. It penetrated the tender membranes there and bounced in turn off the interior of his brain, almost palpable, definitely painful. Within his mind, the groan echoed back and forth, and each tremor of it brought a new spasm of discomfort. Before he opened his eyes, he took an inventory of the pain. His face throbbed with each breath he drew. It felt not his own, a foreign, puffy expanse cruelly cleaved to what was once recognizable. He dreaded seeing it in reflection, if he ever would.

His legs curled under him limply. With another groan, one that again pierced his ears and caused his mind to shudder, he moved his legs slowly back and forth. They moved, reluctantly at first, then with greater ease, but each movement sent a tendril of fire through his hips. In his knees, he heard a cracking sound.

Up his spine, a line of fire burned through the tissue. That was the worst of it. As his lungs expanded, tiny knives dug into his muscles lining either side. The pain did not abate; he could not shift himself into any position that lessened it. The backs of his arms felt immobilized by the fire of it. His shoulders sagged as if trying to crawl back within themselves. His ribs seemed pulverized. He lay for several minutes, moving his limbs slowly, assessing the damage, fearing that he would find something beyond repair. His explorations brought him pain in different forms, but it seemed as if all his limbs could function, albeit reluctantly. He felt as weak as a newborn puppy.

At last he opened his eyes. He knew at once that his face had swollen badly. His right eye barely separated, and more pain shot into his skull. Neither eye gave him a clear view. He gathered, despite his blurry vision, that he was in a small stone cell. The only light shone thinly from the outside corridor in a sliver below the door. He did not seem to be chained, cuffed, or restrained in any way, not that it mattered in the least. He was too weak to move except in the tiniest of gestures.

How long he had lain there he had no way of knowing. He lapsed into and out of consciousness, his mind too bruised to be restless. No window provided the chronicle of a passing day, only the wafery light passing under the door of his cell. No sound penetrated from the corridor. Whispering, elusive images of his father and his brother appeared before him. At one point, he thought he heard Tomas's voice calling his name, but, of course, that was impossible. He thought of Maire, smelled in his mind her distinctive floral scent, conjured the touch of her hair against his skin, then the aches would capture him again. His mind spiraled into an insensate numbness, an intuitive protection against the agony. His body caved once more against the stone, curled in a reflexive defensive posture.

It took some indefinable period of time before an echoing pattern of footsteps joined the light in slipping under his door, one set, walking slowly, sending a muffled clatter against the corridor. Liam tried to straighten his back, but the pain was too great. He slumped against the stone once more and waited for whatever this might be.

A key clicked, and then the door opened to flood the cell in unwelcome light. Liam covered his eyes, the sear of the light adding to the fires of pain. He blinked hard and felt his eyes water. The figure who caused this new pain stood within the doorway, neither moving nor speaking. He waited for the light to work its full effect. He waited for the latest discomfort, small enough on the scale of things, to complete its visit on the wretch that lay across from the doorway.

In the few moments wherein Liam gathered himself against the light, he saw just how small his space was. He would be able to stretch his legs fully before him if the cell were longer and its width provided little more than shoulder room. In a perverse way, his inability to move was a blessing. Had he been in a condition to stretch, he could not have helped but succumb to claustrophobia.

Several minutes passed, or so he thought, and the figure did nothing more than stand in the doorway and look at him.

Liam looked back as best as his vision allowed. It was a peculiar standoff, one in which he held no leverage but his pride.

"You're a farmer, you say?" At last the other spoke, his voice calm and unhurried. Liam perceived that he was not wearing a uniform. He was British, but not a soldier.

"Nothing more. And who the hell are you?"

The figure laughed softly. Liam saw his silhouetted shoulders wave with the laughter. "You may as well consider me to be God, lad. Perhaps I'm as close to your maker as you'll ever come."

"More likely you're closer to the other house," rasped Liam through swollen lips.

"As you wish, boy. If your superstitions give you comfort, then lean on them. But you'll not leave this place except through me. I can give you back your freedom." He paused several seconds. "Or I can take away the very air you breathe. It really doesn't make much difference to me."

"And what would it take to secure the former?"

"Not much, really. A promise. A few knowing words."

"Your boys have already tried to squeeze words from me. You see the results."

Again, the man laughed softly. "Yes. They do tend to get a bit too enthusiastic. For that I apologize." He took two steps into the cell. The close space placed him seemingly directly above Liam, who remained contorted against the floor.

"Unlike them," he continued, "I choose to believe you. If you tell me you're nothing but a farmer and a farmer's son, then I'll believe you. If you tell me you're in town for nothing more than a solid fuck of your woman, so be it.

"But," he said in a lowered voice, "if you say that a man your age, well respected in this town, young and strong, with many friends, has no knowledge of the goings-on of the Fenians, then I may raise a question or two. What say you to that, Paddy?"

Liam took a deep breath, then another. He looked up at the

figure, trying to look him squarely in the eye. "I say," he said slowly through the pain in his ribs, "that in truth I pay no mind to either their politics or yours. I don't give a tinker's damn about the lot of this land. It's all I need to make my own space fertile. And I'll tell you this, you self-important bastard, it doesn't amount to a pile of dung who gets to play the lord in this land. It's all the same. I don't care for any of it. Now, beat the hell out of me, or let me go, or do whatever the hell it is you want. Make up your reasons for it and make them good ones. I'll not play along with you."

The man turned away from Liam and looked out into the hallway. The light from the corridor framed his form, and Liam saw his shoulders move again. When he spoke, his words echoed off the outside walls. "I hate this barren land, boy. I curse the day I got sent here. The air here, it doesn't allow a man to breathe. It's like being smothered in wet wool. Have you noticed that?"

"I've noticed only that it fills my lungs. 'Twould be no different in any land."

"Ah, Paddy, but it is different. Air is meant to fill the lungs, to cause the blood to flow, to stimulate the mind. How the hell can that happen here when you breathe in the stench of the sea, and bogwater, and sheep shite, and dirt? What type of air is that for a man to breathe?"

"Then you'd be wise to leave such air to those that choose to breathe it."

The man turned back again to Liam. "It's not so easy as that, you must know. Even a simpleminded gobshite like you ought to know that. We're here, and we'll stay here, and it's up to me to minimize the doubt of all that. It's 'duty,' or so I've been told. It gives me a short temper, I fear. My wife hates it here all the more for that."

"A pity, then, for you both."

The man turned back to Liam, stepped inside the cell, leaned over, and drew his face close to the fallen man's. "I've got but one demand, boy. If, in fact, your nose is clean, keep it so. The Black and Tans are a nasty lot. You've seen part of their work, but they're capable of much worse. Ask your friend John Flaherty when next you see him. You'll not win this battle, you and your mates. You must know that in your heart.

"But my demand is this: Should you see or hear of any of the mischief of the Fenians' work, you come tell us. If you don't, then we'll consider you an accomplice, and you'll be shot as dead as the perpetrators themselves. Is that clear to your dim little mind, boy?"

"So, you're asking me to be an informer. Very nice." The pain under Liam's ribs seared his lungs. "I would have thought you had plenty of that particular vermin running about."

"There's never enough, boy, as long as your type holds their delusions."

"And that's the price of my freedom?"

"That's the sole cost. It's cheap enough. And you'll agree to it because I've heard tell you're smarter than the average Paddy. You value your own soul a trifle more than the rest of these barbarians."

Liam stifled a groan as the fire along his spine resumed its course. He shifted to ease the pain. "I'll not be your informer, but I'll commit to you this: You'll have no trouble, not a whit, from me or anyone around me. I've told you I don't care for your politics, and I mean it. But I'll not get caught up in the follies that are swirling about. Let me work my land in peace. That's prison enough without your bars."

The man stood and looked once more out into the corridor. He did not speak for several minutes. The cell's only sound was the gritty rasp of Liam's painful breathing. At length, he called down the corridor to a guard.

"Gaoler, bring some food for this man. He'll be leaving us shortly. We owe him a meal."

* * *

Liam's bruised form tottered its way down the familiar lane northward from the town. It wavered from side to side, a dandelion shaft in a bitter wind. It managed itself slowly, each step a conscious response to the brain's befuddled dicta.

The day shone forth brightly, and the light of the sun caused Liam's swollen eyes to blur all the more so that the regular forms of his common route took on dimensions unrecognizable. Rocks jumped at him from the lane's edge then turned to water and receded back into a purplish-black maze. Trees became lumbering mythical beasts with twelve-foot trunks and bristling hides. Sparrows transformed into eagles. The day had maintained the beauty evident at first light, hours before, when Liam had held his lover in his arms. But now the sunlight that had bathed Maire's room in butterscotch shot into his flesh like a torch. Even though it was late in the day, and the sun hung distant on the horizon, its light burned into his raw flesh like the heat from a blacksmith's forge. His head ached from the blows, from the sun, from the very effort of movement, from the air that entered his mouth, blasted heavily into his lungs, and shot up his spine to the back of his skull.

Liam stumbled along slowly, seeing no one and grateful for the anonymity of his disgrace. The police barracks were north of the town as well, so his trip back to the farm was shortened. At this time of day, the lane was empty. He knew where he was despite his blurred vision, the battered mush of his mind, and the dull throb that silently began to rise from his soul.

Within a mile of the farm, his eye caught sight of a small form slightly ahead and aside the lane. He squinted through the pain. It was a child, a small boy, no more than three or four, playing by himself near a copse of trees. The child ran from one tree to the next, then back, laughing the laughter of young children delighted by the freedom of play.

The boy paid no mind to Liam as the lame form passed near him. No father nor mother was anywhere near, at least to the limits of Liam's perception. Despite his pain, he stopped to look at the young boy at his solitary game.

The boy did not stop his play. He continued his joyful running, oblivious to Liam, to the Black and Tans, to the day's sky. Oblivious to the sad and sullen woes of a tearful land. He was a boy—only a boy, and, for one of the few times in his unknowing, unformed life, he could indulge a boy's freedom.

Within Liam's breast, an immense sadness billowed up like a morning fog. It stayed within him and filled his form with a dull, suffocating cold. He continued to look at the playful boy. Tears formed in the corners of his eyes, but they did not run out to make white tracks along his soiled cheeks. He held his tears, but he felt their burn.

No pain he had experienced during this most horrid of days came close to the searing agony of his uncried tears.

CHAPTER VIII

I am half inclined to think that we are all ghosts. . . . It is not only what we have inherited from our fathers that exists again in us, but all sorts of old dead ideas and all kinds of old, dead beliefs and things of that kind. They are not actually alive in us; but there they are dormant, all the same, and we can never be rid of them. . . . There must be ghosts all over the world. They must be as countless as grains of the sands, it seems to me. And we are so miserably afraid of the light, all of us.

—Henrik Ibsen, *Ghosts*

As Liam stumbled back to his father's farm, his brother spotted him first. Tomas saw Liam's misshapen figure edge its way toward the gate, ran from the kitchen where he had sat with his father, and wrapped his older brother in his arms to carry him through the doorway. While Tomas cleansed Liam's wounds and drew water for tea, Liam remained stolidly in the sitting room, caressing his longstanding conviction that some shred of the land's violence would ultimately leak into his family's way of life. Michael Finnegan did not believe his son had perpetrated this violence, had brought it upon himself, or in any way had played a role in its creation. But, in his view, a young man in Ireland would be visited by force and hardship, these days more so than his own. It was the nature of things. And so, his sad prediction all at once validated, he allowed his youngest son to tend to the broken Liam while he tried to absorb the reality of what seemed to have happened.

Liam remained in his bed on Sunday and Monday, seeing no purpose in showing himself. What he would show was not truly Liam anyway. He wanted no part of the sympathies, banal and overdrawn, that would inevitably drip from the mouths of those he might see. Yet, despite his solitary retreat, word of his fate had spread throughout the town almost overnight. No one had seen him apprehended, and no one had seen him released, but no one had to. The British held no stock in the privacy of the natives. It worked to their advantage to let it be known that anyone could be a target, even the most unassuming among them. British soldiers stood in the main square and snickered between themselves.

Maire had gone to Mass with her family the day following Liam's release, spent the day as she always did, enjoyed a wonderful dinner with the family, kissed her father and brothers good night, then returned to her room. Now Monday, she opened Phelan's shop in her customary way. Near ten, Emma Clarke bustled through the door in a near run and went straight to the counter where Maire was rolling a bolt of cloth.

"Good morning, Maire. 'Tis no doubt you've heard. A terrible thing to be a young man in this town these days and have to shoulder your way past the Brits and the Black and Tans and our own boyos, for that matter. Just a matter of time before someone takes a swing at you."

Maire barely heard the older woman's words. Emma chattered wherever she went. Her constant blither made her something of a village institution, a part of the background noise, like the cawing of a crow or the rattle of a cart's wheels. Maire continued about her work diligently and without expression.

"And such a fine lad as to have his head bashed about like that. It seems as if the Brits favor taking the best of our lads to abuse that way. It would do no one a bit of sorrow if they chose to swat the likes of John Flaherty or that tinker's son, Martin O'Leary. They'd be doin' us all a wise favor if they sought out those rounders. But those arrogant bastards—forgive me, dear Maire—seek out our best and think they're sending a message all around in doing so. No, they cannot find Martin O'Leary, but Liam Finnegan falls into their hands and they pummel him senseless."

All of Maire stopped at once—her hands, her breath, her heart. She looked up at Emma, looked her fully in the eye, and dared not move.

Emma looked back, and, cognizant of crossing into some unanticipated land, hesitated before saying, "Surely you've heard, Maire."

Maire replied in scarcely a whisper, "I've heard nothing, Mrs. Clarke. Tell me your news."

"It was Liam Finnegan the Brits assaulted Saturday. They grabbed him in town in the morning and finally let the poor lad go toward day's end. He was beaten a terrible pace."

"And he's recovering now?" asked Maire softly.

"As far as anyone knows. He's not been seen since Saturday, but the word is that he'll be about again soon. And none the worse for it all, I pray."

Maire had enough presence of mind to place the bolt of cloth under the counter before darting out from behind it. She had the presence of mind to urge Emma out of the store as gently as she could, claiming the need to close it for an hour or so. She had the presence of mind to lock the storefront door behind her as she whisked into the street. But those acts were the final shreds of her rational thought, the last gasps of her syllogisms. She fairly ran down the street, heading for the path to the Finnegan farm.

When she arrived, she saw Michael and Tomas at a distance, tending to some chore across the fields. She walked up the narrow wooden steps to the front door and gently pushed it open. Liam sat in his father's chair, a blanket drawn around him, a pillow supporting his head. His eyes were closed, but he opened them as he sensed the intrusion. When he turned his head toward Maire, the young woman gasped. She hesitated for a half second, her heart leaping as she saw the bruised, pulpy swelling of his face.

"I just heard, Liam. My God, man, what have they done to you?"

Liam's voice creeped out of him, raspy and timid, like a rodent sniffing its way out of his hole. "They've done no more nor less to me, Maire, than they have to dozens of others. I should feel fortunate to be so chosen."

Liam felt the press of his woman as she came to kneel beside the chair. One hand reached tenderly behind his head to caress him while her other hand delicately wove itself around his swollen knuckles. He felt the warmth of her cheek lean into the curve of his neck. He felt the first droplets of newly forming tears.

"My God, Liam," was all she said, muttering into the fabric of the blanket wrapped around his strong shoulders. "My God."

Several minutes passed that way until Maire composed herself enough to ask how it had happened. Liam told the chronology of events as best he could remember them. But how, indeed, had it happened? How had it come to pass that a single man from a single farm strives to piece together the illusion of a livelihood, seeks to embrace the love of a stunning young woman, dreams not so much of grandeur but merely of security? How had it come to pass that this solitary man should be singled out by random accidents to be thrown into a stone cell in his homeland and beaten to the point of breaking for the most fatuous of reasons?

How could he answer such a question? How, indeed, had it all come about? When did the process, immutable and omnipotent, a process now of momentum too overwhelming to be altered or deflected, a process that swept him along in its course, a process that swept countless others with him, have its start?

Did it begin with the passion of St. Patrick, the first to stamp the order of a different civilization on these shores? Did it begin with the solitary withdrawals of Columba? Did he unknowingly sow the fruits of his beating when he steeled himself against the relentless winds of the Irish Sea across the rocks of Iona? Did Liam's ribs first break with Brian Boru, or the crossing of the River Boyne by King William? Did his flesh turn purple and swollen because of the Penal Laws, because Cromwell swore a different oath? Was it Parnell that bled with him, and Daniel O'Connell? Lord knows the pain of it predated Michael Collins, was older than the bold workings of the IRA, reached back in time well before the Black and Tans. *When, dear Maire, when did it truly begin?*

Liam knew in his soul that not all the magic of the Druids could wash away those bruises. He could not be soothed by the legends of Cuchulain. The timeless lays of the minstrels could not bring him sleep nor could the exhaustions brought about by a spirited reel. He would never find solace in the bitter satire of Swift or Wilde, in the intricacies of Goldsmith, in the dancing words of Yeats. The pounding that caused his flesh to throb caused a deeper throbbing well beneath the skin. *When, dear Maire, when did it truly begin?*

Liam accepted the soothings of Maire, who stayed near him for the ensuing several days, coming to the farmhouse directly after her hours at Phelan's, cooking the meals, changing the dressings, bringing with her aromatic herbs to ease the pain. All the Finnegan men were grateful for her attentions. Liam accepted her acts and tried to convince her that they tempered his suffering. After a week, he showed her through his increased activity—washing himself, changing his clothes, taking short and slow walks—that he was out of danger. He told her that he was reclaiming his essential self, that within the month he'd be shouldering his fair share of the farm's chores, that the entire incident could well be put behind them. He told her these things, saw the hesitant acceptance of his words in her eyes, and, on that basis alone, felt somewhat encouraged. He himself believed nothing of what he told her.

So days, and then weeks, later, Liam passed Friday evening after Friday evening away from Ryan's Pub, away from those who passed as his friends, away from Maire. She accepted his distance as best she could. She knew him to brood, and rarely did she mind it. Such helped make the distinctive character of the man with whom she teetered on the brink of love. He would give her his Sundays when he could, a few other days of the week on occasion. But Fridays, for reasons neither could grasp, were now often spent apart, Maire in her room reading or perhaps out with her other friends, Liam in silent inspection of a life he had recently come to see as someone else's.

* * *

On yet another Friday night, Liam walked with his head bowed, his hands thrust into his pockets. Although summer, the night still carried a salty chill. He walked with purpose, though still not as fast as he typically could. He had seen enough of this path so that it held no fascination. He did not tarry to inhale the scenery or delve into the sensations of a south coast nightfall.

He entered the town to empty streets. Everyone who might be about was inside, either at the pub, with friends, courting lovers, or merely wrapped around their own solitary pursuits. These streets never bustled, even at the most hectic of times; on a night such as this, they seemed hollow. Their emptiness penetrated Liam's soul to cause an ache within it. It was the ache of a searing loneliness, an abandonment, the absence not only of life but of all life's possibilities. All souls had disappeared. The evidence of their existence—lights through windows, discarded papers lying at the side of the streets, the smell of a cooking meal—was overwhelmed by the signs of loneliness. The darkened front of a haberdasher, the closed and sealed stalls of a vegetable market, the very echo of footsteps all testified to life once present that had moved elsewhere. The effect was worse than staring at a barren coastline, where no life could be expected.

As Liam turned from the main way to the lane that led to his farm, he heard the pattern of quick footsteps behind him. He ignored them for the anomaly he assumed them to be, but their pattern persisted and drew closer. He heard a young man's voice call his name. Liam stopped, a wariness bludgeoned into his instincts, and turned slowly in the direction of the call.

"Liam Finnegan," it repeated, and Liam could see that it was a young man no older than sixteen or seventeen. His brother's age.

"Do I know you?" asked Liam. He sensed his fists clench inside his pockets.

"Not so's you'd remember," answered the man. "I'm one of the boys at Ryan's. They told me you'd be walking through the town or likely on the bluffs. I'm to find you."

"Well, you've done that, lad. What business are you about?"

"A message for you from the pub. A fella is waitin' there to talk with you. He sent me to find you."

"And this fella has a name, I take it."

"Aye, 'tis Devon Coghlin. He sends his invitation to a pint."

"Tell Devon that I'm grateful for his courtesy, but I'm on my way to my bed. I've had enough for one day." Liam turned to resume his walk, but the man grabbed his elbow.

"I was told not to come back without you. I'm sorry, but that's my task."

Liam looked hard at the hand grasping his elbow, then he raised his head to stare the boy directly in the eye. "If I refuse you, lad? What then?"

"You've suffered enough beatings, Liam Finnegan. I'd not choose to add to them."

Liam looked at him hard through the dim night. He was young, to be sure, but he was solid. He carried the body of the land, thick and muscular. Liam silently surmised that his resistance to this invitation would create a fairly even match. But the other was quite right—he had suffered enough beatings. And whatever Devon Coghlin had in mind to discuss would eventually be known. Liam decided that he may as well extend this night a bit longer.

"I'll come with you, then, lad. And as much as I might resent it, you've done your job well." Liam turned fully now and walked silently next to the young man back to Ryan's Pub. The only sound along the street was the muffled stepping of their heavy shoes.

When the pub door opened, Liam took half a stride backward. His eyes squinted and watered, his hands instinctively shielded his face. Smoke and light blasted through his senses, yet the pub was neither overly loud nor dense. The contrast to the dark, dank solitude he imposed upon himself accentuated the liveliness of the pub. It were as if he had walked into a wall and come flush against cold stone. He needed several seconds to adjust himself. His escort seemed to understand. He stood a few feet inside the door and waited for Liam to follow.

When at last he did, Devon Coghlin motioned to the two from across the room, his face spread in a broad welcome. As they neared the table, Devon gestured to the younger man and said, "Jimmy, fetch my friend a pint. Make it quick, lad. And thank you for bringing him here, in spite of himself." Jimmy turned quickly to carry out Devon's request. The two older men faced each other. Liam saw the cultivated charm of Devon's face, saw the eyes set firmly on his own form, regarded the smile he knew to be artificial. He slid onto the chair across the table from his host.

"I'd thank you for your hospitality, Devon, but I have the sense that I have no choice in this matter. And, if it's ordained that I should be here, then what might pass for hospitality is not hospitality at all, now, is it? You've always seemed to have the knack for showing people what they want to see rather than what is truly there." Liam felt himself coiling into a particularly foul humor. He resented being here, resented its arrogance, resented its intrusion into his solitary brooding. He found himself resenting Devon with a sentiment bordering on latent fury.

"Nonsense, Liam. Fridays are nights for the pub. You've been too long vacant. Too long away from this place and from those of us that always enjoy seeing you here. That's all. I'm honored to buy my friend a pint."

"It's grand to see that Ryan's never changes," said Liam. "I could stay away from this sorry place for years and when I walked back in as an old stranger, nothing would be changed—the same room, the same smells, the same people."

"People who you should be with, Liam. A young man has no business squirreling himself away. It defies the natural order of things."

"No doubt your sister has informed you of my moods these days. Something about getting knocked around the head with British oak that drives a man's sociability into the far corners."

The boy returned with a pint for Liam and a fresh glass for Devon. He placed the two ales on the table and, without a word, gesture, or acknowledgment, turned to leave the two of them alone. Devon immediately hoisted his glass and took a long draught. He thumped the pint back down on the table, droplets of the black stout spilling over the side. Liam surmised that he was just drunk enough to have lost the proper gauge of his motions.

"Maire confides in me little, of course. That you must know, Liam. We're two distinct creatures, my sister and I." He leaned forward and said in a low voice, "She adores you, you know."

"Then she's confided in you more than I would have wagered."

"She's told me nothing, Liam. But I can see it in her as clearly.

It's in all parts of her, and I'd be blind to ignore it. For reasons I can't quite fathom, you've charmed my little sister beyond all reckoning. I'd be most disappointed if you ended up breaking the poor lass's heart."

"You brought me here tonight to talk about Maire, then, Devon? I have to confess I'm surprised that a certifiable rake such as you would give a whiff about the heart of a lass, your sister or no."

"You seem to think ill of me, Liam. We've never been close, what others might call friends, but we've had our times. I could be hurt by these inferences."

"I doubt the gods themselves have the capacity to hurt you, Devon. You're not touched by the same things that touch the rest of us. That's been the case since you were a boy, running barefoot over the rocky fields and pulling the legs off frogs. A frog's leg or a woman's heart, Dev. What difference is there, really?"

Devon leaned back. He lifted his pint to gesture with it toward Liam. "You've not touched your ale yet, Liam. So, let me propose a toast, if for no other purpose than to force you to drink. Here's to the play of a boy, whether it be with frogs, lasses, or British oak."

Liam did not lift his glass. He made no motion toward it as Devon took another deep draw of the black stout. The pint sat in the place before him where it was set. Small droplets condensed around the rim, and the white foam bobbed above the ale from the commotion of the room. Liam moved to rise from his stool.

"I'll thank you for the drink, Devon, and you may as well help yourself to it to keep it from being wasted. If it's a game of cat and mouse you're after, find yourself another rodent."

"Sit down, Liam." Devon's command spat from his lips. Liam paused where he stood and looked down at Devon, whose face momentarily flashed away its congeniality. The change lasted just long enough to convey the serious nature of its meaning, a split second, but was sufficient to convince Liam that he had no choice. He sat back down.

"Tell me your business, Devon, and quit spoiling my time."
Liam looked hard at his companion. If nothing else, he had forced
the moment.

"'Tis not really 'business' I'm about, Liam. It's truly more of a
friendly inquiry. Concern for a childhood mate. The Brits treated
you harshly. I'd make myself sure that you're back on your feet,
that you've suffered no lasting damage. That's the range of my
business."

"I told the Brits nothing, Devon. Surely you must know that,
if that's your concern. I have no knowledge to give them."

Devon replied warmly. "The honor of Liam Finnegan has
never been a matter of question, lad. It never could be. Surely
you must know that."

"I've had no part of your doings, Devon. I've made it a special
point to stay as clear of them as I possibly can. But if I had any
knowledge to give them, it would never have passed my lips,
regardless of the beatings."

"Have you recovered from them, Liam? I've heard them to
be quite fierce."

"My body's returned to much of its strength, or so it seems.
And you're right about the bastards knowing what they're about.
They pounded the shite out of me, in various and creative ways."

"I'm sorry for that, my old friend. Just as I'm sorry for all our
boys who've had to suffer them."

"Bones heal, Devon. Bruises dry up, and the flesh becomes
whole again. There's no problem in that. I appreciate your
concern, if indeed it is real."

"*Arra*, lad, it's real. Whenever an Irishman takes a beating
for no good reason, it raises concern."

"For more than my physical well-being, I'd wager. You're
coy, Devon. You've still not given me a clue as to why I'm here."

"What do you mean, Liam? 'Tis merely concern for a friend."

"If my honor has never been in doubt, if, as you suggest,

there's no cause to wonder if I'd been an informer, if, as well you know, I have nothing to inform anyone of even if I were so moved, then why this meeting?"

Devon flashed a thin smile, drank from his ale, and leaned forward to say, "You're a clever man, Liam. You don't need us, and you certainly don't need the Brits. You've steered well clear of anything that could threaten you, yet you've been savaged as brutally as anyone could be. You sit here defiantly, when another man of lesser degree would be either cowering for fear that I'd suspected him of giving us over or begging to join us so that he could get back at the bastards. You're doing neither. In truth, I'd have been stunned if you'd done anything other than you have. All that makes you something of a danger."

Liam stared hard at Devon. His lips drew together into a thin line. Smoke caused his eyes to water slightly at the corners. "A *danger*?" he said.

"Aye," said Devon. "You're your own man, Liam. We take comfort in the fact that you're not the Brits, but we know you'll never be ours. You merit watching, my old friend. You merit a level of concern."

"If I'm not partial to the Brits, then what have you to fear?"

"Your disinterest. You know Tommy O'Dwyer, of course. Do you know that he'll be dead by this time tomorrow?"

Liam felt his heart leap, but he belied no reaction. He continued to stare at Devon.

"Tommy O'Dwyer, who grew up with us, who took his first communion with us as a lad, has seen his last sunset. The Brits hauled him in, just as they did you, and beat him silly over the dead Black and Tan. He knew little about it, although he knew more than you ever could. He knew some names. He took the beatings and told them nothing. Not then, at least." Devon stopped to drink again. He put the glass down with a thud. "But the jitters got to Tommy in short course. Every time he saw a

British soldier, he broke into a sweat. He smoked and smoked, from morning 'til night. He forgot about his lass.

"Last week," Devon continued, "to ease his jitters, he slid a note under the door of the constabulary. Signed it, he did, to make sure they knew who it came from. All that was on the note were two names. One was Terrence Bradbury, the dead Black and Tan, and the other was the name of our lad who committed the act. It confirmed the bastards' suspicions, I suspect. That causes problems for us. More so for Tommy, though. He did it, I'd wager, to clear his conscience, to make himself feel safe. It was a stupid thing, Liam. It breaks my heart to see all this happen."

"Why do you tell me this, Devon? I have no desire to know any of it. It will not change the way I live my life."

"You mean why do I give you this rather incriminating fact, don't you? To indoctrinate you, Liam. To make you one of us. You know now what we're about, at least in a very small way. But it's like an illness that starts first as a sniffle in the nose then spreads through your head and chest until you're totally infected."

"And miserable in the illness," interjected Liam.

"Nonetheless, lad, the illness has been planted. Take it as a warning of sorts. Tommy O'Dwyer said nothing to his captors when they had him at their mercy. 'Twas only after, when his overly active imagination got the better of him, did he fall. Don't let the same weakness afflict you, Liam."

"Goddamn you to hell, Devon. I've no interest in the purpose you're about. All I can see of it is the death of people who have no call to die. You seek to draw me in. Your threat means nothing to me, and I'll save my sorrow for Tommy O'Dwyer. You're no fool, Devon. You know damn well in telling me this that I'll not help your cause."

"Speak as harshly as you feel, Liam. But do so here alone. Our cause is bound to win, boyo. If you don't see fit to help us earn that victory, then make certain that you do nothing to hinder it."

Liam pushed back from the table. "Rot in hell, Devon Coghlin." He turned and walked out the door, his cheeks burning in anger. Devon sat back to watch him leave. He smiled to himself, satisfied that his agenda had been served. He'd have no trouble from Liam. He motioned to the barmaid, who quickly came to his side.

"Ellen, love, let's have another. And clear away this untouched pint. Its taste was too bitter for my old friend."

* * *

Liam did not go home to his family's farm. He did not go back to his headland, now shrouded in a deep darkness. He paced the streets, his cheeks afire, his mind unfettered and bounding in directions forged by its own momentum. He encountered no one. The streets lay as barren as time, as fallow as the days of his youth.

The days of his youth, when he ran through warm fields or raided a nearby orchard between his chores, found patches of grass where he could hide from the world and lie on his back to watch a changing sky, to capture a cloud. The days of his youth, when the greatest prize was a piece of cake from one of the town's bakeries, when the highest honor was to outrun his friends in a spontaneous footrace. The days of his youth, when a hearth fire could banish the chill of any winter's night, when a swim in the pond could alleviate the heat of any summer's day, when the springtime wind blew in from the sea not harshly but in a freshening beckon toward the coming season, when the first chills of autumn hinted at the coming holidays.

The days of his youth, when his father's laughter at the end of a hard working day could justify his heart and beat back childish fears, when he would wrestle with his brother after dinner and then, flush with a fine sweat, they would hustle their way to bed to share stories, fantasies, and dreams. The days of his youth, when a girl's wink could catch his eye and make his pulse race for no other reason than that it was freely and flirtatiously given. The days of his youth, when the land about him vibrated resonantly with power, promise, beauty, and faith, when prayers were made sincerely, the host blessed his tongue, and an Act of Contrition could be honestly offered. The days of his youth, when the gelling of Liam, the creation of his spirit, the forging of his mind, the strengthening of his body, the delineation of his heart all took place in a natural, quiet order, like the rising of the morning sun or the gentle trill of the songbirds in the trees near his bedroom.

The days of his youth played through Liam's anguished mind, and, as they did, he saw them to be idealized illusions of a life he could no longer identify. The essential core of Liam, the certainties that defined the manner in which he approached his days, the faces he met during those days, all faded into an indistinguishable, smoky effluvium. He carried the name of Liam Finnegan, but he no longer had a notion of what that truly meant.

He headed up the street and lane, his mind locked within itself, fevered and frenetic. He knew he had no ready course of action. He could not seek out Tommy O'Dwyer to warn him of his fate. Indeed, that fate may already have been played out. If he were even to try, he would be sealing his own execution. He could tell no one of this turn for fear of jeopardizing whomever he told.

He thought again and again of his father, stoic to the point of detachment. The man had been born to the soil. He had spent his entire life working it, and for what purpose? The Finnegan lands were simple, marginally fertile, and productive enough to assure a secure livelihood in good times. The famines of the last century had affected the family severely, or so he had been told. He did not know the details, but he knew that there should be more Finnegans walking the earth and working these lands than there were. Each spring, the family's collective memory caused them to hold their breath for an instant as they began their inspection of the crops. They knew to look for blight and to fear spoilage.

And Tomas, his honest younger brother. What of this poor lad? Tomas placed himself in diligent and selfless service to the farm. He did everything their father or Liam asked him to do without the usual protests of young boys who would rather be about something else, anything else. Tomas had shown himself to be the hardest of workers, a young man given to the soil and willing to embrace it with an almost religious reverence. *But what will that faith win him in the end?* thought Liam. *Diligence and hard work must have a goal, some glimmer of motivation beyond their own sake.* Tomas was a Finnegan, and therefore his fate was set. He would work a sorry land, strive to survive as comfortably as the land allowed, and measure out his pleasures as parsimoniously as a chemist pouring a dangerous compound onto his scales. In the end, Tomas would die, as would Liam, despite their best efforts, despite their diligence, despite their hard work, despite their honorable reputations, in much the same manner as would their father and their already departed forebears.

None of it made any difference. His strivings on the land made no difference, nor did his love for his family, nor his sense of integrity. His love for Maire made no difference. His assiduous avoidance of the political landscape made no difference. The healing of his battered body made no difference. Sunset might follow sunrise until the next millennium and not a single day would dawn that would author a shred of difference. An overwhelming sentiment of doom, of hopeless, bottomless doom, settled over his troubled conscience.

Liam walked the night away to sort out his fears, obsessively telling himself that there must be some response to all this. He walked the night away to capture a resolution that swam just outside his grasp.

I am a stranger in my father's land . . .

* * *

Two days later, the morning dawned as bright and fresh as a child's breath, one of those rare days when the salty chill of the sea, the moisture in the air, and the sodden, numbing cold it carried abjured any appearance whatsoever. The previous night's pointed bite had vanished entirely.

By midmorning, the sun's warmth had brought most of the town's residents out into the open. They pursued the frolics of a summer Sunday. They went to Mass, skipped away to picnics, took walks through the highlands overlooking the sea, or merely strolled about aimlessly, hungry to ingest the sun, anxious to feel that uncommon sensation of the skin radiating heat. It brought out the very old and the very poor and the very feeble along with the well-heeled, the strong, and the young. This was time too precious to be missed.

So, with so many people about in so many varied pursuits, it was due to be early in the day when someone stumbled upon the body of Tommy O'Dwyer. Shortly before noon, a young man and his lady, off with a midday meal to be taken in the meadow behind the O'Dwyer farmlands, made the unhappy discovery. The lady shrieked in true terror when she saw the body, its mouth agape, its unseeing eyes staring wildly into nothingness, a single bullet hole punctuating the center of its forehead. It had ceased to be Tommy O'Dwyer several hours earlier.

The young man wrapped his arms about his lady and led her back to the pathway that had brought them there. He calmed her with soft words and gentle caresses, soothed her sobbing, brought her head against his slightly shaking shoulder. He pretended, for her sake, to be poised, the controlled authority every crisis needs, but in truth, poor Tommy was his first dead body, too. There can be no adequate preparations for that sight.

The two of them hastened back to town, to the constabulary, where they told the bored and resentful officer of the guard, bitter that he had to spend such a day on duty, of their discovery. He expressed no surprise. With a cultivatedly serious demeanor, he stepped back into the offices to inform his equally bored and bitter partner that he had to go into the field, that something had turned up.

Three hours later, Tommy's body made its final pass through the main thoroughfares of Dungarvan on its way to Burke the mortician. The streets of the passage were lined with townspeople, out for their day in the sun, who had heard the news almost at once that James O'Dwyer would have a lasting need for help with his fields.

But the news of the day had not finished. Later that evening, as the sun lowered itself into a slate sea and the hints of the familiar chill had begun to make themselves known along the horizon, a man with the Royal Irish Constabulary, armed and in the company of three equally well-armed Black and Tans, knocked down the door of the Flaherty homestead north of town. John Flaherty sat at the kitchen table, cradling a bottle of porter, as was his Sunday evening custom. He rose at the intrusion.

"What the hell is this?" he shouted.

The RIC man drew himself to full height as his assistants spread out behind him, each pointing his weapon at John Flaherty's heart. He spoke with a deep-voiced authority. "John Flaherty of County Waterford. His Majesty the King, who demands and deserves your loyalty, accuses you of the murder of Terrence Bradbury, a member of His Majesty's service, for the subjugation of the Irish rebels."

John flushed at the words, then sagged. He shook his head slowly while his heart vaulted into his throat. "You're arresting me then?"

"No," replied the RIC man, and a volley of bullets ripped open John's chest.

Gunpowder smoke filled the room. John flew backward from the impact and sprawled across the table next to where he had stood. The porter splashed against the wall, and, as it dripped downward, it traced oddly shaped lines through the blood that had preceded it there. The Black and Tans stepped slowly toward the body.

"'Tis a solid table not to break with the bastard's weight," said one.

"English oak."

The RIC man stepped to the body and prodded it with his swagger stick. "Let's go, boys. Pile this heap of bogshite into the back. We'll drop it off with Burke. And, should anyone ask, you know, of course, that Mr. Flaherty was clearly trying to escape us. I'll draw up a suitable report, but watch your words even so."

Two of the Black and Tans picked up the corpse by the arms and dragged it to the lorry parked a quarter mile down the road. They lifted it into the back then covered it with a sheet. None of the men spoke a word on the drive back to town. Burke the mortician greeted them with neither smile nor frown. He had no use for this political nonsense, this campaigning and shooting. But he would never deny that it was very good for business.

* * *

A few days later, Liam sat on the headland overlooking the indifferent summer sea. A salty chill was back in the early night air. The lowering sun reached low across the sea-blown horizon, creating a single, giant eye that stared at him unblinking, stolid. He imagined its contempt. Below him the sea maintained a heartless beat. He looked past it, looked past the mists that flew from its harsh meeting with the rocks below, looked past the solitary, burning eye that regarded him past all feeling. He looked past the onslaught of the waves, brutal on this part of the island. He looked past the sky, past the horizon. He sought a solitary point at which he could fix his eyesight, staring at the nothingness until the sensation of sight, of comprehension, was lost, and all revolved around a single, immovable point, randomly selected, defined only by the intensity of the eye that defined it.

And the dark thoughts came to him, as always . . .

It is summer yet again, and I am a stranger in my father's land. I walk lanes I have known since my first teetering steps; they seem as foreign as the plains of the moon. I feel the warmth of a noonday sun; it burns my skin like acid. Birds' songs waft through dense air in tones of lead. The river runs brackish and gray. Along its banks the willows hang limp, flaccid, and near dead. I hear the voices of young men I have known since boyhood; they speak in tongues. Their eyes tell tales I cannot fathom. Their hands make gestures I do not know. I am a stranger in my father's land.

A definable moment, a pass of time, leavened by circumstance and driven by man's deepest demons, to turn the familiar base and to rob the very air of its meaning, after which life itself filters through a strange prism to create colors and shapes beyond our dimension. All that has come before is merely prelude to the reality of the ensuing days.

Liam sat there in a place he had come to regard as more familiar than ever he had wanted it to be. For the duration of the evening, hardly a single cogent thought passed through him, save for the litany that beat its repetition into his consciousness the way a tanner imprints his leather . . .

I am a stranger in my father's land. I am a stranger here, in my father's land.

With that sad litany, Liam at last faced an inevitable conclusion. It was time, then. He rose from his damp promontory and walked slowly back through the town to the Finnegan lands, now as foreign to his unsettled soul as the Siberian steppes or the magnificent heights of the Andes.

A light rain began to fall. By the time he reached the far side of the village, it had grown heavy enough to make his footsteps thick and sloppy. He took the final steps up the lane to his family's farm with effort, the muddy earth sucking back each step. When he reached his gate, the rain stopped.

CHAPTER IX

*I will not serve in which I no longer believe whether it call
itself my home, my fatherland or my church: and I will try
to express myself in some mode of life or art as freely as I can
and as wholly as I can, using for my defence the only arms
I allow myself to use—silence, exile and cunning.*

— James Joyce,
The Portrait of an Artist as a Young Man

Maire rolled onto her side and draped a long arm across
Liam's sleeping shoulders. The bruises there, deep and
harsh, had damaged the soft tissue underneath. The
skin still held a sick green hue, weeks after the purple had faded.
Since the beating, Liam had not lifted his right arm above his ear.
Nor had he spent much time in sport or play in Maire's bed. He
talked little, laughed less. While he had never been meaty, his
frame had lost much of its definition. Maire easily felt Liam's ribs,
protrusions that seemed almost grotesque as they flayed outward
from his resting form. She ran a finger the length of his side and
wondered at the muscles, the bones, the tender organs they tried
to protect. What damage, lad, to all of it. What sad damage.

On this Saturday morning, she regarded the night they had
just spent together as special, a hint of a return to something

the British had beaten away. *Could there be a diminution of the splendid spirit of Liam Finnegan?* she considered. *Is my man frail and flimsy of character? Will the blows and taunts of British strangers drive away the distinctive tone of mind and heart that defined him?*

The bruises would heal, the bones would strengthen. As certainly as the physical processes would overcome that sad day, Maire was no less convinced that the psychological bruises would heal as well. Liam would return. He had to, for she had seen his remarkable character, the inner strength that gave him a quiet confidence and an unshakable integrity. While she knew him to be a handsome man, so overwhelming had been her attraction to his soul that his physicality seemed puny.

She could not deny that Liam had withdrawn from those around him in the intervening days. She could not deny that he had withdrawn from her, although she carried on with her loving attentions, trying not to allow herself to be distanced, convincing herself that his absence, and his silence when that absence was breached, would be temporary, necessary defenses against the trauma he had suffered. Liam had not been gruff with her, nor short, nor rude. He had merely been somewhere else. That alone confirmed in Maire's thoughts that Liam's gentle, caring nature was intact and merely hiding for a while. If hiding, then it must someday reemerge.

But the wait for that reemergence had not been easy or simple. Maire's whole rhythm gravitated to Liam's. She rose each morning with a prayer on her lips for her man, that his day be sweet and full. His image permeated her day, followed her through her responsibilities, stepped lightly behind her own footfall. She had come to count hours between the times they were together. When she saw him, instantly she knew his mood, whether it was buoyant or pensive or quiet or simply content, and it came to echo her own. She adapted her own thoughts and feelings to what she saw in Liam. Maire had always carried herself with an air of pride, bordering on a gingerly assertive independence, but her heart willingly ceded those tendencies to be within Liam's gentle, exciting orbit.

Of late, on the days that Liam would usually come to her in the morning and they would spend their time walking near the headlands, or rummaging through Dungarvan's shops, perhaps taking a meal together, or, if the day were warm enough, splashing along the beaches, he possessed none of his playfulness and little of his wonder. Along the headlands, he would often go on before her, find a pitch of grass, and sit to look out to the sea, seemingly heedless of whether Maire would join him there. When she did, lowering herself next to him on the damp ground, he would often take her hand, wordlessly and without moving his eyes from the sea. There they would sit for uncounted time, until the day drew short and the sun, if there was one, dipped low along the waterline or the clouds' dreary borders blocked the light.

On nights when she made him dinner, they would sit across the table in their usual places, but their talk rang low, subdued, and almost guarded. Liam did not venture into vulnerable territory. Conversation that customarily rang off the walls and ranged freely, joyously, from topic to topic now marched steadily without any of the customary high-stepping, a sodden parade of words cadenced by neither deep thought nor deep feeling. An obligation it seemed. A way to fill the time.

What, then, would Liam really have to say to her? She knew her man well enough to know that his gentle soul percolated, twisting back upon itself, suppressing . . . what? Anguish, yes, but in what form, and for what cause? Humiliation? Disillusion? Or had Liam begun to abrogate the tender core of his proud character? She ached to know what changes lay afoot, but she dare not press him. Her role placed her at his side, to be used, to be leaned upon, to reassure. She would not challenge him to show his thoughts. Her faith told her that it would all be apparent in time, that Liam needed his days to recalibrate what he had seen and what he saw now, to measure once again the length and breadth of the land, the length and breadth of his deeply bruised soul.

Maire would not think to confront Liam concerning these changes. *The man needs time*, she told herself, *and I am here for him. I shall always be here for him.*

When darkness came, the meals were done, and time stood still once more, they would find themselves in Maire's bed, their lovemaking the arc of their evenings, the point to which everything else aspired. Liam had always been a patient, gentle lover. His attention to Maire's body bordered on the reverential. With hushed wonder, he would trace his hands along her curves and valleys, caress her hair, lovingly stroke the side of her face with a single finger, amazed at the marvelous fortune that had placed him once more in the embrace of a woman so lovely, so attuned with his own soul. Their nights had sought no end. There was never a rush, nor a misplaced word or gesture.

In bed, Liam remained as he had been, his adoration for Maire obvious, his movements comforting, at times dynamic. But during the peak of their passion, he drove as much into himself as he did into Maire. At first, this slightly alarmed her, for Liam seemed possessed by a force she had not seen before. His head would pull back as his hips thrust forward, his eyes shut tight, and, at the moment of climax, a cry, a wail, really, would fill the room and rise from some deep, hidden place that housed power and pride and fury, and that most overwhelming of forces, fear.

The night before had followed the recent pattern. When Maire drifted to sleep, her limbs twitched in the aftereffects of such powerful lovemaking, and her thoughts passed backward to the headlands, to the profile of her handsome, brooding lover staring across water at what she could not even hope to see. Now, she raised herself enough to look at his sleeping form, ran her hand down his side, leaned over to kiss his still sleeping cheek, then made her way to the toilet.

Upon her return, Liam had brought himself awake and sat upright, the covers falling around his waist so that his strong chest and arms were exposed to the morning cold. She smiled upon seeing him.

"Good morning, my fine man," she cooed, leaning down again to find his lips. She kissed him gently. Liam grabbed the back of her neck and pulled her around to the bed, where she fell on the covers beside him. He held his hand there, bent down, and kissed her deeply in response.

"So good you are to me, Maire Coghlin, and me so unworthy," he whispered. She looked him fully in his eyes, rubbed her hand along his cheek. "Hush, lad," she said. "There's not a worthier man in this whole sad island. You must know that, Liam. Please, please, please do not doubt yourself. Never doubt who and what you are."

"Ah, Maire, but what is that in the end? Just another gobshite." But he said this with a small laugh. "Where do we go from here, darling girl? What promises make our tomorrows any different from our yesterdays? We're born to this, you know. All of it."

"Then perhaps we are born to each other." She nestled closely against him. "There's comfort enough in that. There's enough in that to make our tomorrows worth treasuring."

Liam did not reply. Instead, he burrowed his face into the curve of her neck and tightened his arms around her small, firm shoulders. *But, no, lass. I'll not press the point. I do not treasure my tomorrows*, he thought. *It is only the present that keeps me alive.*

* * *

Later that day, Liam found himself alone, looking out over the water.

I watch the dark sea, smell its dark waves, and look outward. The land ends to the south, so what lies across these waves is the northern coast of Spain, where it turns its corner with Portugal. Are the rocks that mark that land high, and do they stretch in whiteness east to west? Do the birds there sound the same on cold mornings as they do here, the hushed, quieted chirping that speaks as much of fear and uncertainty as it does of morning light? Does a low sunset bounce off the sand and blind the eye? What truly lies on the other side of this water?

Or if I turn my head to my right, what might lie in that direction? The great Atlantic, the waters increasingly cold, increasingly lonely, near Iceland and around Greenland until they wash against the mysterious coastlands of Canada, and farther south the States. "Amerikay," the land that has already claimed so many thousands of us, a land that may well be as much Ireland as Ireland itself.

I do not believe in the myths I have been told. I hold no stock in fantasies. I cannot believe there is a Land of Milk and Honey, or a Land of Opportunity, or The Place Where Dreams Come True. We build our own dreams, then let time wear them down. We cling to our fantasies and, in our obsessions, ignore the realities around us. I'll have none of that. I do not believe that life in America is easy, or gifted, or that we shall be limited only by our imaginations, hamstrung only by our lack of effort. There is more to it than that. The difficulties I know here cannot be erased by distance.

So, if there are no more myths, I cannot know what is out there. I cannot be certain what lies across these dark waters in any direction, for I have not been there, have not walked the lands nor met the people. I have seen no sunrise that has not warmed an Irish soil. I cannot know what is there.

But I know what is here, of that I am certain. I know this land and these people. I know the sadness that no ceilidh can mask, that no song can drown. We are a fated land, born in the blood of oppressed generations, smothered by centuries of superstition. Character has little worth in the face of such conditions. A single man means no more than a rock along this shoreline and can be swept away as easily, no matter how strong his core. I have seen it too often. I have felt it. I know, too, that what is here now shall always be here. I am what my fathers were and what my sons shall be. I have consigned them, my beloved unborn sons, to my same fate.

As men, we cling to our dreams, but we must also cling to our hopes, which dreams in their fantastic, intoxicating visions can obscure. I seek the clarity of hope, the specificity of potential. I shall not yield to either the stagnation of the day nor the reveries of cultivated visions. The best we can ask for ourselves is that we define ourselves through our own character. All failures and all successes are then our own, and we consign neither ourselves nor our heirs to anything other than the product of their own labors. I shall not pass this sentence that haunts me onto the innocent lives that must follow.

This is a dying land, in which I am now a stranger. And death shall be visited not only upon ourselves. The sins of the fathers, we must expunge them.

* * *

Devon Coghlin stuffed the package into his coat pocket then pulled the coat tightly about him. He placed his hand into the pocket opposite and felt the heft of the Webley revolver. Of late, Devon had made the Webley a constant companion. Tensions had risen, this he knew. The Black and Tans had not gone away, had in fact become more aggressive and less judicious in their choice of targets. Devon was aware of their suspicions, and he had no intention of indulging his vulnerability. So far, they had kept their distance. He tried to remain as visible as possible, both to instill an element of doubt in his enemies and to deepen his presence among his friends. Transparency, or at least the illusion of it, tended to confuse pursuers.

Even so, Devon knew enough to stay cautious. These trips were as necessary as they were regular, but he would cut no corners. His route changed each time, as did his contacts. He left at different times of the day, although almost always at night. He never wore the same set of clothing twice, nor did he stop en route for a pint, a shag, or a conversation. He remained as quiet as he could, would be invisible altogether if he had the power, but lacking that power, he strove to be completely nondescript, just another figure on a lonely country road.

In any war, guns are essential, and this clearly was war. The Brits had a decided edge in armaments. Devon and his mates felt constantly as if they were running uphill, striving to score enough firepower to at least come close to evening the odds. The insurrection carried on through passion and commitment and, for some, a foolish belief in divine providence. Devon prided himself in the realization that he and his band seemed to have an instinctive talent for rebellion.

But they could not satisfy this talent without guns, and guns were always in short supply. Networks existed, though, filled with sympathizers, idealists, and profiteers who saw the chance to turn civil violence into a fortuitous new income. It had not taken long for Devon to penetrate these networks, employing his charm, his agile tongue, and a fair amount of coin, to make himself known and reasonably trusted. He had quickly developed a pipeline for the arms that fed the process.

Most of the guns he procured he exported to other groups operative in the West. He had supplied arms to battalions in Cork, Kerry, and Limerick. Once, several months ago, he had helped supply a ragtag group forming itself as far away as Athlone in the midlands. The market surged, and Devon easily recouped his regular outlays for the arms that fed the fight for freedom. He had, in fact, begun to turn a rather significant profit himself. Still, that was nothing more than a happy byproduct. It was the fight that mattered.

This night, he had waited at Ryan's Pub, where he spent part of most of his nights. He had done the usual things his pub inspired: a couple of pints, some talk and laughter with his friends, slightly louder than normal, a large measure of flirting with the girls. He had been seen by the right people, and the pints relaxed him. From Ryan's he had gone home, where he remained until near midnight. There, he had made his preparations, checking from time to time out his window to ensure that the town's pulse had slackened, that all was hushed and silent.

Now, it was after midnight, and he padded quietly downstairs in the dark, his family asleep and all lights well out. Tonight's trip would not be long. This was local, his contact in Butlerstown, a few miles down the road. He did not know the man's name. He seldom did, an acknowledgment of the safety of anonymity. Word passed in code, and names transformed into cryptic monosyllables—"Ark" or "Wex" or "Cobh"—or sometimes just letters. Transactions always took place at night, in faraway corners uncommonly traveled. This was the way of doing business.

Once the exchange was made, he would make his way back to Dungarvan as unobtrusively as possible. No guns ever changed hands during these meetings. Devon would pay and would receive in turn the instructions for picking up the arms, where they would be left, and how they would be hidden. It would take three or four men to gather up each shipment, wrap them or box them accordingly, then hide them in wagons or carts to be transported under the guise of farm produce, or feed for the cattle, or even manure for fertilizing. Often, he would enlist young women to drive the carts. The Black and Tans were less likely to suspect the women, although they might harass them for other reasons. They never looked into the carts.

Tonight, he would not have to ride, and if he hurried, he would be back well before daybreak. Devon preferred to walk rather than ride. Horses, no matter how well trained, made noise, and he would always have to have a cultivated excuse at the ready should he be stopped or challenged late at night. He'd gladly exchange a few hours of sleep for the insulation of traveling by foot.

The night was well lit, clear, and slightly chilled. Enough moon shone forth to illuminate the path west from Waterford proper. The town's lights blinked off in succession, the streets deserted and no sounds emanated from the shut houses. In the distance, the Comeragh Mountains stood in silent outline, the moonlight tracing their silhouette. Ryan's still carried a clamor, but it was blocks behind him. He was as close to invisible, he thought, as a soul could be. He passed onto Cork Road quietly and made his way through.

The Outer Ring looped the city, and past it were the farmlands, where almost all life shut down with the passing of the sun. Devon considered himself a man of the city, sophisticated, and reasonably well educated, but he nonetheless loved the countryside on this part of the island. The fertile ground retained an abnormal green, seemingly the year round, and the scent of the ocean permeated every breath. Simplicity and freshness, a perfect landscape into which he could be absorbed, became one with the farms and the orchards and the small streams that trickled their way to the Blackwater or the Colligan. Here, he expected to meet no one, to see no face he did not choose to see.

Devon knew the place he was to meet his contact. He had performed this exact run several weeks before without incident, coming away with two dozen Enfield rifles and three Thompsons, a rare find. The arms had been destined for a brigade just over the county line in Kilkenny, and he had overseen their delivery three days later after the guns were secured. That had been money well spent.

For tonight's run, he had specified meeting behind an old deserted stone barn across a field about three kilometers east of Butlerstown. His contact had sent a note indicating that he knew the place. He would wait for him there after midnight. "No particular time," the contact had written. "I'll be there until dawn." Devon had read the note then fed it into the hearth fire.

The barn's black outline appeared to Devon's right after a walk of nearly an hour. He could see his breath in the night air, white ghosts under moonlight. He stepped off the road and headed through the short field to the outline. He crouched slightly and took small strides, peering to the barn to see any signs of movement. He moved like a rabbit, his legs poised to jump in any direction at the first scent of danger. He made no sound until he had crept to within five meters of the southwest corner of the old stones.

"*Whisht,*" he hissed through clenched teeth. "*Whisht. . .* Waterford's passing through."

From around the corner, a tall figure, equally crouched, edged gently forward. "*Whisht,*" came the response while the figure stayed recessed against the wall's shadows. "Butlerstown sends a welcome."

Devon stood tall then, the contact made. All would go well tonight, as it had dozens of times before. He stepped to the shadows.

All of a moment, his head exploded in a blinding white. Devon dropped to his knees then heard again the sickening whack of wood against the side of his skull. He fell prone, the chill of the moist ground seeping at once through his clothing, cooling his back and sides while his head felt nothing but fire. Through his pain, he squinted upward but saw only the blurrings of his now swimming eyes.

"Butlerstown sends a welcome, you heartless bastard." Above Devon loomed a familiar muscular form, a cudgel in his right hand. "So do I. One that's long overdue."

Devon focused on the voice. He recognized it, even if he could not make out the face, and something within him sank. A hollow chill from his heart met the cold of the damp earth.

"Finnegan," he exhaled the word through his pain. "You want no part of this."

"I never did, Devon, and I still don't. But this is for Johnny Flaherty and for Tommy O'Dwyer and the other nameless souls you and your gobs have dispatched." Liam brought down the cudgel again on Devon's head, hard enough to render him unconscious but not so hard as to damage him permanently. He would have neither murder nor injury on his already tattered soul.

Devon groaned with the blow then closed his eyes. Liam knelt above him and reached into the front pockets of Devon's jacket. He first felt the revolver, lifted it out, and threw it across the field. He knelt again and reached back to the other pocket, where he found the thick envelope of money. Liam stood, and in the moonlight felt its heft.

"This should do," he said to himself, "and do nicely." He blessed himself then, dropped the cudgel, and hurried off across the field to meet a new dawn.

* * *

Morning rose through a thick fog, and all lines blurred, all shapes twisted into gelatinous suggestions of substance. Sunrise began as a hint. The air gradually brightened under the sun's obscured watch. Once it fully rose above the horizon, the sun hovered through the haze, an unblinking, menacing eye.

Along the quays, birds appeared from nowhere, squawking over their feeds, diving through the mists into the water or perching on the posts or moorings. Damp air captured the scents of the ocean, fish near the docks, wet ropes, wet crates, tobacco and spit, the scents of discard and neglect. The air breathed thick, heavy, and sad.

A squat merchant ship lay at anchor on a far pier, cargo to be loaded at its base. Dockhands and stevedores worked on the ship, bringing aboard supplies, checking their lists, talking to one another in direct, profane tones. The ship itself was undistinguished, simply another entry in the army of ships that plied the North Atlantic following the Great War, built neither for speed nor comfort, but merely utile in its purpose. It shipped its goods and its people efficiently enough to generate a reasonable profit for its owners, the British and Irish Steam Packet Company out of Dublin.

That morning, it would ship westward, stopping briefly down the coastline at Cork, then heading across the Atlantic to Boston. This was a standard run for the solid ship, one it had accomplished a dozen times before.

Liam walked through the summer fog, past the steamer, and into the shipping office at the foot of the quay. He stopped only briefly to regard the lines of the ship, then strode with purpose to the small office, where a clerk behind a cluttered desk greeted him without looking up. "Mornin', young fella."

"Booking passage on the merchant, if it's taking passengers. There's time enough, am I right?"

"Time aplenty, lad. Leaves in ninety minutes or so. The full run or just to Cork?"

"All the way."

"To the great land for you, then. Well, you're hardly alone in that." The clerk grabbed a passage form from the top of a stack near the corner of his desk. "My own brother took this same trip on this same ship last year. It's easy enough passage. It's what's waitin' for you on the other side that proves the challenge, or so he's said."

"It would be more challenge to stay here."

"I've no doubt of that for someone like you. You've got the fare? Forty pounds for a room, such as it is. Twenty pounds steerage, which is a bunk in the hold. Includes meals, such as they are."

Liam reached into his pocket and pulled out a handful of bills. "I'll take a room," he said, and with that his ticket was issued, his course was set. He retreated to the docks, the air as heavy as it had been all morning. His bag at his feet, he filled his lungs as deeply as he could with the thick Irish morning.

For the next hour, he sat near the boat and watched the activity around it. Gulls swooped and dove near his head, one coming as close as a hand's-length from his bag, curious no doubt at the smells that came from within it promising the possibility of a quick stolen bite. The morning lightened slightly as time passed.

Sitting at the quay, Liam thought no great thoughts. He drew no conclusions other than the simple one that this was merely as it had to be. After a long night that stretched the limits of his capabilities, he felt tired, drained by considerations and conclusions, the hard, exhausting process of coming to decisions. He had arrived at them in due course, and now he recognized the weight of the effort. He wanted more than anything now to sleep.

But rest would have to wait. The stewards were completing their preparations. One checked the names of passengers as they gathered at the foot of the planking, then he sent them up the ramp and on their way to board. It was time.

Liam rose, stretched the tightness from his legs and back, picked up his bag, and headed for the ship. At the foot of the ramp, he gave his name to the steward and was somewhat surprised to see that, despite his late booking, his name was already listed. The steward nodded him toward the boat.

Liam paused. He looked over his shoulder at a misty, unremarkable harbor scene. *Nothing to remember here*, he told himself. *Nothing to forget*. He closed his eyes, tilted back his head,

and drew one last, deep breath, his lungs filling for the final time
with Irish air. He exhaled then turned to walk up the narrow ramp.

* * *

The sea, even when quiet, rocked with a steady constancy,
roiling gently and preventing stability of stride or thought. Liam
hung on a back rail and stared at a thick, grey North Atlantic.
The clouds that covered every corner of the sky hung as grey as
the water. Only a slight breeze, enough to gin the water into light
mist, blew across his face. He inhaled a salty damp air in slow,
unhurried breaths.

Three mornings ago, Liam had walked his farm for what he
knew would be the final time, at least for a good long while. He
could not imagine the circumstances into which he was hurtling,
so neither could he imagine the circumstances under which he
might again see these lands where he was nurtured. He had taken
his time to stand in each field and consciously note the heft of the
land beneath his boots, the uneven texture of the soil, the smell of
the spongy loam. In early afternoon, he had entered the old stone
barn and taken account of the slivers of light that permeated the
cracks, the strong animal scents, the pungency of manure and stale
feed. From there he had walked back to the fields then returned
again as the sun drew lower to regard the changes created by the
dimming natural light. He had spent the entire day ignoring his
chores and breathing in his homeland, his past, his youth.

As the day had worn on, his lack of emotion had become
a puzzlement. He had expected that he would be beset by the
strongest sentiments his soul could muster. He had anticipated
nostalgia, and regret, and identity, and the steady ache of
impending loneliness. By choice, he saw himself abandoning
every comfort he had ever known and the lovely souls who
authored those comforts. His past could be overturned, his very
self-definition adjusted, his family relegated to the past tense, his

Irishness neutralized. All of this could happen, and he himself would be the sole determinant of the process. All of this fell to his thoughts, to his preferences, to his temperament, and as it loomed, Liam had felt no different than if he had been selecting a cut of ham at the village butcher.

A decision had had to be made, had in fact been made, had been beaten into him against his will. The agony of the decision itself would overshadow its aftermath. In the final hours before he would be called upon by his own character to enact it, his thoughts, emotions, and reactions had turned outward, away from the inherent pain of his choice and toward the practical considerations that would have to be met to put that choice into motion. As a result, his emotions throughout the day had dulled. His accounting of the time, of the space, of the single arena that had crafted his core and fiber had proven to be more intellectual than emotional. The sights, sounds, and textures he deliberately sought to etch into his psyche had assumed the guise of sepia photographs, colorless and devoid of dimension.

At day's end, Liam had sought his brother. Tomas's days were set in routine, and Liam had known that he would be in the barn as the sunlight ended. There, Tomas would be putting back his loy, clearing his boots, paying attention to the animals' feeds, finishing the work of his hours.

Liam had come to love his brother deeply and instinctively, the protective, guiding visage of an alpha wolf watching the younger pup strengthen and grow. Though Tomas was only a few years younger, to Liam he was of a newer generation, purer, and to be shielded as long as possible from the complications that eventually come to call on every man. After consumption had claimed their mother two years ago, the three Finnegan men had forged their way without the gentle influences a woman could offer, but no one in the county would ever have characterized them as brutish. Liam, in fact, had showed early and often the sensitivities that would set him apart. But he had become increasingly reflective, perhaps fueled by the loneliness imposed by the absence of a mother's love and the relentless obligations of farming soft, wet land. Yet even before his mother's passing, he had concluded that he would not bow his will to any man's expectations. Peer pressure did not exist for him.

By the same measure, he would not have imposed his own thoughts or approach on any other man, most significantly Tomas. Rather, Liam had sought merely to show Tomas the alternatives his own life offered and to illustrate constantly the benefits of the simple virtues that Liam held dear, the sole lessons that Liam could teach. He had trusted Tomas to make his own decisions and to make them wisely. The young man had inherited a strong measure of the innate wisdom that had permitted the Finnegans to survive several centuries and countless traumas. While never wealthy or highly esteemed for anything other than their character, Finnegans had been a fixture for generations in a land that flowed and sluiced its people through the grinding mills of harsh times.

Tomas, to Liam, combined the best qualities borrowed from himself, his father, and the other Finnegans he had occasionally seen over his first twenty years. Tomas methodically approached every responsibility, limning its demands, gauging the resources needed, and pursuing solutions in measured steps.

Perhaps more so than Liam, however, Tomas showed evidence of great compassion, that rare capacity to empathize rather than sympathize. He felt his own hurts deeply and saw the pain of others as natural emanations of a shared destiny. When Liam had spent his days recovering from his injuries, it was Tomas who had shared vigilance with Maire, bringing him his meals, changing his dressings, and often reading him to sleep in the evenings. Tomas had no more formal education than did Liam, but Liam interpreted Tomas's gentle, giving, supportive tendencies as a sign of uncommon intelligence. He only hoped that these sensitivities would not be beaten out of the young man and that empathy's antithesis—the callous indifference of the selfish soul—would ultimately emerge.

On Liam's last day at home, he had found Tomas in the barn and stood quietly watching him go about his day's-end chores. He had regarded his emergent character and felt satisfied that Tomas's future would ultimately be his own. He had stepped forward from his corner, and Tomas had raised his head in surprise. He had not seen his brother there.

"Could you not lend a hand instead of skulking in the shadows? Christ, Liam, you're useless these days. Have a go with these buckets."

Liam grabbed two from around Tomas's legs then lifted them to the shelving near the pens. He adjusted the loys hanging on the edge of the shelves, pausing enough to feel once more their heft. *The loys define this land*, he thought. *They cleave it, break it down, level it—the same thing the land does to us. I'm nothing beyond a clump of Irish dirt.*

"One of the cows has come up lame," Tomas said. "She's an old girl, but she could barely move this morning. I've left her in the field, and I ran out some straw for her. She'll not be running off. But Lord, we're about to stand another loss."

"A farm's a hard thing, Tomas. It's always been so. It's a wonder any of us are still at it."

Tomas looked up and nodded without expression. "No wonder at all, Liam. What else is there for us to do? We're farmers. I don't see the world bearing down on us with offers and opportunities."

"Ah, Tomas, but have you never thought about getting out? Has it never occurred to you just to throw the whole thing over and leave?" Liam turned and looked out the barn's doorway into the gathering night. "Da could sell the land, and you and I could head off in whatever direction we want—Dublin, Paris, New

York—makin' a go of it on our wits and our courage, nothing else. Exploring the whole damn world. The whole damn world, Tomas, is right out there, and we're in here, with no thoughts of leaving. We've no need of purgatory after a life like that, I'll wager."

Tomas regarded his brother and spoke slowly. "Your discontent again, coming back like a spring rain. It grows tiresome, Liam."

Liam faced him fully and placed his hands on his shoulders. "Listen, lad, there's no assurance for any of us, for any day. Each of us might drop off the face of the earth itself at any time— especially these days, when death carries a gun in every village. I've not been one to offer advice, and God knows I've little wisdom to send your way. But tonight I'll tell you this: Don't sit quietly by and allow yourself to be strangled like all the others. Don't, and if I could beg you, I would. You're a bright man, Tomas Finnegan, and you're as curious as I am if you'd only admit it to yourself. You owe yourself a life lived within that curiosity. I'll offer that it's not that hard once you set your mind to do it." Liam's words caught in his throat and burbled back down within him. Wordlessly, he collapsed his arms around his brother and hugged him tightly.

"Damn, Liam, what's captured you tonight?" But Tomas hugged him back. He could not remember ever hugging Liam, and the pressure of the other's strong frame felt strange, reassuring, like a promise. "You're talking more nonsense than usual."

Liam patted Tomas's back twice then released him, smiling quietly. Like Tomas, his work here had run its course. "No nonsense, Tomas. Merely a thought for the future. You're strong enough to face whatever comes. I only pray that I share that strength." With their arms around each other's shoulders, the two young men walked across the short pathway to the Finnegan house.

Later that night, Tomas had lain behind him, a sleeping form the final memory for Liam, who had peeked his head into the younger man's room as he snuck softly and silently toward the front door. He had done the same with his father, customarily in bed as soon as the sun set. No goodbyes. No promises of letters or return visits, although Liam anticipated each. No final benedictions either given or taken. Liam had no call for rituals, which had never served him well. He had no call for the formulas of leave-taking. What would they matter, all the fine words and sentiments? Would they change an ounce of it? Or would they merely attenuate the inevitable, lengthen the time needed to step off and exaggerate the pain of it?

So, there had been no last words. He had simply left a brief note: "Da, Tomas, I've gone, and it should be no surprise to you. I'll write when I get settled, perhaps in the US. I'll be well. You be well, too, and take good care of each other until we can be together again." Liam had left his home, the place where the scenes of his boyhood had been played and ultimately lost, moved through his village, the place where the doorway to a brutal, bitter adulthood had been crossed, and went about the desperate business of the night. If one day he returned, so be it. If not, then, he told himself, he had left on his own terms, in his own way. It was time, that he knew. If not then, if he had not cultivated the courage to act while he could, the remainder of his days would have no chance of meaning.

But this did not mean that there were no regrets. Liam had stared into the black brine surrounding him and felt the knives of loss. His brother, his father, his farm . . . his land. His youth. Time. Certainty and a sure course. The sweet sunsets of summer and the quiet songs of winter nights near Christmas. The salty sea breeze that blew north from Spain and flamed his lungs with distance. Pathways that led to homes he knew.

Maire. The sharpest knife of all.

That he was young made no matter to him or to her. He had never envisioned a woman like Maire, all strength and beauty. He had never before known either sensuous touch or the deep kisses of genuine love, never before been made to feel worthy of another's devotion. She had redrawn him by breaching his defenses and caressing his soul. She had done it intuitively, sensing in Liam something distinct and gentle, wise and sad. She had seen into him clearly, had known his discontent, known it would come to no good end, yet she had continued to love him. This young love had never been halting or hesitant. Both had immersed themselves in the discovery of marvelous new terrain, and both had explored the rhythms and curves of this new land with joyful wonder. What they had rose above youthful lust, mundane sentimentality, or romanticized longings. Maire and Liam had blended in one motion, danced inside each other, and loved the music they instinctively shared.

We are young once, he told himself, *and each of us falls in love for the first time only once. It cannot be replicated. The feelings that arise with our first love stay with us, burn like fire deep within us even if we cannot see their flames. I shall never know another Maire, never know the freshness of a first journey, never feel again the unfolding of my own soul.*

She will be fine, and no doubt better off without fretting over the likes of me. She can run free, follow broader dreams than mine. She can be the lady she is and not consign herself to a dirt farmer, to a Finnegan. She's better than that.

But, God in heaven, I shall miss her fiercely. On lonely nights in a strange land, I shall think of her behind me, think of her thick hair and darting eyes, smell her floral scent, feel the soft press of her flesh, and curse myself for being a fool. There is no getting away from that, and there will be no exit from the pain for as long as I walk this sad earth.

CHAPTER X

Did you know that secret? The awful thing is that beauty is mysterious as well as terrible. God and the devil are fighting there, and the battlefield is the heart of man.

— Fyodor Dostoevsky, *The Brothers Karamazov*

Liam looked into a handkerchief and saw a sandwich with thick brown bread and days-old cheese looking back. A sun warm enough to raise sweat from his morning's trek to the building lot baked his neck, and he sat back against a pile of carved bricks, pulled away the cloth from the sandwich and held it. He had little desire to lift it to his mouth, little desire to bite into the rubbery cheese and dry bread, little desire to do anything beyond close his eyes for a few seconds while his workmates found their own spots to eat what passed for a midday meal.

The summer heat here was unlike anything Liam had known. The air hung low, palpable, a heavy, thick animal that crouched on the shoulders and stole the breath from his lungs. Rain, on those days it came, lent little relief. Rainfall cooled nothing and often fed the animal so that it came back hungrier, the air a wet blanket that could not be thrown off.

It seemed like weeks since he had felt cool. At the end of each day, Liam dragged back to a small rooming house near Back Bay, where he shared a single bedroom with three others. The second floor held the heat, and with every window wide he would lay on his pallet searching for air, each of his pores open and flowing. Noise from the street, from the alleyways, from the sky itself it seemed, broke the night, and there was no quiet. There was no rest. The nights were little more than punctuation.

At times in his restlessness, Liam would walk down to the harbor. Leaning against a railing, he would stare at the water that had brought him here. Brackish and bold, the harbor lapped into the shore and hinted at tranquility. Through his youth, he had spent hours watching from the other side of it. He had been seduced by the waves flowing offshore, away from Ireland and its sad, poor farmlands. A siren had penetrated his tender conscience, and in the end he could not resist it. The rocks he had crashed upon were no less solid, no less crushing than those that brought sailors to the bottom. The water in his silent watch offered neither relief nor justification. The summer droned on.

Still new here, and still unknown in this unknowable place, Liam leaned back and nibbled at the thick, stale bread. The dust from the bricks mingled with the food, lending grit to the surface of the sandwich and overwhelming its faded taste. He chewed silently, looking sightlessly at the common scene of an urban workplace. A flask of warm water drew more heat from his back pocket. He took it out, unscrewed the top, and drank deeply, his thirst throwing itself in front of any possible relief. As he drank, he thought of the cool stream that ran through the Finnegan farm and emptied into the Colligan and the greenery that surrounded it. No workload on the farm could not be lightened by a drink of the water there or a sniff of the sea air that wafted in even in the dead of summer.

He thought of Tomas, as he often did. The lad must be burdened now, the sole pair of strong arms to man that property. Still, he had made his choice; let the flotsam that bobbed behind him in his wake find its own level. *Every man has the obligation to choose.*

Liam finished his sandwich. He wished he had something more. An apple, or a cucumber, something sweet and wet. Done with eating, he leaned back and waited for something to change. The heat continued to beat him down, and he draped his now empty handkerchief across his nape. Eyes closed, he waited the minutes away until his foreman gave the customary shout.

"Okay, boyos, back to it, back to it," he said, and he clanged a wrench against a sheet of tin as he walked through the group. Some groaned, and one or two cursed him, but everyone gathered themselves. Liam, who always ate alone, was among the last to stand. Before heading back to the staging area, he refilled his flask from a barrel of water they all shared. Bits of wood and insects floated on the surface, but what matter? Water was water, and, damn, it was hot.

"Finnegan, will you deign to join us? Always the last bastard in, and this thing won't build itself."

"Let a man get some water, jocko. I'll carry your damn bricks." The afternoon resumed.

* * *

The Batterymarch Building would be Boston's highest when it was completed. Only the Custom House Tower would stand taller. With an elaborate design, replete with ornamentation that spoke to the city's past—a codfish, a bean pot, a clipper ship—and the city's current pace—a locomotive, an airplane—the building was touted as a showpiece, one of the finest new buildings the country would see, a splendid example of modern new Art Deco.

To get it built, the city needed cheap labor. The work was hard, hot, mindless, and dangerous—lifting materials, putting them in place, securing them, scaling up and down small spaces, the usual heavy construction—and the pay was minimal. The Irish were perfect for it.

Blessed with a strong arm, a strong back, and the conviction that he could get by through his own labor, Liam had signed on the day after he had disembarked from the merchant ship. How hard could it all be? He had worked farmlands all his life, and he had never slacked, at least in his own mind. When he made his way from the docks to the Irish quarter in South Boston to find lodging, he had found a job to go with it, approached at the head of Boylston Street by a large, hairy, smiling man whose teeth shone through a thick beard. He had placed a confidential arm around the newcomer and told him there were riches to be made through the sweat of his brow, just sign here and show up at Batterymarch tomorrow at seven and ask for Eamonn.

Perhaps the streets in Amerikay really were lined with gold.

Rooms were plentiful, but they were as crowded as they were simple. Liam had asked around, and he was directed to Malone's Hostel, an elegant title for a flophouse of seven bedrooms, each shared by four Irishmen. There was room for another, at one dollar a week. Liam had done the math in light of his newly promised employment, recognized that even if he had no job at all the wad of bills locked in his belt would carry him a goodly distance, then had walked the few blocks southward to his new home.

Emma Malone ran a loose house. "Rent's payable in advance at the start of each week. Ya get a pallet on the floor and a towel. Meals are on yer own, and if ya want me to cook somethin' up fer ya, ya'll pay for it. Keep the common areas clean, and don't break anything. Beyond that, I don't give a rip what ye do here. Ye can fight, or fuck, or fuss. The boys here set themselves straight, so if ya get out of line, ya'll have to answer to them. I stay out of it and collect my rent. If yer more than three days late with the rent, a constable will be callin' on ya to help ya with yer next move."

That day, Liam paid his dollar and took his bag to a third-floor bedroom with the promised pallet. The doors had no locks, and when he entered, no one was there. Four flat wooden slats on the floor were lined with thin blankets. Discarded dirty clothes sat on three of them. Liam had put his bag down on the fourth blanket and looked around. There was no other furniture except for a table in one corner, nothing on it, and there were no closets. A single window looked onto the twelve feet that separated Emma Malone's house from the one behind it. When Liam had moved to look around, the floorboards creaked loudly, an animal twisted by the tail. Three or four small holes punctured the near wall, and on the opposite wall a wide sheet of dark paper covered a larger wound. Home.

The three who shared the room were Tommy Clarke, Devon O'Neill, and Xavier Barry, but they were interchangeable with the others who lived there. They might as well have had no names at all. Each was like the next, and all were hard, hard men. Liam's roommates introduced themselves with grunts. This was not Dungarvan, these were not the farmlands, and the men at Malone's were not pastoral laborers.

The first night, Liam's sleep was unsteady, interrupted by snoring from throats that had scarcely acknowledged his presence and the sharpness of solid wood that held little comfort. Shortly after midnight, or so he thought, curses roared up from the second floor near the stairs, preceding a fistfight. When the fight's loser was thrown against a wall, the whole house shook. Liam's roommates continued to snore while Liam rolled over to face the tattered, broken wall.

A bit later, a tiny pair of legs scrambled across Liam's thigh. He sat with a start and felt around. Coming up empty, he lay his head down again. The intruder returned, and Liam, more alert now, grabbed the hindquarters of a mouse as it scampered toward one of the holes in the wall behind him. Liam held him firmly, and two dribbles of excrement wet his hand as the mouse flailed for escape. Liam relaxed his grip so as not to hurt the mouse, then slowly raised his captive to eye level. The mouse was a young one, tiny, very fragile, very much afraid.

"I see you, laddie," he whispered. "No worries. I won't hurt you." He lowered his hand toward the wall and let the mouse run off. "No doubt I'll be seeing you again. The first of my roommates to shake my hand."

Liam woke early enough to find his way to the job site the next morning. When he found Eamonn, the foreman signed him up at three dollars a week, payable on Friday at the end of the shift. With the ink from Liam's signature still wet on the crumpled workmen's roster, Eamonn pointed the newcomer to a pile of hods and told him to use one to start hoisting bricks up to the third floor. Liam did as he was told, and the rest of the morning he lugged heavy loads of untreated brick up three floors of wooden ramps. By the time he broke for his half-hour lunch, his now-strong shoulders felt weak and the imprint of the hod had ground away the flesh near his collarbone. He had not thought to bring a lunch. His break was spent leaning against an unfinished wall and massaging his aches.

The afternoon was no different, and at day's end, when the foreman finally yelled at the men that it was time to wrap it up, Liam's back was on fire and his shoulders bled. The sun was low enough to cast long shadows as he made his way back to Malone's. No one on the site had spoken to him all day other than to give him orders for where to place or load his bricks. No one had asked his name. On the way back to the rooming house, he passed several inns, but he did not go in. There was no one with whom he could badger, no one he knew enough to find. All he wanted now was some rest for his stunned muscles and fibers. And some water, perhaps. Some cold water if he could find it.

So, it continued, each day to the next, for one week, then two. Liam worked, slept poorly, ate more poorly still, and spoke to almost no one. He kept as much distance as he could from his roommates, who unnerved him with their brutality. Fights were common—sprawling bare-knuckled rampages that most often were acted out on the street in front of the rooming house. As ready as they were to fight each other, the roomers were cowed by Emma Malone, whose squat physical presence, supplemented by a cudgel she was no doubt unafraid to use, was enough to keep them busting up one another indoors. Any furniture they broke they would have to pay for, or find themselves in the street. The occasional pock in the walls was fine, but the furniture was too dear to replace on a laborer's pay. For the most part, they obeyed the house rules and waged their battles in the street or the alleyways. Liam steered clear, neither combatant nor peacemaker.

The Friday night of his second week, he felt the need for a drink. He had had none since his arrival. Part of that was due to the law of the land. Prohibition, one of the damndest, stupidest things he could have imagined, had shut the legitimate trade. Even so, Boston teemed with places where a workingman could find at least a beer. Despite the law, in this new place Liam had little stomach for drinking. Most nights, he wandered down to the harbor, delaying his return to the rooming house to answer an instinctive call to the water. The sea calmed him as it always did. There were no headlands to sit on there, and the breezes blew warmer than those that whispered to him off the Celtic Sea, nor was he alone as he liked to be. Others crowded around him. Lovers walked by arm in arm, children scampered around his legs. But it was the water, nonetheless, and despite the distractions, something timeless stirred within him when he was near it. Much better to spend time overlooking a fetid harbor than rubbing elbows or throwing hands with the group at Malone's. Beyond that, there was no place else Liam knew to go.

This night, well beyond the harbor's calming influence, Liam sniffed down the back ways around Tremont Street, halfway on his walk to Malone's. He had heard his workmates talk of a place. In South Boston, no one cared, really. The cops turned a blind eye to the dark corners, themselves benefitting from a strong drink now and then, and the owners of these places took good care to pay for their indifference. Down an alleyway between Tremont and Shawmut streets, Liam found what he thought he was looking for. Men walked in, a few stumbled out. There were no windows, but the door was wide open. Liam walked in.

His body as sore and drained as his spirit, Liam had no grand scheme beyond a quick pint if he could get it. The bar was there. He had found it and turned in. Once inside, he blinked to accommodate his eyes to the dimness. As he did so, two broad-shouldered men whose eyes were tuned to the place pushed their way in, jostling Liam to one side.

Adjusted now to the light, Liam walked the few steps to a long cedar plank that served as a bar. The man behind it looked his way and raised his brows. "Mate?"

"Ale. The strongest you've got." A pint appeared, Liam's first in the New World. The taste bit his lips and matted against his tongue. A soft familiar flame trickled down his throat, and, for the moment at least, all was well.

The man who poured the pint came back to Liam and leaned across the plank. When he spoke, his Irish was apparent. Liam noted that almost all the voices in this place carried a brogue. He may as well have been back at Ryan's in Dungarvan, for all that. Except for the darkness, the strong-armed strangers, the simple fact that he was drinking beyond the law, the lack of music, the absence of pleasant conversation, and no women in the place at all, it was exactly the same.

Damn, what have I gotten myself into?

"You're a bit young for this crowd, aren't you, lad?"

Liam raised his glass. "Old enough to know what to do with this. My first glass in Amerikay." He took a deep swallow.

"Then recognition is in order. Let me stand you to the next one."

"I'd be pleased," said Liam. "You might be the first friendly voice I've heard since I got off the boat."

"It's not so bad after a while. You get used to the hard edges. It's not as if our kind is ever warmly received here, you know." He reached across the plank and offered his hand. "My name's Conlan, from County Mayo."

Liam shook it firmly and introduced himself. "Liam Finnegan, from Dungarvan, County Waterford. Two weeks fresh and wondering where the hell I really am."

"You're in Boston, boyo, on your way to Hades along with the rest of us." Conlan took a sip from his own glass. "You know, you hear all these tales of the Great Land. You hear the myths, that every man can make a fortune if he works at it, that there's nothing you can't do across the sea except drink." He chuckled again. "It sucks you in. The lies seduce you, and you want to believe it all so bad that you lie to yourself once you get here. You tell yourself you're not seeing the things that are right in front of you. But it's all just the whisper of the faeries.

"The truth is, there's poverty, and there's hard knocks, and there's a barrel of hatred. No one gives a damn about those getting off the boats. If you can get through a day with something in your belly and no one taking a swing at you, it's a good day. That's what I've learned about the Great Land. There are no streets lined with gold. You've got to spin your own the best way you can. There's no one about to help you do it. Does that sound like paradise, young fella?"

"It sounds like bloody hell. But I can't say that I've seen anything to disprove it."

"Where are you staying?"

"Emma Malone's, on Albany Street. Me and about two dozen of my best friends."

"As good a place as any, I'd reckon. But that's a rough lot you're with, and in a rough part of the rough part of town. I have a friend here who tells me that one Irishman in a room will make a poem, but two Irishmen in that same room will make a fight. Watch yourself."

Conlan walked back down the plank to pour for the others holding out empty glasses. He spoke to one or two, but most had no desire for conversation. They were there for the beer, for the whiskey, for the Friday release of a week's worth of tension. In time, he returned to the fresh face near the end of the station.

"So, why did you make your way here, Finnegan? Did you come with your family?"

"I came on my own," said Liam. He drank deeply again. The second pint wordlessly appeared in front of him. He emptied the first glass and poured the dregs of it into the second. "Christ, I just left them a short note. They must think I'm dead."

"Jaysus," Conlan said as he expelled a low, throaty breath. "Jaysus, Finnegan. What led you to do a thing like that? They don't know you're here?"

"I mentioned I might be going to the States. They might assume it. I hinted at it for a while, but no one seemed to be listening. With the Black and Tans running wild, and the fighting amongst ourselves, and the goddamned dreary day-to-day meaningless way we live, it seemed like the time to go."

"Your ma's bound to be worried, don't you think?"

"I've got no ma. Just my da and my younger brother. They'll do all right without me. Just a little farm outside Dungarvan. Fruits and some cattle. Christ, there's little I added to things as it was."

"Still, that's a bold move."

"Was it? Listen, I suppose deep in my heart I knew there was no such thing as a promised land. I'd heard the stories. I'd heard people talk in wonder about the States and what you could get done here. I didn't believe it.

"But," Liam continued, "the first day I landed, I got a job, even before I had a place to live. They practically grabbed me from the boat. So, maybe parts of it were true, I told myself. Maybe it's not all a myth." He drank again, deeply. The ale was beginning to have an effect. The darkness of the place dissipated in the illusion of light, and his head began to spin.

"Then I find Malone's, a place for my head, any place, but it's no better than a workhouse. I'd be as well off sleeping in the alleys. There might be fewer rats, and I know there'd be less fights. I get to the job site, and it's brutal. The work damn near breaks me every day. I can't see how the older guys can do it. Lift and sweat and haul and climb. Don't fall, don't stop, and, for God's sake, don't take too much of the water. Get on with it.

"I haven't spoken to a friendly soul until tonight, and I haven't even seen a woman worth speaking to. I walk back to Malone's each night with my eyes open, because you never know when you might get dragged behind a bush and beaten for a few coppers.

"But when I think about it, Conlan, none of that really matters. I was dead in Ireland. I was just taking up space, and everything I could do there wouldn't amount to shite. I was living just like my father, and my grandfather, and probably every last Finnegan since we learned to walk upright. And any sons I have would be condemned to the same sentence. So, I was dead there, and here I'm not. Even though it's not pretty, it's not comfortable, and it's certainly not what I wanted. But at least it's mine."

Liam drained his second pint then stood with a wobble.

"Are you okay, lad?" asked Conlan.

"No worries," said Liam. "Damn, that was fine."

"Come back any time," said Conlan. "You're always welcome here. And tell your friends."

"My friends . . . ," muttered Liam. "Thanks for your kindnesses," he said, "and good night."

It was a warm night, like all the others, and Liam shambled back toward Albany Street and the hovel he was forced to call home for the moment. He kept his head down, feeling the warmth of the ale within him, feeling it rise to meet the heat of the summer's night. No breezes blew, and thin lines of perspiration condensed on his upper lip and across his brow. The exhaustion of a hard week's work, the comfortable drain of the alcohol, and the press of a too-hot night made movement thick and slow.

He walked through rutted, dirty, rank streets, dark to the sight and dark to the senses. Loud, angry voices carried curses around the corners, and piles of rot sat at the walkway's side. He was here in Boston, with an aching body and an aching heart. It was a Friday night on the edge of the New World, and no streets of gold.

Near Albany Street, three men roughly his own age walked his way. As they approached, they laughed loudly. Liam could not make out what they were saying, nor did he particularly care. They were like all the others, those he lived with and those he worked with. Christ, did they even have souls inside them?

The three came up to Liam, smiling and in good humor. "Boyo," said one, perhaps the biggest of the three, "come join us for a drink. We know a place."

"No thanks, lads. I've had enough for the night."

"Come on with ya, then," said another of the three. "It's too early to turn it in, unless you're soft." Then the third joined in. "If ya can't come drink with us, then maybe you can set us up for a round. Maybe two rounds, unless you're soft." The three laughed again, loudly but with no humor.

"Not tonight, I'm tellin' ya. And I'm not soft." Liam moved to step around them and make his way to Malone's.

Suddenly, the world exploded in bright lights. The sound of broken glass was the last sense he had before darkness flooded in, and he collapsed onto the stones beneath him.

He woke to the wet nose of a stray dog sniffing along his neck, where broken glass had embedded itself into his collar. Slowly, as he opened his eyes, his mind took inventory to see what might be broken, or, worse, missing. His head throbbed, but his limbs responded as they should, and his breathing evened out. He felt what was probably a thin line of blood run down the back of his neck but no real damage beyond that.

Sitting up, Liam shooed the dog away, who slinked off reluctantly, looking over his shoulder as he did so. Whatever possibilities this strange and broken young man might have held to change his street-hard existence, or at least lend some light to it, would come to nothing.

He could not have been out long. The street looked the same, still empty, and the fall of light had not changed. The three young men had, of course, vanished.

"You feckin' eejit," Liam muttered to himself. "You bloody feckin' eejit." He searched his pockets although he knew he would only find emptiness. The three had taken his week's pay from his belt, which hung now, ripped open, off the rear of his pants. They had even taken a cheap ring Tomas had given him two years ago at Christmas. It had no value beyond a younger brother's love. Now, it was gone along with the three dollars earned this week and perhaps two dollars more that he had carried with him. Gone.

"Bloody feckin' eejit. Why didn't you just empty your pockets for them and save them the trouble of bustin' your head? Jaysus, Liam, you ignorant jackass." He knew he shouldn't have turned his back on them. Best to have crossed the street when he saw them coming or change course and go down another way. He knew better. A couple of pints, an actual conversation, and he had gotten lazy.

What was this place, then? A strange new land, built in his mind on mythology, that now grew too real. Under his feet lay hard stone, and around him rose buildings that rotted and stank.

The sky itself was different. The geography of the stars, which he had come to know as a boy and had always reassured him of his place on this planet, were out of place, obscured by too much light and too little air. Hard for him to believe that these same stars shone now over the Finnegan farm. He may as well have been on the sixth moon of Jupiter.

No air for the stars, no air for the soul. That was why he had come here, wasn't it? For the soul. To save himself from an earthly purgatory that had flamed for generations and promised to consume his own flesh in drudgery, poverty, and lost hope, that promised to consume his best parts and the best parts of anything he might be able to produce. The thought of it had nearly made him mad.

But on these shores now, he missed the open sky. He missed the voices and touches of the pub, where even if he drank nothing he still had a place to sit and someone with whom he could banter. He missed Tomas's hopeful innocence and his father's steadying strength. And in his deepest core, he missed sweet Maire. Above everything else, he had struggled most to put her out of his mind, to wash away her imprint on his heart. Yet each day as he dragged through his backbreaking work and trudged back to the slum he shared with his brutal, unthinking housemates, she flitted before him. He saw her thin form, the glint of her eyes, the fall of her thick reddish-brown hair. He smelled her intoxicating floral scent and recalled how he would roll himself into it in a passion tempered by youth and tenderness. The memories of times and places they shared, the simple walks, the laughter, the nights sitting on a stone wall listening to the ducks chatter and the cattle groan would not leave him.

Perhaps if this place were different it might have all come together as he imagined it could. Liam had known the risk he had taken. Now, tonight, he had been confronted with another piece of evidence that the risk had consequences, that the world revolved in real time and not according to the fancies of stories or idolatry, or the deceptions of the faeries that had lured him to the waters and the wild.

This was Boston. It was real, and it was mean, and he saw precious little milk and honey here. In two short weeks, he had been consigned once again to the outskirts, to the margins, where he might work his life away and no one would notice, except perhaps those who chose to steal from his labors. He saw too clearly that in seeking to escape the fatalism of his days in Ireland, he had found something deeper and harder.

Liam pulled himself up and walked unsteadily the rest of the way to Malone's. His head pounded from the blow, and occasionally his vision made loops around the street. Once, he had to stop and brace himself against the side of a storefront to keep from falling over. He had no notion of time. The walk may have taken five minutes or fifty. He had lost the capacity to count anything beyond his losses. In due course, he dragged himself up the stairs as silently as he could and collapsed onto his pallet.

The next day was a workday. The site did not close down on Saturday, and men were expected to keep pace. Foremen were usually understanding on Saturdays, giving allowance for Friday night celebrations of payday. A concession for a nine-hour day was balanced by a six-day week. Workers could take it or leave it. There was always another Irishman to fill any void.

Liam's roommates groused themselves awake at dawn with snorts and grunts. It took them almost no time to pull on work clothes and head down the stairs. Liam sat up, his head sore, but his thoughts clear.

There was no seaside to stimulate his thinking, to reach inside him and raise a spiritual mirror so that he could calmly and truly see who he was and what was needed. This morning, there was no need.

Liam moved slowly enough to allow his mates to precede him

down the stairs. When he was dressed and alone in the room, he took his bag from the corner and filled it with his few things—a change of clothes, an extra pair of shoes, a jacket, some scraps and rags. He lingered longer, listening to the work boots hitting the stairs, the landing, then leaving out the door. Liam knew no one here and had spoken not even a greeting to anyone other than his roommates, but he saw no need to draw attention to himself.

When enough time had passed so that he was sure that almost all of the men at Malone's had left, he walked softly out of his room. Emma Malone was in the dining area boiling something for a lone figure slumped over the table there. Liam walked down the stairs and out the front door but then quickly turned around the house to the small back area separating it from those behind it.

He looked quickly around to make sure he was alone then checked the windows on either side to see if anyone was watching. It was unlikely on a Saturday morning, but he had already paid the price for loose vigilance. When he was reasonably assured that he was unwatched, he walked to a corner of the small yard and bent down over three large stones that abutted the back wall. He moved the stones to the side then dug into the ground beneath them to find what he had buried there his first night at this rotting place. Finding what he sought, he lifted it out of the dirt, tucked it into his front pocket, then replaced the stones as they were before.

He waited several minutes, standing against the wall, looking in each direction, breathing softly, just waiting. After a time, certain that he remained unseen and that no one was likely to turn the corner into this dingy patch of black earth, Liam took out the envelope from his front pocket, peeled it back slowly, then exhaled with relief. It was all still there, all of it that he had buried, and with it his release. Devon Coghlin, still in service to the spirit of Ireland.

Liam put the envelope back in his pocket and walked back into Malone's. No one was in the front area, so he hurried up the steps, grabbed his small bag, then just as quickly hopped back down to the street. Instead of turning to the right as he had done each morning, Liam turned left. It was several blocks to South Station, but he covered them quickly, and as he hustled along, he caught a deep scent of the sea blowing toward him from the harbor.

Where shall I go now? What shall I do?

* * *

Liam knew almost nothing about his new country. In Ireland, all he had heard were the myths, and all the myths played out in the big cities—Boston, New York, Philadelphia. But he knew, too, that this country had its riches, and that those riches lay in part beyond the dense, thick turbulence that consumed the past two weeks. This country had farms, he knew. Liam was a farmer. He would find a farm.

In his mind, a plan took shape. A farm, and he would work it as a laborer, work it hard, and put by what he earned. In time, he would buy his own land. There, he would raise himself again, without the undue assumptions and violence and castings that locked generations into the same places in the land he had left. He would tend his land and explore the possibilities it enabled, peacefully, contemplatively, and above the nagging smolder of poverty. This might be the best he could do—and if not the best, it would at least be the truest.

Liam took the envelope from his pocket, quietly counted how much was in it, and walked to a ticket counter in South Station. His heart began to race as he approached the clerk.

"This is an odd question, man, but where would I find the best farmland in this country? Where would a man have to go?"

The clerk looked up, puzzled. "That's not for me to say, friend. You make your own choices."

Liam noted the Irish in the clerk's voice and drew closer. "Listen, I'm just off the boat. I don't know what the hell I'm doin' yet. I just know I can't abide this city, not now. We're kin in our own way, and I could use your advice."

Customers had formed behind Liam, and the clerk noticed. He was older than Liam, in his forties, maybe older. He paused a few seconds, then said, "Step aside, lad. Let me do my job. But if you can wait a couple of hours, I'll talk with you on my lunch. You're buyin'."

"I'll buy ya the biggest damn steak in the city."

"Wait by the clock, and I'll get to you when I can." Then he called, "Next in line."

Liam went back into the terminal and found a seat on a bench near the central clock. Anticipation crowded away the soreness in his head. He still had not cleaned the wound, nor had he washed his face or hands. *I must look terrible*, he thought. He would clean up a bit in the toilets here before he left, before he left for wherever it was he would be going.

In the early afternoon, the clerk walked into the central terminal, looked around quickly, and spotted Liam. He walked his way.

"There's a stand on the far side. Let's get some food, and I'll tell you what I know."

They walked together, and the clerk stepped up to order a thick sandwich of beef with a boiled egg. Liam ordered nothing but paid for the clerk. They walked back to the bench, and the clerk began to eat. Between bites, he talked.

"I've heard there are farms you can't imagine," he said. "Land that goes on and on and on, all of it green and growing. Corn, barley, hay, vegetables you've never seen before. And great sheep and cattle farms, with land enough for the beasts to eat from dawn to dusk and never come close to trimming it all away. I've heard of this. I've not seen it, but I know it's so.

"And," he continued, "these lands are so vast that no one man, no one family, can tend it all. A strong back, strong hands, and a little knowledge of how the land works will stand any man well. If you want the farms, lad, you'll find no place on this earth as rich as these."

"So, where do I find these wondrous lands?" asked Liam.

"You have to go a ways. The Midwest is the heart of the farmland, although it goes on for miles and miles, all the way to the western mountains. Go to the Midwest, lad. You'll find a farm."

"Let me ask you then, why have you not done this for yourself? You're a train clerk in Boston, and you talk to me about paradise."

"Each man has his own paradise, son. I'm a city man. Always been. I grew up in Dublin, near Ringsend. I've a wife and two sons born on these shores. This life is all I could have wanted. You're young, alone, and born to the land. Your Eden will grow different fruit than mine. Go find it."

"I'd be honored if you sold me a ticket to where I need to go."

"Let me finish my lunch. Come to the counter in half an hour. Now, go wash up. I've no idea what you've been up to, but you look terrible, and if you're bound for a long train ride, you should smell better than you do. There's a washroom for employees, but I've got the key. Use it, and bring it back to the counter. The room is around the corner, marked for official use only." The clerk pulled a single key from a vest pocket and placed it in Liam's hand. "I admire your youth, son. And I admire your courage. That'll serve you no matter where you go."

Liam took the key and in so doing shook the clerk's hand firmly. "I'll be back." In the washroom, he drew cool water and let it run down his face. He splashed the back of his head, slowly rubbing out the dried blood and checking for pieces of glass. In his bag sat a shaving kit, and Liam took it out for what he knew would be his last shave for a while. He combed his hair, pulling through the tangles, and fixed his shirt collar. Then he drew himself before a mirror, and, considering the circumstances, liked what he saw. He found himself ready for the next step.

At the counter, he returned the key. "You've remade me," he said with a lilt.

"Someone had to. Now, where will you be going?"

"To the farms," said Liam. "To the Midwest. What city lies at the heart of it?"

"Chicago. The city's an island surrounded by fields of plenty, or so I've been told. You'll need to change trains in Albany. That's in New York, along the way. Two-day trip. Coach fare is seven dollars, with meals extra, unless you want a Pullman. But you don't strike me as the luxury type."

"Coach is fine." Liam drew the money from his envelope. "You've been a great help. When does it leave?"

The clerk handed Liam his ticket. "You've got some time. Four thirty on Track Four. Check the boards. Now, get on to it, lad, and greet the cows for me."

* * *

Liam rested his head against the window. By the time his train pulled out of South Station and crossed away from the city sprawl, he lapsed into a deep, deep slumber. Postponed exhaustion becomes narcotic, and Liam was indeed exhausted on all levels. His body suffered aches, his mind suffered confusion, and his soul . . . his soul just suffered. At the first opportunity he found himself outside the struggles of his days, he had collapsed. He slept steadily until the train neared Albany.

In the Albany station, he roused himself enough to change to a train that would take him across upstate New York to Buffalo, then around the lakes and through the rich fertility of Ohio and Indiana. Liam did not know this, of course. He had no internal map of his new country, knew nothing of the states, knew nothing of the geography. He sought the farmlands only. This train would take him there. As his train left Albany in the dark, he let his sleep claim him again.

He woke the next morning to a bright sun that warmed the window against which he rested. Shaking himself alive, he stretched the tired muscles in his legs and arms. A sharp pang of hunger knifed through his abdomen, and he realized that he had had nothing to eat in more than a day. He had been told that there was a car here that sold food. The walk to find it would do him good, revive his blood, and bring him back.

Liam rose from his seat, and as he did he looked out the window toward the sun-warmed glass. He gasped and fell right back in his seat at the sight before him: farmland, unlike any he had ever conceived.

There were broad fields that swept to a horizon with a lake that had no far shore. The lake spanned the length of his view, and before it crops were growing rich and thick. He did not know what those crops were, but it did not matter. The land here was so fertile that all he could see were growing things—no roads, no pathways, and only a single farmhouse with a high barn behind it.

He wished he could open the window and smell the air, which must be as full and scented as the land itself. He wanted to stop the train, get off, and dig his hands into fertile, fecund American dirt. Liam Finnegan's God had recreated for him a personalized Eden. With this land under his feet, he would need nothing else.

Hunger forgotten, Liam kept his seat and looked hard out the window, transfixed and rapt. The train sped on with a steady pace as he pressed his forehead against the glass and sought to drink in everything he could see.

A conductor walked down the aisle announcing, "Cleveland next. Next stop is Cleveland, Ohio. Thirty minutes to Cleveland."

Liam imagined Cleveland to be a farming community large enough to be recognized, perhaps like Limerick or Kilkenny. When the land broke up and gave way to houses, shops, and factories on Cleveland's outskirts, however, Liam grew puzzled. His puzzlement grew to alarm as the train pulled into the dirty, congested downtown depot and scores of people got on while scores of people got off. The freshness of the vast fields had given way to smoky, greasy, noisy chaos—another Boston. Liam began to sweat, and he closed his eyes. Perhaps he could sleep it away like before.

When the train pulled out and had gone far enough to clear the city, Liam saw the farmlands return, as wide as before. The train cut through them like a plow. Liam went back to looking out the window and stoking his dreams. For most of the rest of the way, he slept quietly and let fanciful reveries play though his still restless soul.

* * *

"Chicago next. End of the line at Chicago." The conductor repeated the call as he walked the length of the car, opened the gate at its end, and walked into the next. Liam did not hear it. He heard nothing but the roar inside his head as he tried to decipher the cruel joke unfolding before him.

For the past hour, he had pressed himself against the window once more, but this time not in fancy or delight. He had watched instead with a rising horror. The farms were gone, had been gone for a while, replaced with old buildings jammed together, broken-down stores, and huge sky-high stacks belching smoke and flame. People along the tracks looked up with nothing in their eyes or shuffled along the rail bed with aimless steps, heading nowhere, coming from nothing. The horizon, so limitless a few miles back, closed in like a dark curtain. He saw no water, nothing growing, and very little light. And as they neared what he knew to be the final stop, as they neared Chicago, it all got denser, more congested, and darker. Had they just ridden in a great wide circle back to Boston? No, of course not, but it felt the same to him. What had he fled, and where had he finally pointed himself? Where did this exile lead?

* * *

Liam was the last man off the train. He made his way out of the coach and into a sprawling railroad station. He paused inside the door to the track to gather his bearings. What he also gathered was the conclusion that he was stuck here, at least for a while. His money was running low, and he dared not spend a chunk of it on another ticket to someplace he did not know. He would have to get by for a bit, pay for a room, pay for some food. He would need to replenish his funds before he took the next step, whatever that might be.

On the railroad platform, he approached a porter who had just loaded a cart with suitcases and boxes. "Say, friend, where can a new man in town find a safe place to stay for a week or two?" Liam asked. The porter looked at Liam, took his measure from top to bottom, and in a glance regarded his clothes, his bag, his posture, and his tone. Finally, he replied, "I'm no travel agent, pal. There are boards all around where places post notice. Find one, then take your pick." As Liam thanked him and began to walk away, the porter added, "You'll want to look for the Irish part of town. That's in the south, but there are some neighborhoods in the north that might be right for you, too."

Liam found a board and looked at what was posted. He had no way of judging one from the other. Almost all of them advertised rooms near the station, in a city he knew not at all. North, south, how could he tell? One ad, though, caught his eye. "Clean room for a single man. Irish preferred." It gave an address on a street called Irving Park, along with a weekly rent that was slightly higher than the others. *Trust your instincts,* he told himself. *My guess is that you get what you pay for. No more flophouses, or I'll be damned to hell. Let's go see Mrs. Kilpatrick,* for that was the name of the housekeeper. He stepped outside to find a cab.

An old black car was so marked. Liam stopped. An American

cab, so different from the very few cars he had seen in Ireland. This one looked beaten and worn, as dirty as the city around him. This thing belonged here.

He climbed in. "1440 West Irving Park," he said, and the cabbie turned to face his new fare. "Pay the fare up front, Mick. It's seventy-five cents to get you there." Liam, who had absolutely no idea whether this was a fair price, handed over the coins and they were off through dense streets that grew only slightly more relaxed as they headed north. Liam was relieved to see the cityscape soften a bit. Factories and plants gave way to residences, some of which were quite nice—single family, or so they appeared, and many with plants lining small lawns. Emma Malone's still haunted him. He would need to find a room where Malone's ghosts had no place to land.

At 1440, the cab stopped, and Liam looked at a tall, narrow, very well-kept house. The windows had shutters, and the paint was fresh. A stone walkway cut through the small patch of grass between the house and the street. He got out of the cab and approached the front door.

Elizabeth Kilpatrick and Emma Malone hailed from two separate species, or so it appeared upon first impression. Mrs. Kilpatrick dressed well, stood tall, and smiled. When she spoke, her voice came forth soft and civil. She did not swear.

"Yes, the room is still available. Let me show you, if you're interested."

Liam walked inside to a well-kept parlor with clean turn-of-the-century furniture.

"I have four rooms, four boarders . . . well, you'd be the fourth. All are young men like yourself, and all from Ireland. I prefer it that way. I can look after you all, and there's none of that nasty 'No Irish' sentiment. No fighting, and if you drink, keep it quiet."

At the top of the stairs, they entered a small bedroom with

a single high bed, a dresser with a mirror, and a window that overlooked the small lawn in the rear of the building. "This would be yours."

"And who would be my roommates, ma'am?"

Mrs. Kilpatrick gave a gentle chuckle. "No roommates. You'd have the room to yourself." But then she grew serious and looked Liam directly in his tired eyes. "You've had a hard time of it, haven't you?" She paused, still regarding the young man. "I have just one question for you. Are you running from the law? I'll not have you if you are, and I expect you to be honest with me."

"No, ma'am. I left Boston two days ago of my own accord. No one's chasing me. No one really knows I exist on these shores."

"I'm sorry. I had to ask. I try so hard to avoid trouble with my boys. Do you have a job here?"

"Not yet, ma'am, but I'm after looking for one as soon as I find a place. I've got enough money with me to cover the first month's rent at the rate stated on the advertisement. If I've not found work by then, I'll move on."

"I have a friend who may be able to help you with that. He owns a grocery store a few blocks on, and he's always looking for strong young men to stock shelves and deliver products. If you're willing to work hard, you'll do well here."

"To be truthful, I had no notion of where I was heading when I got on the train in Boston. I had hoped to find some good farming land and hire myself out."

"There are no farms in Chicago, my young friend, but they *are* close by. You'll have something to work toward."

Liam looked again around the room, heard the soft tones of Mrs. Kilpatrick's voice, and realized he had stumbled upon a minor miracle. He drew himself to his full length. "I'd be pleased if you'd consider me for this room, Mrs. Kilpatrick. I promise to you now that you'd not be disappointed to have me here."

Mrs. Kilpatrick nodded. "I have no doubt. But I don't even

know your name. How will I introduce you to the others if I don't know your name?" she chided.

"Liam Finnegan, ma'am. My family's from Dungarvan, in County Waterford."

"Welcome, Mr. Finnegan. I hope you like it here enough to consider this your new home."

Indeed, Liam felt as if he had found a haven, a place to gather himself again. He would stay here a bit, he reasoned. He would get a job in this city of nearly three million souls and work it hard. There was honor in that. The farming could come later.

CHAPTER XI

There were Irish there on Irving Park. Elizabeth Kilpatrick's house sat within a neighborhood filled with Flanagans, Doyles, O'Byrnes, Dooleys, O'Fihillys, Cullinans, and a hundred other names common to what Liam had left behind.

He fit in culturally at least, if not socially, and that comforted him. He heard the lilt of familiar intonations as he walked the streets, stopped at a pub (or, as the Yanks would have it, a "bar"), or sought work. The sounds soothed him, and he could conduct his days without the angst that permeated his first weeks in the country.

The neighborhood itself was residential, so none of the hard edges that he had seen in and around his former workplace in Boston were apparent. The Kilpatrick house exuded a gentility that never surfaced. He shared it with other young men, but,

unlike his previous housemates, they were largely quiet, not given
to drunkenness and fighting on the weekends, and perseverant
toward whatever it was they were after. Liam knew one of them
to be a student and two others to be working office jobs—a postal
clerk and an accounts manager at a small firm downtown. Liam
slept with his door unlatched.

In a week's time, he had scoured the businesses in the
surrounding blocks to see who might need an able-bodied, strong
Irishman. He could stock shelves, move furniture, clean and wash,
or even drive a hack. Nothing opened up immediately, but those with
whom he spoke were almost universally polite and encouraging.
He would find something, he told himself and was told by others.
He needed to stay at it, and good things would follow. With each
day, he drew a wider circle farther into the surrounding blocks and
spoke to whomever would listen to his request.

Liam calculated the days his remaining cash would buy. Given
Mrs. Kilpatrick's reasonable rent and his penchant for cheap
living, he had no pressing worries. He would be good for several
more weeks, and, if it came to that, he intuited that he could
appeal to his kind landlady for a delay or possibly even a loan.
Her actions and words implied trust, and one night at dinner
she confided to him that she would never have allowed him to
stay if he had not exuded an integrity that she had felt instantly.

Still, Liam needed a job. He needed to plant himself at least
to a limited depth. The restlessness that had driven him here had
taken its toll. The fury of his flight from Boston had exhausted
him and exhausted his dreams. Farmwork would be ideal and
would feed his soul, but there were no farms here. His flight had
dropped him amid tall buildings, crowded streets, and businesses
he sometimes could not recognize. Nothing grew here, certainly
not in large measure, and so there would be no farming. Let that
dream settle a bit while he made his way in this new, strange,
comforting place.

In the evenings, he would take a place in the sitting room after dinner, usually alone but often with one or more of his housemates. There, he would watch a night unfold through the front windows, regarding the strange new angles of a setting sun, the fall of light on city streets, the glint of windows from the houses across the way. He would listen to the voices of children running up the sidewalks, playing their games, chasing one another, being children. The occasional car motored by, sometimes kicking up a loose stone that clattered behind it. Couples might walk by, some holding hands if it was pleasant and warm. A neighborhood dog, a scruffy little terrier, often pranced up the steps of the Kilpatrick house looking for the scraps that his kind landlady would leave for him or a scratch behind his ears from someone coming or going.

His life having played out so far away on a farm and rural village, then against the unforgiving streets of Boston, Liam considered what he saw now with wonder and a hint of awe. He was here, then, in this distant place, the other side of the world from everything he had known, and he needed to know what it was and how it fell to him to wander this new land.

This new, strange, comforting place . . . his reflections on those quiet nights took him here. What constituted his comfort? Where, he asked himself, can a man be who he was meant to be?

I have come here by chance. I did not know such a place existed. I could not conceive of a sprawling city, of its height and depth and breadth, of the thousands and thousands of people who have jammed themselves into it to create their own lives or perhaps to have those lives thrust upon them.

That's it for most of us, isn't it? We have our lives thrust upon us and either we accept it to do the best we can with what we're given or we struggle and kick and flail. For all the flailing, we end in misery more often than not. We lack strength and purpose and vision. No one tells us these things. No one tells us that we can do better. We must find it for ourselves, if at all.

I left what I left, and I'd do it again. I had no way of knowing where I was headed, but I knew damn well what was behind me. Rot and violence. Despair. The hopelessness of knowing every day would be like the one before and the one after, if in fact I could even manage to survive it. Our gentle isle of green, where I'd been arrested for no reason, beaten for sport, threatened, told to hold my peace, seen my mates go missing. Erin go bragh, indeed.

The comforts there were never comforts at all. My father did not tell me nor did he tell young Tomas. He did not know enough to tell me. To tell me that there was no point to it there. That there was nothing to be gained through all the struggles. That all hard work meant was staying in place. No one moved forward. No one grew comfortable.

He will die there, my poor father, with the same sad humility with which he lived. His days draw down even now. His step is slower, his back more arched, bending under years of too much labor and too little reward. He seems smaller. He seems frail and weak, and he grows more so every day.

But is not a father's greatest purpose the preparation of his children? Is there nothing better for him to do than to launch his children someplace higher? In his own way, he did this. I love my father for his sacrifices, although he would not call them so. I love my father for his perseverance, and his loyalty, and his gentleness. I love my father for showing me that I had to go and for bestowing somewhere within me, in a corner of my soul I could not recognize, the strength to break away.

Tomas must learn the same lesson. He must find the same space. I believe he will do so, but it will be difficult for him, especially now. I regret leaving before I could tell him that he must stay out of it all. He cannot choose sides. His only loyalty must be to himself alone.

At the time, I could have told him all this, but I was too weak to do so. If I ever return, it will be for Tomas alone, to tell him these things and to see where and how he is faring. He merits better than what is at hand. He merits better than that sad land.

And sweet Maire stays there still. She walks in the space of her childhood, and she will never leave it. But I know, too, that the only times I ever came close to comfort were the times I spent in her arms, in her gaze . . . in her heart. From the days of my boyhood, these were the only times. No sunset beyond what I saw reflected in her eyes, no dawning more spectacular than the fall of her hair. Those fleeting moments were where I belonged. The only place, and the only time, and all of it destined to crumble away like dry parchment.

I could not stay. For all her beauty and peace, she was not enough to overcome the rest of it. She could not create a land or a time or a future. Our children, even if they lived, would be stillborn. There was nothing she could do.

Yet I would be lying to myself if I did not acknowledge the deep pain of the parting. Better that I left her without words or a proper farewell. I'll be easier to forget, and much easier to disparage. Memory will rise up and swallow the bliss. She'll see me as selfish and weak and too bold for my own good, for her own good. She'll tell herself that she's better off with someone stable, who'll stay by her side and help her build a life in that sad land. She'll believe it. It's best that way.

But, Lord, it does burn within me, this absence. I'll never know another Maire.

Two nights later, as Liam took his place in the sitting room at day's end, one of his housemates came down from his room and sat in the chair opposite. Liam knew him to be quiet, another who kept to himself and kept tidy. They had not spoken more than fifteen words since their introduction, so Liam was a bit surprised when the man sat down near him and began to talk.

"You're down here quite a bit in the evenings. Mind if I share the space?"

"Not at all . . . John, is it?"

"Yes. John Flynn, from County Roscommon."

"Ah, yeah," Liam recalled.

"So, what do you think of the new land so far, Liam? It's quite a place. Quite a bit different from where we come from, right?"

"Different, to say the least. But here we are, and now it's what we make of it."

"And what are you making o' it? Good or ill?"

"It'll take some time to put a judgment on it, don't you think? But for now it's good. I've no complaints since coming to Chicago."

"From Waterford, as I recall. Some fine farming land there."

"Aye, but there's no farms here. I may have to adjust to being a city man for a time."

"It's not so bad, Liam. There's a whole new world here. Around every corner is a story, or someone who can tell one. More to be done here in a week than we'd find in two years back home. I have to say that I'm taking to it rather well. And there are women here, of every sort." He paused with a shy grin. "Sometimes, I'm amazed at all the beauty walking nearby."

Liam found himself warming to this man, who seemed kindred. Liam had not been the first to make this odd journey nor had he ever supposed he was. But no one in Boston had spoken like this, and no one there had expressed wonder or surprise or curiosity beyond their next job or their next drink.

"I've seen the women," Liam replied, "but I'm in no state to pursue them. I need to settle myself a bit to begin."

"Ah, I'm not certain that matters, Liam. We're all after company and comfort in this new place, aren't we? Another body to warm us, another soul to make us feel less lonely. That's all it is."

John paused to look out the side window as a horsefly buzzed against it furiously. The fly banged hard into the glass, backed himself up, and did it again. He saw the forms and colors on the inside, but he did not see the impenetrable glass that blocked his way, the barrier glass, mute and cold, that would never break.

"Did you leave one behind you?"

"How could you know?" asked Liam as the image of Maire, always at the ready, wafted again through his soul.

"We all did . . . we all did, Liam. But that's what we do, isn't it? Leah Durgan was her name, and she was my best friend since we were six. Then we grew up. That was the beauty of it. We were already so comfortable with each other. We knew each other so well that it was no challenge at all to cross the line from friend to lover."

"So, why did you leave her and all the rest of it?"

"My father played the role of rebel. He marched off one morning with the IRA, and we never saw him again. They set him to rig a bridge to blow when a British lorry was passing over. But the eejit had never worked with explosives before. He blew himself to bits getting the sticks and wires in place. He's gone, but the bridge is still standing.

"Anyway," he continued, "with him gone, my mother gave up the fight. We had a small shop in Castlerea that sold dry goods. I worked it with my two brothers, but with Da gone and Ma lost at the bottom of a bottle, I could see that things were going to go to hell quite quickly. And so they did. Most of the customers were used to seeing Da. He was a character. You know the type. Every town has one—the smiling, talkative, funny, compassionate shopkeeper. Christ, he should have owned a pub. But he owned a shop instead, and when he was gone, and the inventory faltered because no one gave a damn enough to account for it, and when the books no longer balanced because Ma couldn't add two plus two to make it four, and when the customers stopped coming in to buy their goods and hear my da's stories, we sold it to the bank. I took my share, small as it was, and got out. One of the lads from Castlerea had come with his family to Chicago, and I had heard it was a right enough place. So it is."

"You're with the post office, as I remember it."

"Indeed. My friend works there, and he brought me over my first week here. It's not much of a job—stacking and sorting and carrying heavy bags. But it's a start, and the pay's not bad at all, more than I could ever hope to make back home. I'm saving up, even though I'm sending a bit home every week or so. In two or three years, I'll buy a place of my own. Until then, this is home, as long as Mrs. Elizabeth extends her welcome."

"I find it quite pleasant here," said Liam. "I had a stay in Boston for a time before I made my way out here. I slept in the rooming house there with one eye open and a club by my pallet. It's a joy to sleep in a real bed, in the house of a woman who knows your name."

John laughed quietly. "She's a jewel, she is. We're more than rent money to her, I tell myself. We're safe here, she'll see to that.

"But listen," John continued, "I need to ask you, are you working now, Liam?"

"I've been looking," he replied with a sigh. "It's a bit tough not knowing where to go, or even what you can do. I've never been anything but a farmer."

"There's no injury in that, and it makes no matter with what I'm asking now. Would you be interested in coming down to the post office with me come Monday? We've had two people quit in the last two days, and we're terribly short. The work's not glamorous, but it's solid. And, to be honest, I think I'd enjoy the company."

* * *

The next night, a Saturday, the two men ventured into the neighborhood to spend the evening at a hidden pub three blocks over. They bought each other rounds, told stories of their youth, flirted with the girls without any intent of real pursuit. At the end of the evening, they walked back to the Kilpatrick house, drank enough to feel the warmth of a fine night and the glow of a new friendship, but they were still and ever respectable in appearance and speech. Elizabeth Kilpatrick would have been hugely disappointed if her boys had come home staggering.

Two weeks later, again on a Saturday, Liam wrote his family a long overdue letter, his first correspondence from the new land.

> *Da and Tomas,*
>
> *No doubt you've spent too much time wondering about me. No doubt, too, that you've spent equal time cursing my name, or ruing the day that I first drew breath. I'll not explain my reasons for going. That simple note I left said all that needed saying. The land is dying, and I was dying with it. A man is more than battles and work and struggle, of that I'm sure.*
>
> *But I know for myself that my leaving gave you more hardships, and for that I deeply apologize. In truth, I gave little to the farm other than a small measure of my labor, and of late that was not much. Since the beatings, I've been useless to you on the land. You've had to make do without much contribution from me. At least now there's one less mouth to feed, saving you enough perhaps to hire a man who'll really work for you—so I tell myself, and I hope it's true. You remain my family, and, despite all I've done to make you think otherwise, I love you both deeply.*
>
> *I would guess that there are rumors circulating the village about me, and if Devon Coghlin has his say, my life in Dungarvan would be short in any event. Set them straight. What I did gave me my escape, but it also was my way of pissing on what's taken place in our once quiet part of the island. I take no sides in this madness. I curse both their houses. They've destroyed the beauty of my home and bludgeoned its future beyond my capacity to bear it. So tell them that I did not act on behalf of the British or the Black*

and Tans. I acted solely on behalf of Liam Finnegan, to whom I owe my sole allegiance.

When I left Ireland, when I left you, I spent days and nights on a boat rocking westward, looking at an ocean that is now between me and everything I had come to know and cherish as a boy and a young man. I reflected deep and hard on what I was doing. And in the end, it was nothing more than instinct. Survival instinct, or a will to live by my own terms. A casting off of the pains and shackles of a limited existence with no future. But I am not a violent man, you must know this. It was not easy for me.

The boat docked in Boston, and I stayed there for two weeks or so. I found Irishmen and took a room in a boarding house where many of them lived. Boston was large, dirty, and rough. I worked at a construction site but took no satisfaction in what I did. I found myself there surviving as I had back home. I lived day to day, with some fear and no plan. The Irish I found there were not at all like those around whom I had grown up. They were not like you. They fought and drank and whored, and any of them would break your leg for half a dollar. In two weeks, I heard no friendly word, nor did I ever see a smile except at some other man's misfortune. So I left. Again, I left.

I took a train west, and when it stopped in Chicago, I got out. Find it on a map if you don't know where it is. It's in the middle of the whole damn country, surrounded by green and farms and fields so rich that anything would grow in abundance. But I'm in the city and see no farms, and I'll see none for a great while.

This city is three times as large as Boston, and I have no illusions that it is not just as dirty and rough. But I've found a part of it that suits me. Again, I found the Irish. I'm staying at Elizabeth Kilpatrick's rooming house with five or six others, most from the island. They're a decent sort, though. They work hard, they have their own dreams, and together we provide some comfort for one another, if only a familiar tone of voice. One of them has become a friend, or so it seems. He's a smart lad, slightly older than me, and he's shown me what he knows of this city.

I've taken a job with the postal service. It's basic. I load things onto trucks. I take things off. I carry bags around and occasionally do some sorting. The pay is good, though, and here is some of it. I'll send what I can when I can. At least this way I can be with you in part and take some of the burden off my leaving.

Go see Maire. Tell her these things and try to make her understand the flawed soul that made these sad decisions. Tell her that I love her no less, that she will always be the first and greatest of my loves, no matter how long I live or whom I shall know. I do not have the courage to write her myself to tell her these things, and if I did I doubt she'd hear them. She may tear up the letter upon its arrival, with no blame from me. I left her in a cowardly way, and that's a scar I'll take with me to my grave. I have no right to ask her forgiveness. But my love for her will not leave me, tomorrow or ever after.

I do not know when I will come back. Perhaps when the cruelty and loss there dies down and Ireland becomes a nation of some standing where a man can walk down the street without looking over his shoulder, where he can harbor a realistic dream or two, maybe then I will return. But for now, I will build my life here step by step, so I cannot plan what lies too far ahead. Right now, I am here and you are there. With my deep, deep love, and a plea for whatever forgiveness you might spare, I write these words tonight with you both in my thoughts.

Liam

Young Tomas Finnegan did not read Liam's letter when it was delivered to what remained of the Finnegan farm outside Dungarvan—that would be something to fall to their father, Michael Finnegan, alone. When Devon Coghlin's boys had come to the farm to take restitution for the theft of their money, they had expected to kill the family's three cows and set fire to the barn. They had not expected that Tomas would be in the barn helping his favorite cow during a late-night birthing. The commotion the boys had made as they stormed up the pathway to the farm—for they had spent the evening drinking at Ryan's and had roused themselves to a boisterous, vengeful fury—had drawn Tomas out. He had then broken for the house to fetch the family's gun, but the stone that Jamie Francis threw caught him hard on the side of his head. As the boys burnt the barn and the cattle bolted inside it, Michael Finnegan had rushed out of his house with the gun Tomas could not fetch and fired shots at the dark forms running back down his pathway. He thought he hit one of them, perhaps in the leg. The running forms stopped long enough to pull up a comrade, who was dragged along as they made their escape.

As Michael ran to the barn, he called for Tomas, but in hearing no answer he grew frantic. Small buckets of water could not douse this fire, which had been properly fueled as it was lit, and the old man answered the horrific agonized cries of the cattle within with his own deep wailing. In the light of the growing flames, as he knelt there by his loss, he saw the form of his younger son lying prone on the grass near the pathway. With a cry, he ran to him and saw at once the pooling of blood spreading out from his head. The gash along his temple was ripped wide. Bits of flesh curled along its edge. The father smoothed them back into place and took a rag from his back pocket to try to stanch the flow. There he sat, rocking his son's head in his lap as he pressed the rag into place, weeping with intermittent indistinguishable shouts, the kind an animal makes when it feels the pain of a slow knife. He stayed there the remainder of that long night.

As the sun came up, he wrapped Tomas in a blanket and loaded him into the cart, but there was no longer an ass to pull it. He dragged the cart the two miles to town, and with the help of two shopkeepers who were opening their stores, took him to the village doctor, who was woken by the loud pounding on his door.

Tomas had yet to regain consciousness, but his breathing was steady. The doctor cleansed and stitched the wound, wrapping the young man's head in thick bandages. For the rest of the day, Michael sat next to his silent and motionless son, gently weeping.

Three days later, when Tomas finally stirred, he woke to blindness.

His small holdings destroyed, his barn in cinders, his elder son vanished, and his younger son crippled, Michael felt that all was lost, and so there was nothing more at stake. He knew, too, that the town's constabulary would do nothing, fearful of being caught in the middle of unreasoned vengeance. So, on Monday of the following week, he had called upon the Auxiliary Division of the Royal Irish Constabulary office in Waterford to let them know what had happened and who they might look for, mentioning the names of those in Dungarvan who had moved against the Black and Tans.

* * *

Liam carried on with Chicago. Over the next few months, his life unfolded sweetly, and although it required hard work, long hours, and a devilish commute on rail lines to the city's center that ate up two hours of his day, he found his place in the postal service. In short order, he gained a reputation for efficiency and reliability. Promotions loomed, or so he was told.

In the evenings, he would still spend time in Mrs. Kilpatrick's sitting room or sometimes at the local bar, drinking quietly alone or with John Flynn. John had taken a liking to the American sport of baseball, and so on days off they would often make the short walk to Wrigley Field to watch the Cubs. Liam knew almost nothing about what was taking place in front of him, but he marveled at the wide swath of green with its clear sharp lines and tight cut. He fancied the colors of the uniforms, the contrast with a blue sky, the tints and hues of those in the stands. He breathed in the smell of cigar smoke and the warm meats they sold there.

In time, he came to feel something special as he sat in the stands. Although he did not understand the flow and purpose of the American game, he took pride in cheering on the Chicago team. Sometimes, they won, and he joined in the collective yells of those who sat around him, celebrating not the game but the city that had drawn him. More often, they lost, and he would pause to let almost everyone else file out before he did. He would stand then and take a few minutes to look around—at the field, at the houses beyond the outfield walls, at the taller buildings in the distance, at the sky, at the emptying stands. As he did so, he invariably said a quick and silent prayer of thanks to whatever forces had placed him here.

When his father's news reached him from Dungarvan, he let forth a deep moan that grew into a wail as the torment he had caused became clear. He withdrew for several days, emerging only to go to work and to take his meals in silence. His work diverted him from the avalanche of guilt that cascaded his thoughts into jumbled debris. He worked to sort through it all, to pull away anything of value he might salvage from the disaster of his former home.

* * *

In a pub, dimly lit, smoky, and woody, Liam sat by himself in a corner, snug, drawing on his fifth pint, his eyes focused on distance, his heart as numb as the tip of his ale-soaked tongue. He licked his lips and felt their cracks. Felt their small dry furrows. Felt the arid broken spaces. With a snort, he reached down to his pint, warm and thick, and took another tasteless swallow.

Around him were voices he did not hear and light and shadows he did not see. Liam sought only numbness and dead time. Thoughts came, tarried a bit, and he let them go. Time passed without notice or care. Liam recognized his special knack of slaying time and thought. He recognized the peculiar and perverse alchemy of turning the most precious into the most foul.

What is bravery, then, and where is the line crossed toward foolishness? Toward self-indulgence? Toward cowardice? His blurry thoughts could only coalesce around questions. No answers dared present themselves. It was a night of questions only.

Nothing gained without an outlay. No victories without casualties. Everything dearly won comes with a cost. But why must those costs be accounted from the souls of others?

I am no hero. I sit here beyond danger or threat, beyond poverty, in a new place rife with comforts and pleasure, heated by the incandescent fuel of promise. But behind me lies a trail of sorrow, heartache, loneliness, and broken bodies, of those I despise and of those I love most dearly. I am as guilty as the man who threw the rock that blinded my brother and the cold bastard with the warm torch that fired our barn. I am more brute than hero, more Fingal than Cuchulain.

What is bravery, then? Whatever it is, it falls beyond my grasp and sits buried under the debris of a frozen soul. I define myself now only by what lies at hand. What lies behind me are shreds and tears, tatters and blood—in Dungarvan, in Boston, in sweet Maire's fair bed, in my brother Tomas's dead eyes.

I have spent too much time running away. I have no choice but to go forward, and I know that I'll never set foot again in the land that bore me. I'll never go home. There is no home to go to. In exile now, I can run no more.

Liam motioned to the barkeeper for another stout. It would be his last this night. The coins in his pocket were too low to do much more, and it would only take one more to blot out the sour, inconsolable questions that danced in his psyche like black-shrouded Druids at the solstice.

When a man has lost himself, where does he turn? Where in the broken, floating flotsam of what used to be whole do new dreams lie? When does the energy rise to identify and pursue those dreams through a spirit shipwrecked on a rocky and forlorn shore? Floating in this flotsam all around, bobbing in unclear waters. Grab hold of the debris. Float and kick hard. Keep your head above water, and feel the rich new air fill lungs not yet flattened and empty.

* * *

On weekends, Liam continued to explore his new city. Believing that he could not truly know a place until he felt the whole of it beneath his feet, he would walk without a map or purpose, following the streets by whatever name captured his fancy at the moment—Ashland or Marshfield to the east, Waveland or Addison to the south, or the blade of Clark Street that cut diagonally across them all, and a hundred other avenues and lanes, each with its own feel. As he walked, he imagined the fabric of strange lives behind the narrow brick facades of small homes or the worn storefronts that sold tobacco or dry goods, newspapers or stale fruit.

He listened to the voices that came from within or rose from the sidewalks around him. He heard arguments between lovers and heated discussions about Prohibition. He heard the coy hagglings between buyers and sellers and listened to the boasts of friends trying to outdo one another about what had happened the night before with this woman or that shy girl. He heard the laughter of children echoing down sandstone and brick.

Each sound, each voice, linked Liam to something that had come before, and with each linkage came comfort or regret. His walks told him that while Chicago might be immensely larger and more complex than Dungarvan, the flow of life in each place followed similar rhythms. A child's laughter in Lincoln Park took him to Walton Park, where on Sundays after Mass, children freed from their parents ran and played, pushing hoops or throwing balls or racing the boats along Davitt's Quay. Irish voices in Chicago argued American politics, and in them Liam heard Devon Coghlin and his gang bullying the nights in Ryan's Pub. Around a corner, he might see an old couple, hair white and shoulders slightly stooped, walking slowly and delicately with each other, perhaps hand in hand, and he would hear his father's voice stab a deep wound into his ambushed heart. One afternoon, he passed a hospital on the North Side and looked into the sightless eyes of a young man being walked by his nurse, pale and blind but otherwise strong enough to work a farm, or so it seemed.

But the pain of remembrance ebbed through the consolation of continuity. Places and accents might differ, faces might take different hues—black, brown, and white—and the light of days might wane at different angles. But Liam saw that the struggles and joys and wonder and loss, that the infinite permutations of the mind, the body, and the spirit, rang true in this new land, that he was part of something constant, and that, no matter how hard or how far or how fast he might run, he could never outrun his own soul.

* * *

Fall and winter had passed in the city, and on the Sunday twilight of a warm April day, Liam sat on a promontory overlooking Lake Michigan. Behind him the sun sank gently in pinks and oranges and indigo, changing by the minute over the wispy light clouds of spring. He had spent the day wandering again, all the way downtown where he looked into store windows and considered the women who sold clothing, fabrics, hats, and lace to young ladies and matrons. He thought of Brendan Phelan's millinery store in Dungarvan, Maire behind the counter in cotton and smiles, as much an attraction to those who entered as the goods she tried to sell them.

He had no thought of purchase, nothing that he needed other than to see the faces and hear the voices. That was enough. After walking the afternoon down Michigan Avenue, he reached the Chicago River underpass and stood for a few moments against the railing. A few boats sailed beneath him, and upriver a smallish freighter trailing grey smoke chugged toward the near West Side. A gull landed next to him on the railing. It turned a white head to give him a curious glance then lifted its wings to stretch itself. Liam saluted the bird with a finger to his cap. "Better luck to you today than for me," he said, then turned and headed north again. He stopped for a pint at a place he knew on Randolph, ate two hardboiled eggs, then resumed his way to the shore.

This was not his first time at the lake. Liam had sat on this rock before, had seen sunsets and late winter storms, had felt the rain on his face and the sun on his shoulders. The water always drew him. That at least had not changed. He valued the constancy of the water. He valued the fidelity that spoke of distances and place.

Water so vast that you cannot see the other side, and yet it is just a lake. Cross it, and you'd still have half a continent to travel to reach its end. Different depths. Different currents. Different life beneath it. Different life above it.

I sit here now and watch the same sun that shone on my father wind low behind me, the same sun that shone into my brother's sightless eyes. Different life beneath it.

I have no notion of crossing this lake. I've done enough crossing for a lifetime. I have done what I have done. The time for running is over.

Ah God, I am no hero. You of all should know that. You see my cowardice, and You see what has made my heart cower. You see why I am here. And I trust that in time You will share with me a hint or a clue, perhaps a whisper, as to what it all really means behind the false hopes. Perhaps someday You will tease me with an answer.

But right now I see You only in these waters and hear You only through the lapping of these waves. I am still a young enough man. Impatient. Discontent. Still afraid after all this running. Afraid of my sins and what they have wrought. Afraid of who I really am beneath the illusion of myself that I carry so well that I even sometimes believe its substance. But at heart I know what's really there. And I know what isn't. There is no bravery and nothing close to valor. My soul runs cold and shallow.

Gulls swooped high to low in the late-day sky, diving for fish. Their cries wailed sharp and mournful, piercing the quiet city noises into distant rumbles. Their plaintive shrieks pierced Liam's heart, banshees and lost spirits carried on the soft air. Nightfall loomed from across the water, both gulls and Liam himself oblivious to its dark creep.

"I don't want to bother you, but are you okay?" He heard a trilling of Irish winds.

Liam turned with a start. A woman no older than twenty-one stood ten feet behind him. "Are you okay?" she repeated. "You haven't moved for as long as I've been here."

The young man dropped his head with an embarrassed grin. He looked up again into eyes so blue that the lake paled under their brightness.

All he saw were the eyes. It would only be later that he would come to regard the thick mane of black hair that circled a face so delicate and fair as to remind him of the china in Mrs. Kilpatrick's dining room or the white of a priestly alb. Only later would he come to marvel at the firmness of a trim body and the curve of legs both strong and fine. The lilt of a gentle and graceful voice would forestall his sleep that night and for nights ahead. But right now, there were only her eyes.

"I'm sorry, lass. Lost in my own thoughts, I suppose."

"They must have been deep thoughts."

"Are there any other kind? I find this a useful place to clear my mind sometimes, especially at day's end."

"I do, too. This shore reminds me of home—sunsets and water on a warm April evening. And for a bit of time, I can fool myself that I'm back where I once belonged."

"But no more, I take it. We're here now, both of us, for whatever it means."

"It means what we make of it. My name is Molly, or Miss Morrissey, if you prefer to be formal."

"I've never been one for formalities. Liam Finnegan, Miss Molly, and very pleased that you disturbed my dreamings."

"I come down to this shore many nights, Liam. This is my escape. I may have even seen you from a distance once or twice."

"And what is it you're escaping?"

"The same as you—drudgery, boredom, and that awful foreign feeling you get when everything seems so wrong. Or am I being presumptuous?"

Liam rose from the rocks and picked up the light coat he had brought along. He crossed the short distance to face this new and wondrous occurrence. "A bit presumptuous, yes," he said lightly. "I just find this to be a place where no one expects anything of me and where for a time I don't mind being anonymous or even being a stranger."

"Ah God," said Molly. "We're constant strangers. I so much miss the sense I had as a girl, that sense of belonging and *knowing*—knowing where I was, who I was with, and what I was supposed to be doing. There's none of that here, is there?

It's too big, and too close, and too loud, and not enough music or dance. But here we are."

"And where are we, Miss Molly? Where is that?"

"Why, we're in Chicago, Mr. Liam. We're both of us lost in Chicago."

So it began, this small act that grew by the day into something deeper, into redemption. Liam and Molly walked away from the lake together that night and learned what there was to learn about each other at first meeting. Her family of Morrisseys came from Schull in the west of County Cork, following a mythology of work and riches. Molly's father had been a farmer. Now, he was a laborer, perhaps little different from those whom Liam had seen in Boston. She was twenty years old, rebellious enough to walk the city alone and bold enough to speak to strangers who intrigued her. She had sensed Liam's brooding nature and intuited a hard story that she wanted to hear. Liam shared it, and from that point there was no turning back for either of them.

Three weeks later, after several end-of-day meetings on the street where Molly lived with her parents and five younger siblings, after walks back to the spot on the shore where they had met, after Liam found the nerve one night to steal a kiss that in truth did not need stealing, he took her to meet Elizabeth Kilpatrick.

They chatted, the three of them, in the parlor for more than an hour. Mrs. Kilpatrick served tea and biscuits, asked all the right questions and a few of the bold ones: "What do you think of young Liam, Molly? He's a special lad, no?" and "Where do you stand on the IRA and unification?" and "Do you ever miss a Sunday Mass?"

Later, as Liam walked her home, Molly laughed and rested her arm against his shoulder. "Your Mrs. Kilpatrick is a character, Liam. She has few qualms about interrogation, that much is clear."

"I'm sorry about that, lass. I didn't quite expect that she would go as far as she did. She's a dear heart."

"Oh, I had no mind of any of it. She wants to protect her boys, and you're the one she wants to protect the most. I could see at once that she deeply cares about you." Molly stopped walking and pulled Liam around to face her. "As do I." She kissed him gently on the lips, there on the sidewalk on Diversey at day's end. "As do I," she repeated and kissed him again.

When he returned to the boarding house after delivering Molly to her family, Mrs. Kilpatrick was waiting in the parlor, seemingly unmoved from where she had been when Molly and Liam had left two hours before. "Have some tea, Liam. It's just made."

"Thank you, Mrs. K., but I think I've had enough for the day. I'd just as soon say good night and head on up."

"This will only take a few minutes, Liam. Please sit." There was no denying a command from Mrs. Kilpatrick. Liam sighed, then said gently, "In that case, I'll take the tea." He sat in his favorite chair as she hurried to the kitchen to bring it.

When she returned, Liam took a sip and felt the heated liquid flow the length of his throat and settle into his stomach. Mrs. Kilpatrick pulled her chair close to his then placed her hand on his knee.

"I'll be direct, Liam, with apologies for my boldness and if I'm speaking out of turn. I'm sure I am, but there are times you need the wisdom of someone older, now that you're away from your da and anyone else you can trust. But you can trust me. Am I right?"

"I always have, Mrs. K. You've taken good care of me here and given me as close to a home as I could want."

"Well then, let me care for you one more time." She leaned in close. "What I have to say is simple, but it couldn't be clearer to me." She paused.

"And what is that?"

"Marry that girl, Liam. Don't let her get away. Marry her, and make a life for yourselves. You'll not find anyone finer than Molly Morrissey. This I know."

"And how do you know this, Mrs. K.?" Liam asked with a grin.

"It's obvious to anyone who cares to look, Liam. You're perfect for each other—two souls stumbling along and groping about for something to hang on to. She's bright, and beautiful, and has great spirit. Yet there's a gentleness about her that she could never hide. She's a good person, Liam. A grand person. And she's crazy about you. She couldn't take her eyes off you, Liam, and she hung on every word you said, although God knows why."

Liam laughed in spite of himself. "God knows why. I've not got much to offer, I suspect."

"You have the best to offer there could ever be. You have a heart that is bruised and torn but stronger in the broken spots. You have kindness, whether you see it there or not. And, Liam Finnegan, you have more courage than any young man I've ever known here."

Liam's giddiness turned sober, and he looked intently at his landlady, who saw courage where he did not.

"So, be courageous one more time, Liam. She's precious. And so are you."

* * *

Six months later, after presenting himself and his intentions to Molly's father, who had stared at him wordlessly over a glass of beer and said nothing when asked for his daughter's hand and then walked out of the room, after Molly's mother had apologized to Liam and hugged him to tell him that he was the best thing that had ever happened to Molly, who, she said, was very lost and on the verge of doing terrible things, after nights spent on cool porches just holding hands, after stolen kisses and stolen beers, after conferences with Father James O'Halloran, a local parish priest, to assure the good padre of their faith, their devotion to each other and their ultimate purity, after writing a letter home to Michael Finnegan explaining that his son was about to be wed and would most likely never return to Ireland, at least for the foreseeable future, after the subtle agony of being so close to what was one perceived as paradise, Liam Finnegan and Molly Morrissey became husband and wife on a late morning in the company of Molly's parents, a handful of Liam's friends from the post office, and Elizabeth Kilpatrick. Father O'Halloran presided.

The world is what it is; men who are nothing, who allow themselves to become nothing, have no place in it.

—V.S. Naipaul, A Bend in the River

CHAPTER XII

We work in the dark—we do what we can—we give what we have. Our doubt is our passion, and our passion is our task. The rest is the madness of art.

—Henry James, *The Middle Years*

A night in March, too soon warm and filled with the discontent of an unsettled mind. I settle now into a chair in the quiet. Always, there is the quiet, and I share my space with no one. I hear the tick of a clock, the whirr of the refrigerator, and take a glass of wine with me as I sit in a room with no pulse. The only rhythms of this place are what I can lend to it, grudgingly and joyless, until I absorb them back into my own restlessness. I sip the wine, surrounded by music I cannot hear, and think back to better days.

I see her again and again, but her face is interchangeable with others I have known, others of different colors and different contours. I feel again the touch of her hand as I held it there, or rather, as she held it in lock with mine. I could not let her go; she would not let me. Now, she has me still in her grasp. *Votre chérie* indeed.

Always the questions come back the same way. Where is she now? What has happened in that place where fate lay down with human nature and bred a misshapen childhood? Who was she, really? What in her young and tatty life had already died, and what could be reborn? What do I do? What, please God, must I do?

The wine burns its way through the immutable, unwavering questions, and I come back to her eyes, which never left me. Her eyes, which regarded me with wonder, and suspicion, and chance, and loss, and so much more than I could ever discern because I could never burrow myself behind them to see what was really there. Her eyes, that have seen panoramas that can dwell only in the realm of my fantasy and fancy. Her eyes, again and again, larger than what befits a tiny girl. What have they seen that I need to see?

Votre chérie.

Please, God, what must I do?

* * *

If April was to be the cruelest month, March that year was its herald. Conor drank his wine, stirred the embers of an unquiet mind, and held tightly to an unarticulated conviction that there must be something more to him than he could see. He thought that some of his Grandda Liam's fighting spirit must be somewhere in his DNA, part of his constitution, part of what would help him find his own way, find the answers that would solve his life's riddles.

As he pondered this, he saw the fabrication of who he was, the flimsy facade shielded by a legislative portfolio that lent a validation to a self-absorbed and isolated community. Shallow and meaningless in the warm spring night, fallow and alone, Conor saw the hands of time rushing too quickly. How to make it mean something again? *Please, God, what must I do?*

On nights when sleep came slowly, Conor would lie in his bed and think of how Grandda Liam had set his mind on a specific course and never looked back. He would think back to his fantasies, the ones that had filled his youth. He would remember the basketball games, the sound of the ball flicking through the net after he had launched a flawless jump shot, then the cheers of a crowd long since dispersed and gone away. He would remember the hot sand beneath his feet as he headed for the surf at Newport and the initial cold splash of the salty water as he dove in to find a wave to ride back to shore. He would remember the first autumn breezes that shuffled the trees on Queens Mall when he knew, *he knew*, that a proud and celebrated life lay just before him and all he had to do to grab it was just continue to be Conor Finnegan. He would remember the voices of his roommates, the tromping of their footsteps on the stairway, their laughter, and their faith in the simple fact that they all belonged together there, in that small and dirty apartment, sharing with one another the best they had to give.

With those memories, those gentle fantasies, he would try to quiet himself to sleep, to peel away the veneer that coated who he really was, who he still had to be, somewhere under there, under all that debris. Find the purest parts, the ones unspoiled. The ones that survived the derailment. Maybe then sleep would come.

* * *

Outside Conor's apartment early one morning, well before sunrise, a homeless man was staggering about. He woke Conor first with his anger, a profane ranting that barked like a dog's snarl. Conor couldn't make out the particulars. All he heard was anger—vicious, violent, and helpless. All the homeless man had were his words, whatever they meant and wherever they arose.

He kept at it for at least half an hour. Conor thought about peeking out the window to see where the man was and what he looked like. It was easy to entertain a vision. So many homeless wandered around this city, and so many looked disheveled beyond the point of all loss. Conor imagined a youngish man, perhaps in his twenties but not older than forty, long hair, unkempt beard, and clothes that fit inconsistently—perhaps a shirt too large or jeans with more than a few tatters.

Conor didn't look, though. Even this display deserved some dignity and the shield of anonymity. *He lives in his own private swirls and eddies. I have no call to invade them.*

After a time, the man's rantings changed. The anger faded, perhaps expunged, like a panting breath. What replaced it was a guttural moan that rose from deep within, the bellow of a wounded animal. Conor could not know what bore it, nor the precision of the agonies he roared out. A loss of time, of youth, of power, of relevance, of sanity . . . gone, and forever gone in his shredded psyche, his unstitched heart. The man roared, and moaned, and cried from the throat.

At last spent, he sobbed rhythmically then softened his breathing in a regular pattern. Conor heard in it a comfort, almost as if he were pleasuring himself, his hollow moans transformed into quick and definite breaths.

Over an hour, Conor heard outside his window what he could not feel. *But I know it is human,* he thought, *and because it is human, it is shared. There is no fear in that. There is no peace, either.*

* * *

Conor proclaimed himself on his Committee on Foreign Relations business card. After Rwanda had reawakened a dormant sense of purpose, he had resolved that there was indeed something he might be able to do about the complexities and sorrows of those that most people chose not to see. At least he would make the effort and see what would happen.

The list of countries whose dirt soiled his shoes continued to grow. Most were countries that Conor had never envisioned seeing. The highlights of his travels were never the tourist sites or the romantic locales. He visited Cambodia and did not come within 100 miles of Angkor Wat. But he did see some of the most remarkable slums imaginable and children running naked down an unpaved road divided by a free-flowing open sewage ditch. In Thailand, with its four-star restaurants and luxury hotels, he ate dried frogs in a bamboo hut, served with pride by a woman in incalculable poverty whose sense of hospitality he could not ignore. In Egypt, he drove into the desert to watch young boys work limestone quarries in 123-degree heat with neither shelter nor clean water at their disposal. Conor saw the Pyramids and the Sphinx from a train window as he sped up to Alexandria. He got no closer than dusty images through smeared glass.

Each trip had a purpose, usually in conjunction with evaluating some development or rehabilitation project funded by the United States Agency for International Development or possibly investigating work that could be done in a country where human needs and US foreign interests overlapped. Conor eagerly volunteered for each assignment. His duties in Washington became an anchor that weighed him down as he envisioned new venues for his fragile idealism and the small victories he might hope to win. In the field, he perceived an energy, a movement, that did not exist in the District, where protocol and power remained the dominant values.

He had no illusions. Children would still starve, young women would still be trafficked, curable diseases would still claim young lives that could easily be saved. Yet he also knew that a program here or an initiative there—well conceived, sufficiently funded, and strategic—could do some good, might change some lives, and could possibly create models that others could regard and replicate. A few minds might come to new conclusions about the humanistic potential of relief and development. No mountains would be moved, but those who lived in the shadows of those mountains might enjoy a bit more sunlight.

On nights when he did not travel, at home in his apartment across the river in Virginia, Conor closed most days at a living room window that looked out back onto a patch of woods spared the soulless suburban development of condominiums and retail. The dark woods cast shadows that sparked a fancy, especially on unsettled nights of wind or rain. Music would play, and Conor would watch the woods, the interplay of dark and light, of solidity and flux.

He tried to empty his mind, breathed in rhythm with the music he played, followed the flow of the trees and the walkways and the night sky with eyes that held no expectations. On these rare nights, Conor thought no great thoughts, and if they had come to him demanding entry, he would have rejected them, telling them to come back later.

And they came again—the boy in Cairo who died before his eyes at the paupers hospital. The street children singing their songs in a school in Vietnam. The young girls wearing bright saris in rural India to welcome his delegation. *Votre chérie.* They came again, quietly, persistently. They never went away, really. He knew they were there, and he would deal with them. *But not tonight, when the sky is black and the busy city is so quiet that you can hear the night birds rustling in their branches.*

Only the night sky mattered, and the trees, and the wind. Only the sense of place. Only the peaceful sense of emptiness. Empty, at last and for a time, although he could not stay this way. The questions were still there, would always be there. There were no certainties, no assurances; life itself was as transient as the wind that fluttered through these trees. He would have to deal with all that, in whatever new and irresistible forms this transience demanded. He knew that.

Empty on these nights, but for these moments. That was enough, these few moments of reflection. That was enough.

* * *

"Hey, Finnegan." Annie DiFrancesco dropped herself into the chair next to his overly cluttered desk. A junior minority assistant, Annie had started as an intern two years before. When she graduated *cum laude* from Villanova, her internship had transformed itself into a job offer to fill a new vacancy that came about when the previous junior minority assistant found herself with an unexpected and unwelcome child. She left suddenly to tend to her life's new chaos, the first step of which was to hunt down the unsuspecting father. Annie came on board after a very short and perfunctory search, the living and breathing beneficiary of an aggressive sperm and a welcoming ovum.

Annie was pretty enough to enter Conor's occasional fantasies—dark hair cut short and styled around a heart-shaped face, dark eyes, and the petite, firm body of pulsating youth. Conor had noticed, as he usually did when something worth noticing came into view. While there was technically a policy against intraoffice dating, no one paid it any attention. Every happy hour or staff party carried the potential for random alcohol- or hormone-induced couplings. It happened all the time.

Conor looked up from his terminal. "What's up, Miss Annie? I'm assuming this isn't a social visit."

"You work too hard, Finnegan, do you know that? You used to be a lot more fun."

"Why, thank you, Annie. I'm flattered that you dropped by to chat about my social failings." Conor couldn't help a teasing grin. *Damn, Annie is cute.*

"I mean it, Conor. You could use some socializing. We should go out for a drink sometime."

"Are you old enough to go into a bar, Annie? Have you ever

seen the inside of a tavern or publick house with the likes of a degenerate like me?"

"Well, you are considerably older, that I admit. And I've been in plenty of bars. It might be an act of charity to force you from behind your desk to come with me."

"Ah, the enthusiasms and generosity of the young. I'll consider it. I promise. I might even buy the first round, given that you're so newly employed and I'm a seasoned old bastard."

"I'll hold you to that. But that's not why I'm here."

"What's up?"

"Africare is having a leadership retreat next week. Among other things, they'll be trying to devise a legislative strategy, and they're interested in seeing if redevelopment in Rwanda might be worth an emphasis. They want someone to come out and talk about what's happening there, what else is needed, and what it might reasonably cost. They want to see if Rwanda is worthy of being an arrow in their lobbying quiver."

"And I'm the guy?"

"Yeah, you're the guy. You've been there, and you can't seem to stop talking about it. If you're going to bore everybody with your obsessions, then we can at least put you to work. Besides, they might give you dinner."

"When and where, Annie? I'll see if I can fit it in."

"Next Wednesday, from four to seven. It's at the Aspen Institute Wye River Conference Center, on the Eastern Shore."

"Jesus, that's a two-hour drive from here, through the Maryland swamps. Dinner should be the least of my compensations."

"That's the cost of being a seasoned bastard, Conor. They'd never entrust this assignment to my young and firm ass." Annie stood and dipped her hip as she walked away, smiling over a well-shaped shoulder. *Damn.*

The following Wednesday, Conor and a sketchy PowerPoint illustrating the still unmet financial, social, and cultural costs of

Rwanda's genocide left the office shortly after noon. The autumn sky shone bright blue, and an early chill kept the air tart. Conor allowed two hours for the drive, another hour for the vagaries of DC traffic, and a final hour to arrive without rushing and to compose his thoughts before addressing what he assumed would be the typical gathering of people with high intentions and low capacity to act on them.

Conor had spoken often to groups about various global situations that he had seen directly. He had addressed a Coptic church about Egypt and spoken to a rural development association about Bangladesh and half a dozen nonprofits about their targeted interests in India, Vietnam, and Cambodia. But Rwanda remained special, and whenever he could, he stepped up in response to the passion his time there had engendered. The genocide was years ago, and people had forgotten. On to the next crisis, the latest headlines of despair. Plenty more to worry about now that Rwanda had had its day. Conor, though, could not let it rest.

Votre chérie.

Conor knew little about Africare, but it didn't matter. He would not tailor his remarks to the nature of his audience. Facts were facts, or so he thought, a lingering vestige of the unyielding idealism that had brought him, for better or worse, to where he now was. He would talk about educational access and literacy rates, the demographic gap between genders, water and sanitation issues, communicable diseases and a paucity of treatment programs, community-based economies, and, in the end, the tens of thousands of people still living as refugees at the mercy of whatever aid agencies might spin their way.

And this group would react as all the others—intense eyes that never left him as he spoke, bodies arched forward to hear the facts that they did not know or to ponder within their own futility those they did.

There would be questions, too. They were usually well meaning, but Conor still recoiled at the memory of a gentleman in a three-piece suit at a panel discussion about Sub-Saharan development who had sanctimoniously asked, "They're Africans. Do you really think they possess the capacity for social rehabilitation?" and a young woman, no more than twenty-two or twenty-three, who had asked at a presentation to a church group, "Would it be possible to conduct a continental evangelical movement to bring those who suffer to Jesus?"

So, Conor would speak with his usual passion, the phantoms of his time there still haunting him, but he recognized that his audiences came from disparate perspectives, had limited resources, and most likely even more limited interest. Still, it was what he could do.

The Africare presentation and discussion only differed slightly. The board was well-informed and merely needed confirmation of what they had already considered. They had a network in key countries that could get a few things done, and they wanted that network to do more, supplemented by a newly aggressive lobbying effort to bring attention on Capitol Hill to their points of emphasis. Rwanda was one such point. During the course of the evening, Conor gave them ammunition to construct a rationale that more public dollars might help this country meet its humanistic obligation to vulnerable people, especially women and children, who could be easily helped toward self-sufficiency. All it took was a bit of vision.

He concluded in the usual way, "Among the casualties of Rwanda was the enormous loss of potential. How many thousands of children, even though they survived the horror itself, had whatever promise they might have possessed snatched away? Education, home, family, identity, self-esteem . . . gone. Every death has a ripple effect, and the children and young people of Rwanda, and of every country that suffers natural or

manmade cataclysms, suffer those ripples at their core. They
are no longer children but rather some hybrid link between our
purest and basest forms. They have lost more than we could
ever calculate. We owe them our best efforts at reconstruction
and at redemption. In the process, we perhaps gain a measure
of redemption for ourselves."

At the dinner following, Conor sat next to a public relations
advisor whose name he did not remember and a board member
who seemed particularly engaged in his remarks. He had been
reluctant to stay but felt obligated to his hosts despite the long
drive back home that now would be postponed for at least another
two hours. No matter, really. Tomorrow, he would still find his
way to his desk at the usual time, albeit a bit bleary-eyed.

The board member, an attorney with a major law firm
representing multinational corporations with African interests,
captured him as soon as the salads were served. "Your remarks
hit home," he said. "I've spent a good deal of time in Nairobi, and
I've been able to hop over to Kigali from time to time. No real
business there, but the country fascinates me. Such trauma, and
how does one really recover?"

"One doesn't," said Conor. "The challenge is to process it in
some way that allows you to move forward. As I tried to stress,
the country needs some investments in infrastructure. They're
surprisingly stable given their last fifty years of turmoil. All
they need is some time, space, and resources to put things back
together."

"But the psychological costs are immense. I recall you saying
that everyone in the country had a story, that their families were
either victims or perpetrators, and that there were almost no
innocent bystanders."

"The reconciliation councils are a great step," replied Conor.
"They'll be doing their work for the next generation. It's a start,
and a good one, but in the end there has to be a consensus that

the country cannot withstand more violence, more hatred, and more separation. They're tired of fighting, that's apparent. You may have noticed that Kigali is one of the quietest big cities you'll ever see. No one raises a voice, no one honks a horn, no one yells at their kids. There's a collective depression that's going to take a couple of generations to overcome."

"I'm trying to decide if your view is optimistic or pessimistic."

"It's neither. I try to keep myself firmly based in reality. Idealism only goes so far."

"But it's an essential component in all this, don't you think? We have to be idealistic and allow ourselves to reach beyond what might be possible."

Conor paused and looked down at a half-eaten salad. He looked up again and met his companion's eyes. In the next breath, the hard lessons he had learned about life crystallized in his response. "I think we need to marry idealism with pragmatism. That's the only way forward. We have to recognize that we will never, ever reach the finish line. I'd say most people would call that pessimistic. But there are those of us who think that reaching the finish line isn't as important as running the race."

"Excuse me," said the board member, and he left the table to go back to the conference room. When he returned a few seconds later, he handed Conor a business card. "My name is Richard Jakande. My information is on this card, which I want you to have. I want you to consider what I ask now.

"I am also on the board of a small nonprofit organization," he continued. "You have not heard of it, I imagine. It's young and just getting its legs. We founded it three years ago to provide grants to community organizations in Sub-Saharan Africa working in education and health. That's the only way to do it, you know. The only way to change a system is from the ground up. I believe you alluded to that yourself in your remarks tonight, that change cannot be imposed by broad-scale programs if those programs are brought in from the outside. A people with a history of colonization will see such efforts with even the best intentions as another form of social conquest. So, we try to empower those few visionaries on the ground who are addressing their community's problems in their own ways and within their own cultures. So far it's worked, I think."

"I'm assuming, then," said Conor as he regarded the card, "that you'd like to find some avenues of public funding."

"Not at all," continued Richard, earnestly. "We can't support these fragile communities if we're perceived as part of the US government. All our funding is from private sources—individuals and foundations—and I'm trying to convince our corporate brethren that such investments are good business. That part of it is slow going, but it will come. In the meantime, we need to convince as many people of means as we can that we are a good investment that offers the best promise of bringing about lasting change for the poorest people of Africa . . . for the forgotten people of Africa.

"So," he went on, "I'm not asking you to be a representative of the Foreign Relations Committee or to do anything that that position entails. Frankly, young Mr. Finnegan, anyone can do that.

"We're looking for a new executive director, someone who is articulate, passionate, and knows the ground. Someone who knows how things work. You said it yourself—marry the idealistic with the pragmatic. I am chairing the search committee, and your presence and words here tonight have told me that I may have found exactly who we need. I'd like you to consider this very seriously."

Conor stayed silent as the servers cleared the salad plates and brought out the entrees. In the clinking of tableware and the low hum of a dozen separate conversations, his own thoughts had come to a halt, made inert by a diversion sudden, unexpected, and promising. He looked from the business card into the face of Richard Jakande.

"Take your time," said Richard. "Think it through, and call me later in the week with your questions. I know you have them. But don't ask them tonight. Tonight, let's just enjoy this wonderful meal and the wonderful sense that there may in fact be something we can do together that could brighten this dark world a tiny bit."

* * *

In the heart's deepest caverns, dreams dance with fantasy, and the dance goes on, even if the music should stop.

Votre chérie . . . you dance inside me still. Dance, child, and reach your hand to me, across all time and through the deepest distances. I shall grasp it again. This time I will not let go.

* * *

Conor sat by his window late on a Friday night. Where scotch had been his regular companion for day's end brooding, tonight he was drinking wine. He knew little about the finer points—the vintages, the nuances of each grape, the ways that they might blend—but he knew that wine calmed him more than even the finest scotch. A good viognier drove him deeper than a fifteen-year-old single malt.

But how deep, really, did he have to go? He had never looked at his career as something that needed to be built. He had never had a strategy for advancement. *Do the right things for the right reasons*, he had always told himself, *and the right things will happen*. His entire working life had been spent on Capitol Hill, and he had come to see the tatty, self-serving shallowness of the clutch for power and control.

Conor had neither the tolerance nor the talent for the machinations that passed for negotiation. Compromise most often left him cold, nursing the wounds of lost opportunity. Ethics and balance were for the weak. The real movers and brokers had no use for such petty considerations while they steamrolled their way to the perquisites of power. And power was the end in itself, that was all. There was no room to think about what one might do with that power, what might be accomplished for those on the outside, or on the downside. Despite the trappings, the momentary and shallow victories, the very occasional passage of anything that might actually change a life or two for the better, that was the nub of it all: Power. Power and control.

That said, the Committee on Foreign Relations was not something that could be easily dismissed. It was really a plum assignment, near the top of the legislative food chain. He had done some good work there, and his instinctive passions had brought energy to it. The victories were sparse, and the impact of his work on the conditions he had studied and seen were minimal, that he knew. Still, there was something to be said for pursuing it all and, in his own way, representing those on the margins. He could keep doing that, keep walking in measured and careful steps, his ideals mitigated by the need to get things done, even if those things were negligible.

But to do so, Conor reflected, would mean preserving a subdued version of himself. He sipped his wine, looked out at the trees, and remembered what he used to be.

His undergraduate days, where every morning launched new opportunities and he plunged headlong into each day with a sense of the possible, acted out in security he had never known before or since . . . The presence of friends as close to him as brothers . . . The intertwining of their hopes and ambitions into a thick cord that bound them together, nurtured by bright lights and the driving beat of deep, persistent rhythms . . . Moving outward, always moving, and exploring, and finding . . . Every day an adventure waiting to be crafted . . . Every day a wonder in itself . . . Everything ahead and not much behind . . . Everything ahead.

In the drunken euphoria of youth, he had known no destruction, no loss. He had perceived the world as his own, to be shaped and sculpted in accordance with his own grand design.

This would not die, this impetus to blaze a trail unfettered by convention or expectation, this conviction that he breathed a special air and walked on special ground.

But time and structure had brought his youthful intoxication to heel. He had become part of a system that he had expected to change but that instead had changed him by stripping away each illusion that he had nurtured and that had nurtured him since boyhood. What he had expected to be pliable was intractable, as solid as concrete and as timeless as cold granite. He had become an ant on the pavement, scuttering frantically but doing nothing more than preserving the species.

Conor sipped his wine. *What's it been, really? What have I been? I've done nothing, and when I'm gone, there will be scant notice and no loss. I've let myself be seduced by all the wrong things, and I've grown comfortable with the seduction.*

He stood and walked around the small room to look at a photograph that he kept on a side desk. It had been taken his final year at Rutgers, and in it he stood with his three roommates, their arms around one another's shoulders and each face radiant, smiling in unvarnished joy at their youth, their strength, their promise. Of the four of them, he alone had let that joy evaporate, turned to mist by the fire of hubris. He alone felt wrung out.

Conor thought of them now: Dan Rosselli, with a vibrant practice in a field he loved, with a clientele that loved him in return, and with no regrets about how he had conducted his personal life; Lanny O'Hanlon, ever the operative, pleased to be back in Boston after translating a political career into a new role as a venture capitalist, making money on the big deals but reserving a bit for social capital projects that had received notice for making the city's marginalized a little less vulnerable.

And Tom McIlweath. Dear Tom, whom he had known longer and better than anyone, one of the strongest souls he had ever met. All Tom had needed to do was find that strength. When he did, everything that had weighed him down came not to matter. Tom, working now in London, married to a beautiful Irish woman he had met during his graduate studies, more at peace with himself than any man had a right to imagine.

Conor had not seen Tom in more than half-a-dozen years, and then only for two days when Tom had come stateside with his new wife to show her a bit of his American roots. They had stayed at a hotel near Conor's home and had spent their time wandering the city's museums and monuments, then eating and drinking far into their too-few nights. Conor had been amazed at his friend's quiet self-confidence, his sense of balance and place. After years spent in a psychological and emotional wilderness, Tom had found where he belonged, the purpose for which he had found his way there, and the person with whom he wanted to pursue that purpose. He had done it by not listening to the voices telling him where he should go and what he should do. In the end, he heard only the single call that rose within him, in defiance of all demands, conformities, and expectations.

Thoughts of the departure of Tom and his wife back to London triggered a deep sadness in Conor. The contrast between his friend's well-won contented, focused purpose, and Conor's own miasmatic drift would not leave him, and he tried to recount all the missteps that had placed him where he was. It would be easy to blame those who had come at him with expectations he could not meet or to diminish their intentions as less noble than his own. It would be easy to blame an aggressive boss who did not like him much or a senator who was in office for all the wrong reasons.

It would be easy to blame a shattered love affair with the perfect woman.

Even now, Conor brooded over all these things. He recalled the stubbornness that buttressed a misplaced idealism, an inflexibility that caused him to break when he wouldn't bend, the conversations that had gone wrong, a push here and a pull there that had not been well received and in fact had stoked resentment and bitterness. He recalled as much of it all as he dared, and as the wounds reopened and the tender flesh bled once more, he knew that he had done it all himself. There was no one he could blame.

At the window, Conor sat back down and sipped again at the wine that had grown too warm. The trees outside continued to sway gently, the harbingers of a night where nature held no rancor or disturbance, giving space enough for his own.

Conor took the final sip of his wine. He rose then and stretched his full length, the warmth of the drink drawing through him. He looked out the window at the trees, at the quiet street, at the frayed end of a suburb near a city that did not care which street he walked or which hand he shook.

All the potential of the dead years, all the cultivated illusions that had sustained him through a youth too callow by half, all the vibrant and electric streams of promise . . . iron filings, all of it, weighing him down and pressing him into a form he no longer recognized.

* * *

Two weeks later, Conor interviewed with the search committee, chaired by Richard Jakande. He went into the interview relaxed, not that he thought there was nothing to lose. To the contrary, he felt assured that he belonged there, and that, if for whatever reason, they chose not to pursue him, the fault lay with the organization's perceptions and not with him. For an hour and a half, he was composed, articulate, and thorough.

Three subsequent meetings with the outgoing executive director, a public relations consultant, and the small staff confirmed what everyone already knew. Within about a month of the address and dinner to which Annie DiFrancesco had sent him, Conor accepted the position of executive director of a fledgling international nonprofit that no one had ever heard of and that fed itself on dreams.

* * *

The night Conor accepted the job, he sat in his apartment with a glass of wine and reminisced about Glynnis. He thought of how his life had changed, how he wished he could share his news with her.

It's the simple things that call to my mind now. I've had years to consider the profundities. I've become familiar with the depth and the dimension of who we were. Now, it's the details that hold sway, that bounce through my thoughts like feathers in a windstorm.

Your head sleeping against my shoulder as we sat on a tatty green couch watching a movie . . . A silly giggle on a hot summer afternoon . . . Walking together without saying a word under trees blazing with autumn . . . Throwing snowballs at squirrels in the park.

Tonight, I remember your kiss. A simple thing, and common, but worth noting now that it's gone. Different kisses for different times. The first kiss the day we met, on the slope of a hill beneath your dormitory, where I nestled myself into the curve of your neck just to be there, to be close to the softness of your long hair and the rich forever scent of lilacs. A kiss of discovery days later, when our souls felt the first trillings of the distant lyre that drives the dance, eyes closed and lips carefully limning new territory. The deep, raw kisses of passion, the plunging ahead against all fear or timidity into the maw of lust. The blind and blinding kisses that devoured us as we made love. The soft brushing kisses on cheeks or chins or hands, quick notes of passing. All different, the only commonality being the beauty and fire of the participants and all embedded now in psyche and memory that cannot, can never, burn away.

One last kiss, outside Union Station, years ago, as I was dropping you off after a weekend too short and too contentious. Slow death of love hung in the air like the scent of rotting leaves. You turned in your seat to look at me, and there was something in your eyes, something deep I noticed only later. You looked into me in a way you had not done before or I had never noticed. I see you now regarding me, evaluating just who this man was, all you had come to learn and know about this accidental lover condensed into a single glance, and in it I saw admiration, and sorrow, and loss. And love. In this blend of spices, most definitely love. But it was quiet, overwhelmed by the complexities that had come to bury it. But in its quietude was purity. I had not seen that look before.

You leaned in, and I kissed you, with no rush. An unspoken ending, but something we both knew intuitively. This would not come again. No rush then as your train steamed toward its gate and our futures darted further and further apart. The press of your lips extracting every measure of time and passion and hope, the boundary now of where we could no longer penetrate. It was the lust of souls, this last kiss, for what could no longer be and a benediction for all that it ever was.

We ended that kiss and everything else. You looked into my eyes once again as you reached for the door, the wisp of a smile unable to mask the finality of your beautiful deep gaze. I squeezed your hand and said nothing. The door opened, and you were gone. You did not know it, but I watched the station swallow you up, drawing for myself as much of your form and stride as you moved through a crowded walkway to the great doors, then inside to join the myriad everyday faces that consumed you and pushed you down alleys and pathways I knew I would never be able to find nor follow.

Tonight, I remember this kiss above all the others. I hear a quiet wind and find myself glancing one more time backward before another departure. And, as I change myself again, I cannot help but wonder where you are.

Sweet Lorelei, Singing on the Rocks of Time.

CHAPTER XIII

*Why do they not teach you that time is a finger snap and an
eye blink, and that you should not allow a moment to pass
you by without taking joyous, ecstatic note of it, not wasting
a single moment of its swift, breakneck circuit?*

— Pat Conroy, *Beach Music*

Conor stood motionless for several minutes while a cold
wind whipped against him from behind. The sharp
stinging nips of air made insensate his neck and cheeks.
After a time, he lifted his well-covered hands from his pockets
to turn up the collar of his raincoat. He had underdressed, not
anticipating that a rainy day could bite so deeply.

But the rain had stopped, at least for a bit, and he stood now
before a small grey marker on which were etched the dates of his
grandfather's birth and of his death nearly a century later. Clouds
hung low without opening. Still, the wind persisted.

Conor had expected that he would be able to talk with his
grandfather in a type of silent prayer. He wanted once again to
share thoughts with the great, good man whose life had dwarfed
his own. Liam Finnegan's desperation to create some lasting

meaning to who and what he was had exiled him to this land, where he had built a family and, in so doing, grown a legend. Conor saw in him courage, adventure, and wisdom that he could only hope someday to approach.

His grandfather had died not long after Conor's last visit, now more than seventeen years ago. Today, the younger Finnegan told his grandda that he, Conor, was still finding his strength, negotiating what it was he was meant to do and who he was meant to be. Despite all his youthful self-assurances, the ones that had vanished, Conor Finnegan was still a work in progress. He would always be unfinished. This no longer troubled him, and he thanked his grandfather for the role he had played in showing him this simple, final truth.

Conor reached into his wallet for the letter his grandfather had sent him weeks after they saw each other for the last time. He started not at the beginning of the letter but toward the end, for it was a long letter. Over the years, Conor had read this part many times, but in recent months, he had finally reached a maturity that allowed him to comprehend it.

> *I came to this city nearly eighty years ago, an exile, hiding my fears behind a conviction that I would do whatever needed doing to survive, and once surviving, to carve my own place in my own way. I saw myself as brave and full of dreams. In truth, I was a child, running manically in flight from what I saw as preordained suffocation. I see it now for what it was: More cowardice than bravery. More self-indulgence than courage.*
>
> *I fled, and I left what I loved behind me in flames. I lost a father and blinded a brother. My father sold his farm at great loss and died a pauper. My brother, younger and stronger than I was, turned to the streets of Dungarvan and lived through the kindness of a town that had no quarrel*

with the Finnegan name, giving him odd jobs suitable for those with few skills and no sight. He died before he reached the age of forty, no doubt tired of a life that had no luster and no purpose. I never saw either again.

Ireland faded into the discomfort of unquiet memory, and, if I could, I would have erased all traces of the soil that gave me birth. I strained to speak without my native lilt and to dress like every other American lad. I learned to love baseball and followed national politics. I adapted my profanities to my new land and learned to swear in creative Americanized jargon. I sought to emulate the swagger and boldness of this immense, dirty city, and of this new and wondrous country. I wanted to scrub the Irish off my skin.

But I could not do so, not entirely. An Irish pulse still beat beneath this well-scrubbed skin. I would still find myself wandering in the evenings, restless, searching for what I could never find, could never even define. Through the streets, or to a pub for a quick, unsatisfying draft, or to the lake to sit and stare at water that would never touch my homeland. Restless. Afraid to be still. Irish.

Yet I should be thankful for this restlessness. It was an evening during one of the early years that my disquieted spirit led me to the lake and led me to Molly. All at once, the vapors were quieted.

She saved my life. Without her, the sharp edges would never have softened, and I would have spent the rest of my days without faith. For who can believe that we truly have no purpose, no reason for drawing breath, when each day begins in harmony with the one who cherishes the unvarnished soul? How could I not come to believe that I drew special air into my lungs and that rare blood pulsed through my veins? I was loved without reason by the perfect woman.

In the early years, we had no need to feed ourselves on dreams. We had no dreams beyond the present day. Instead, we reveled in reality, in the clear, glorious reality of each other. We rose together, set our days together, and, as the obligations of work and place ended, came home to each other's arms, to each other's hearts. At night, there was the closeness of our bodies, the warmth of touch and breath. We cherished what we had and where we were. What need did we have for anything further?

Through the years, we continued, assuming always that what was meant to be would come along properly and in due course. My work progressed with promotions and small raises, but that didn't matter except as a means to an end, and the end was always Molly.

She gave me three sons, and we raised them, regarding each as an almost holy emanation of a spiritual union. But they were neither spirits nor symbols: they were boys, and they ran the streets of Chicago, skipping school when they could, sneaking into ballparks and testing the limits of their curiosity for mischief. The streets did not corrupt them. To my limited knowledge, they committed no crimes. No petty thefts, no dealings in the bad things, only a few minor scraps. In the evenings, they would find their way back to a home they knew would welcome them always, despite the ends of whatever mischief their day might have conjured. There is something in that. Perhaps that is all that one needs to raise good sons—the security of a warm bed where they might always lay their head, no matter what.

The boys grew up, and they grew away. One joined the army and made a career of it. Another sold insurance in Indiana, and the third, your father, moved to California to find something new for himself, emulating his own father in much milder tones. Where once we had a bustling flat filled to overflowing, Molly and I found ourselves almost all at once alone again with each other. While I missed my boys, I took pleasure in the aftermath of their leaving. Perhaps there might be space to dream the dreams we had deferred.

Something in the rhythm of our time, something that whispers satisfaction, and belonging, and ultimately peace.

But then the cancer came. It began with a slow ache in Molly's stomach that moved to her back like an invading army. She could not get rid of it, nor could she find anything that would lend her comfort. For a week, she did not eat. The doctor ran the normal tests and came back with the abnormal results. Six months later, I placed flowers on her newly covered gravesite.

How have I come to this place now? I am an old man in a dingy, shabby flat on the North Side, surrounded by tatters and memories.

After Molly left, the neighborhood changed. I changed with it and became more resolved. This small, once crowded flat was where my family was born. Where I was born. I will not leave it.

These walls hold the energy of their past, and I will complete my days amidst their comforts, amidst their reassurances that what I once had in richness still resonates here. I touch the walls where my boys hung their posters and sit in the chair where Molly once rested. I eat at the same table where crumbs that touched her lips once fell and where my boys spilled their milk. I open the door to a hallway that once echoed their footsteps, and in the far corners of my dwindling consciousness I can hear their laughter, their excited cries, their disappointed shouts, and sense the timber of their scattered lives.

What I have done with my life, how I have lived, is my province alone, and I take responsibility for its glories, for its failures and brutality, and now for the peace that comes to me at the end of it.

I have felt the waters on my face and heard the wild cries of anguish, pain, and sorrow. In flight, I came to a quiet place, and there I stay until all sorrow has passed and breath itself is drawn down to nothingness.

I am exiled no longer.

Conor placed the carefully folded letter back in his wallet and put it in the front pocket of his slacks. He knelt at the grave marker, crossed himself, then kissed his fingers and laid them across his grandfather's name. "I love you, Grandda. Sleep well. I love you forever."

He rose again, mindful of the wet splotch at his knee but not caring, then turned to walk slowly back down the hillside. With tears in his eyes, he stopped one last time to look behind him to where his grandfather slept in a peace he hoped one day to know himself.

Then, finally prepared in mind and spirit, he turned his head forward.

* * *

After the plane touched down at LaGuardia, after the harried shuffling plod to the baggage claim, then out into the noisy and noxious channels for arriving and departing passengers, after standing in a cab line next to a gentleman with pungent oniony breath that seemed to change the color of the air, after finally climbing into a cab for the creeping, crowded ride into Manhattan, Conor at last put back his head and closed his eyes. One more day of this, then home.

He had flown in from Chicago, where, after visiting his grandfather, he had met with an advisor to three of the country's largest family foundations, one of which had an expressed interest in African development and children's issues. Advisors, he had learned, were the gatekeepers for wealthy family conglomerates—two or more generations sharing the same name yet holding disparate visions of how the philanthropic sliver of their vast wealth should be dispersed—and Conor had met with one of the most prominent. She was an abrasive, no-nonsense woman who had not smiled once during their ninety-minute meeting. There was no small talk and not an ounce of levity. But at the end, she had requested that Conor forward a proposal focused on community health in central Africa, specifically Uganda, Rwanda, and Burundi. She would discuss it with the one family whose foundation took an interest in such things, but she would also share it informally with her other two major clients. No promises.

It had been worth the trip. Every month, Conor would bring himself through doors his board members had opened or he had opened himself through persistent and charming entreaties for a quick exploratory meeting. That was how it was done. So, he had flown off to Chicago, and before that Houston, and Los Angeles, and San Francisco (twice). There had been periodic train trips to New York, where many of the great foundations were housed.

When Richard Jakande had reviewed the organizational budget with Conor his first day on the job, now more than a year ago, he had asked Conor what he saw as the disproportionate travel line. "You'll need every penny of it," Richard had said, "and that's with traveling coach and staying at dingy two-star hotels. No one knows who we are. You have to go introduce us to the right people. The right people with the right money do not live in Washington."

So far, it had all worked well. Entirely through private support, the organization's budget had nearly doubled by the end of Conor's first year. In the early months, when he was still finding out what was in the file cabinets and formulating a long-term strategy, he had discovered within himself a new kind of charisma. His boyish charm had reemerged, and he had found that he could effectively relate to potential donors by channeling his passion for the cause into rational, lucid arguments, then backing them up with a warmth that was not entirely contrived. His trips placed a very human, well-considered face on the organization, one that was remembered well when artfully crafted, thorough proposals were submitted and discussed.

In some ways, it was an act, one which he could turn off and on as needed. To people of means and financial representatives, he presented a compelling blend of reasoned thought and unvarnished humanity, all the while making very certain that his organization was being run efficiently and transparently. He reviewed accounts daily and kept his financial officer on speed dial. He had had no idea that he could be an effective business manager, and that discovery did not displease him.

But none of those nascent business skills would have mattered were it not for the passion that drove the work. During his first nine months, he had taken two site visits to observe the small groups his organization was funding. His first had been to Zambia, where his destination lay down a dirt road at the end of a bumpy, often unpaved four-hour drive from Lusaka. When the car finally arrived at the small village on whose outskirts his grantee lay, his back ached from both the torturous ride and a nine-hour flight from London in a cramped coach section middle seat.

There he was met by the group's director for the short drive to pastures and farmlands dotted with dormitories, a recreation barn, a dining hall, and a school. All of it was the property of his grantee, which collected AIDS orphans from the city and brought them together in makeshift families in the countryside, where they were fed, received medical care, and attended school, all things that they had come to lose with the death of their parents and subsequent consignment to life on the streets.

"We had to come this far out," explained the director, a soft-spoken former teacher in his mid-thirties named Moses who spoke English with a Bemba accent. "We had to get them away from the bad influences there. You know, most of the orphans end up selling whatever they can to survive—whatever they steal, drugs, or their bodies. All for sale for a few pennies. Very sad. We had to try to give them purity, a fresh start."

"How did you come by so much land here? Tell me how you put all this together."

"No one wanted the land, so I bought it very, very cheap. I convinced a local builder to put up the structures. I had some money. My family, *ndume*, has some money, too." He said this last shyly, using the Bemba word for "brother." "The rest I asked for from the village and from friends in Lusaka."

"You grow your own food here?"

"Yes, and we grow enough to sell in the village. This gives us income. We are doing well enough. All the boys have tasks. Some grow the food. Some help teach the classes. Some do maintenance on the buildings. They learn their skills, then they can make a life for themselves. We have two boys who will go to university next year. But every boy will have something to do when he reaches the age to leave here, *ndume*."

That day, after lunch in the dining hall, Conor walked the grounds with Moses. As they passed the school, a group of young boys no older than ten came rushing out on break. They tossed a soccer ball between them as they ran, but when they saw the director and Conor, they changed course and hurried to them, surrounding them with laughter and excited cries that Conor could not understand. Moses spoke with them, then he turned to Conor. "They are excited to see you, *ndume*. They think a white man must be very important, and this is a very good omen that you are here." He chuckled. "They want to know if you play football."

Conor recalled the impromptu game at the Rwanda camp,

what now seemed like so long ago. Mud had splattered his pants so deeply that day that he'd had to discard them. No regrets.

"I do, but on one condition. After we play, I want to sit down with these boys for a bit. We can talk about whatever they want. Deal?"

Moses translated, and before he could finish, the boys grabbed Conor to push him toward their field. Conor took off his shoes, tossed them clear, then chased the boy carrying the soccer ball, who yelped with glee before dropping the ball and passing it to one of his mates. The game was on, even though Conor was unsure of who his teammates might be. He ran to a wing and for the most part just tried not to run over anyone.

They played for half an hour. He thought the score might have been two to two, but he couldn't be sure. No one cared, no one took note. There was grass, and sky, and the sweet smell of springtime, and laughter. That was enough.

At the end, Moses drew the boys around him while Conor caught his breath. Another pair of pants looked to be beyond salvageable. *No matter*, he thought. *I can always buy new slacks. But when will I ever get to play soccer in Zambia again?*

They gathered in one of the classrooms and brought their chairs into a circle. The boys, so energized and excited on the field, grew quiet as the strange white newcomer explained who he was and why he was there. "My organization gave you a grant last year to buy school supplies and farming equipment," Conor said. "Now, I want to meet the young men who are making such beautiful use of these things. I want to get to know my new young friends."

They told their stories. One, who was no more than nine, had spent months sleeping in an alleyway and scrounging for food from throwaway bins. He had no other family besides his parents, whom the disease claimed within three weeks of each other. Moses had found him when he had solicited the older man for sex.

Another had run away from his home as his father weakened. His mother had run off, as had his older brother, and he couldn't bring himself to watch his father die. He had been fortunate enough to apprentice himself to a woodworker who fed him and housed him after a fashion. Meals were thin, and his bed was a wooden plank with a mealy blanket in the back room of the shop. Moses had convinced the woodworker to let him go, that the expenses of keeping him and the need for years of training outweighed any value of his work.

Conor asked him, "You have no idea what happened to your family then?" and the boy replied, "My family is here. These are my brothers. I live for them." The other young boys nodded, and one next to him put his hand on the boy's shoulder.

Moses whispered to Conor, "They *are* brothers in a very real sense. When they come to us, we place them in units, with the older boys as big brothers who look after them and care for them. These boys learn to care for one another in ways no one ever cared for them. They are safe here, and they know this. It is important for us to build new families when their old ones have disappeared."

"Now," one of the boys said to Conor, "you are our brother, too." When he said this, and Moses told him what it meant, Conor turned away to look out a window so that the tears that built would remain hidden.

There are lights in this world, he thought. *Bright lights that cleave the constant darkness and youth, hope, joy, and promise that do not die.*

Votre chérie—the silent, immutable call of sleepless hauntings.

Soon after this encounter, Conor had found himself in South Africa in a Cape Town township as dense and fetid as anyplace he had seen. His group had made a grant to an organization providing recreational opportunities and sports leagues for young people provided they show proof that they were still in school and doing well in their studies. As well, they offered regular health checkups, meals and snacks, and counseling for those who thought they could use a friendly ear.

The program had been started by a white banker who walked away from a vice presidency at South Africa's third largest bank "to do something that mattered," as he put it. He had put together the elements of the program after rather confidently going into the township to introduce himself and his ideas to the community's leaders. His white colleagues at the bank thought him mad.

"But it's madness that can change the world, don't you think?" he had laughingly explained to Conor. "They told me that if I brought the money they would bring their kids. They really wanted to, but they were a bit suspicious of an *mlungu* like me offering to do something for people like them." So, the banker, Kevin, had arranged a grant from his bank to be used to purchase two adjacent vacant lots and rehabilitate them into a soccer field, then to build next to it a clubhouse with sound equipment, musical instruments, and a stage. Once done, Kevin had quit the bank two weeks later to direct the program himself.

"Did you ever feel threatened when you went into the township?" Conor asked.

"Oh, all the time, especially at first. But I trust that most violence stems from fear and threat, and I presented neither. I think those who might have been tempted to rob me or beat me up sensed this somehow. Nothing ever happened. Then after a time, I gained the confidence of the leaders, the ones who took their votes and gave whatever jobs they had to give. After that, I had no qualms at all."

"You must be a man of inestimable faith, Kevin."

Conor's trips had confirmed his sense of the groups that his organization was already supporting and provided introductions to other groups worth considering. With the increased revenue he was generating back home, he knew his organization had the wherewithal to expand its support. It could build a network of these small groups and make them stronger. *This could work,* he told himself. *We can do this.*

And now, Conor was in New York. His cab darted through Midtown Tunnel and into Manhattan's netted, webbed streets. The tall buildings obscured the last of the day's sunlight as the taxi arrived at Conor's hotel. The day had been long with its miles and emotions. It was finally time to alight and rest. Conor paid the driver and took his bag through the narrow entryway to find a room at once too small and badly worn. It didn't matter. Once in it, he would not go out again. It was time to sleep.

The next day, Conor headed to Wall Street, destination Goldman Sachs. He would be meeting with a dozen senior managers and directors, connections he'd made through a former colleague from the senator's staff, the man's economic advisor who had since gone on to work as the African project director for the World Bank. A few months before this trip, Conor had visited this former colleague, Steve, with a request, but first, he had explained what his position with his nonprofit entailed. Steve had then asked Conor, "So, do you think this work can change the world?"

"No. We can't change the world," Conor had replied, "and I've long ago given up trying. We live in a snapshot, and all we can be concerned with is the here and now. I'll leave systems change to wiser minds and stronger personalities. But what we can do is change the lives of those we reach. We have that capacity, each one of us. And that should be enough."

"That may be one of the most cogent defenses of idealism I've heard."

"It's not idealism. It's practical as hell."

Conor's comeback had surprised—and impressed—Steve, who recalled Conor as a man who lived in the clouds. It seemed Conor had changed.

"So, how much money are you seeking, Conor? And before you answer, you must know that the Bank is fairly deliberative. We'd be happy to learn more about your group and what it does. It sounds promising. Just know going in that any investment request will take months to evaluate and several months more to process, even if we come to a positive conclusion."

"I don't want your money, Steve. I want your network."

"A bit of chutzpah there, Conor. You think affiliation with your group brings a special shine?"

"You know the second-tier people at all the major financial services firms. At least you did years ago with the senator, and I expect they've kept in touch with you since you migrated over here. I'm asking if you could pull some of them together for an informal, no-strings-attached coffee or cocktail reception. I want to meet them."

Steve had sighed, recognizing again Conor's persistence, a fire that had been constantly evident when they had worked together years ago. Conor was a pain in the ass, but there was something infectious about it all. "Let me see what I can do," Steve had said at last. "Maybe we can do something here through one of our informational programs. I can target it to the J.P. Morgan and Goldman Sachs boys. Both of 'em want to know what the other is thinking, so if one group attends, the other will, too. But that's as far as I can go."

Now, the cab deposited Conor on the corner of Vesey and West streets, shadowed by steel and glass. He gathered his briefcase, swept his card through the meter, and stepped to the curb. He would be heading into Goldman Sachs to meet with some of its top executives and others from the World Bank and J.P. Morgan, the gathering Steve had made happen. For a second, Conor recalled the feeling he had before every basketball game he had played, every competitive match he had entered on a tennis court or baseball field, the amalgam of confidence, focus, and nerves. It would go well, this he knew. It always did, at least lately. And it was worth doing, no matter who was there or where it led.

Conor, the new man, stepped through the glass doors into the immense lobby to present his identification, to register, to go through security, and to be escorted upstairs.

Votre chérie.

CHAPTER XIV

And in the fall of light from heaven to earth perhaps all our stories were told, all actions of the living and dead explained, and all time past present and future there revealed.

— Niall Williams, *The Fall of Light*

From Grandda Liam's letter:

What is it that the last harsh breezes of winter sweep away? What do the gales and gusts of the last cold days blow into oblivion?

In the renascent warmth of new spring, we find ourselves again, find the best, lost parts of us that had been forlorn while icy winds bite across our necks and kill the senses on cheeks and eyelids. It is in those days, the days that dawn darkly and end quickly, that the world seems entranced in black and adrift. The days hopeless in scope and despairing of relief, bracketed by blown snow, ice, and winds that never seem to die.

But spring puts the lie to this despair, and once more we emerge from our frozen stasis. In the celebration of our rebirth, when our limbs grow once again strong, our blood flows high, and there is joy and purpose in our days, we are once more as young as we ever were, as alive as we ever might be.

So, do not think of the times when the bleak and desperate days will once again hold dominion over our time, over our souls. Do not choose to remember the lonely dark nights and the short grey days where clouds press down like damp, cold cloth and breath itself comes hard. Do not remember the barren times. Not now. Be willing to forget for a time, to embrace the delusion that life is warm and full and grand, that the soft new grass will feel full beneath our bare feet, that the reclaimed sun will infuse comfort and wellness through each pathway until it descends into a gentle nightfall.

Be willing to forget for a time, even within the certainty that the cold days will come again, that nothing on this earth ever truly dies, that power and beauty and grace and strength and pleasure and love itself are forever haunted by flesh that grows weary, by spirits that seep into nothingness, by souls turned as numb as uncovered hands on a snowy winter night.

Be willing to forget for a time the lost faces left behind through a comet's fleeting arc.

Believe for an instant that the virtuous and the holy hold sway forever in the newborn warmth of springtime, that gentility governs each action, that an abiding nobility beats within each breast and welcomes each new face into a community that will never die. Grasp the hand of God Himself, clasp His shoulder, and look deeply and fully into His infinite eyes.

Do this in the rebirth of the warm and breathlessly golden days. Nothing on this earth ever truly dies.

* * *

In Boston in April, now about two years after joining the nonprofit, after the first saucer magnolias had bloomed along Commonwealth Avenue and mallards nested once more in the Common, Conor took his place on a stage in a lecture hall that sloped all seats in his direction. He sat in a chair facing the fishbowl while the dean of Boston University's School of Global Studies poorly articulated his introduction. The dean stumbled through each sentence as if he was reading it for the first time, and perhaps he was. The immense lecture hall was less than half-filled, maybe no more than a third. To politely tepid, hesitant applause, Conor stepped to the podium to speak about the complexities of community development in Sub-Saharan Africa.

He was no stranger to such addresses these days. As his organization's visibility grew, so did the invitations to take part in symposia and panels with academics or other practitioners who bandied various ideas, theories, and approaches to Africa's socioeconomic mysteries. Occasionally, Conor received an invitation to speak to a class in international development, or, in this case, to a school of global studies. The best professors looked to augment academic approaches with practical perspectives, and Conor found that he was quite effective in expressing his passion for the young people whom too few people chose to see.

Often, despite himself, his remarks took flight almost beyond control, his very few notes becoming totally pointless. In such addresses, he had most often been expected to speak about the gaps in current international development models and how community-based initiatives could fill the empty spaces, but Conor learned that he had little patience with sterile academic theories and development indices that translated very human struggles into impersonal formulas.

Instead, he circled back to the images that still burned clearly behind his sight—the young boys desperate for some semblance of play, the women who graciously took Conor into their very simple homes and shared whatever they had, the men who strived once again to assemble some construction of pride and value.

Conor took the poverty, the despair, the disease and loss, wove them together with the inherent and undying spirit of hope, and let his rhetoric soar. He told stories of women banding together to challenge the barbaric traditions of their homelands—child marriage, female genital mutilation, and bondage. He recalled the beauty and innocence of the boys who had coaxed him into a muddy game of football, then went joyously to the only school within twenty miles, built by a group his organization had funded. He related the delicate precision of paintings drawn by young people in South Africa's most desperate townships that illustrated an abiding faith that life in all forms and in all places carried with it a subtle beauty and the delicate conviction that such beauty was worth pursuing.

He told of a tiny girl who did not speak but whose voice carried to him across time and distance to demand attention, to demand that she not be forgotten and that the circumstances that placed her in such a silent, lonely, untouchable space be addressed.

When he did so, his audiences most often sat up. They had not anticipated what he brought. They had not expected passion and raw emotion. They had not expected a clear and pitched voice demanding that they consider their shared humanity and daring them to use their privilege and achievements to find new answers to old problems.

Tonight, at Boston University in the early blaze of a radiant springtime, Conor spoke again, not solely to the students who sat before him, but to the ghosts whose faces would not die.

He concluded his remarks, "In South Africa, before it was fashionable for a politician to confront apartheid, Bobby Kennedy said, 'Each time a man stands up for an ideal, or acts to improve the lot of others, or strikes out against injustice, he sends forth a tiny ripple of hope, and crossing each other from a million different centers of energy and daring, those ripples build a current which can sweep down the mightiest walls of oppression and resistance.' Oppression comes in many forms, not all of it political, and what I have seen throughout an Africa we brand as poor and underdeveloped is that constant fire of economic and social self-determination. We have an obligation to these people, whom we will likely never meet nor ever truly know. But know that their fate is inextricably linked to our own and that in authoring effective solutions to the challenges within their remote and distant communities, we are at the same time securing our own humanity."

Following those remarks were applause and a somewhat stunned dean, who shook Conor's hand before stepping forward to invite questions. Conor responded for another fifteen minutes before the session closed. Several students came up to the stage to speak with him personally, and it was another half hour before the hall cleared. He expressed his thanks to the dean, who invited him back next term, gathered his notes, tucked them into his briefcase, and walked up the long aisle to the door at the top of the lecture hall.

As Conor turned the corner into the hallway that led out of the building, the flood of twenty-three years swept him into deep and roiling waters.

"Conor," she said softly. Her face was as it ever was, and the gaze that seemed almost secretive, hiding bemusement or fear or furtive wisdom, the same gaze that dominated those dreams that were driven by the depth and warmth of her infinite brown eyes or the gentle, scented pressure of her touch, beckoned him.

"Glynnis," he whispered in reply, as soft as a prayer, as subtle as the shudder of a soul.

They embraced, then, in that hallway, a strong, clutching embrace that pressed their bodies together, corporeal and sensate, and very real. Neither spoke. Conor would not recall how long this embrace lasted or who at length stepped back from it. But he would recall the firmness of her still slender form, the feel of her hands gripping his shoulders, and the long-lost scent of lilacs. These details would never leave him.

A million flashes of partial thoughts, careening without restraint, and the torrent of images that exploded within Conor confused him. All he could do was shake his head in a wordless, bobbing nod.

"Oh, Conor," Glynnis spoke softly as she dabbed a newborn tear. "I'm sorry. I should have contacted you earlier to let you know I'd be here. But I lost my nerve a dozen times. I didn't mean to ambush you."

"Glyn," Conor managed, "what are you doing here? In Boston, I mean. I never imagined where you might be."

"I teach here—the School of Visual Arts, painting and composition. After all these years, I'm still junior faculty, nothing but an assistant professor."

"So, you come to boring presentations on nights when you have nothing else to do?"

She laughed. "A colleague of mine specializes in African art. He's from Kenya, and he told me about it. I brushed it off, but then he showed me the notice, and I saw your name. He was here tonight. I stayed outside the hall and listened to you from out here. I thought you didn't need a distraction while you did this. Conor, you were brilliant. You were wonderful. I want to hear everything you've done and everywhere you've been. I love your passion. It's still there, Conor, and I'm so proud of that."

Conor continued the struggle to compose himself. He felt his blood returning to flow again, and consideration began to replace shock. Still, the best he could do was to look at her, standing there now in front of him. Words came slowly. "Passion took a long hiatus, Glynnis, and I still don't trust it, but there it is, probably in spite of myself." He paused, then said, "I'm guessing there's a lot of catching up we could do. Is there a place we could sit and talk for a bit?"

"There's a wine bar down the street. It's fairly quiet, and we can talk there if you have the time."

"That sounds perfect. And I believe a very large glass of wine might be in order. I certainly need it now."

Glynnis led the way, and as they walked, they began the awkward and stilted task of rediscovering each other. "So, tell me," Conor said, "the path that led you here. When I knew you, Boston wasn't part of the equation."

"You go where the jobs are, Conor, especially in a field with minimal commercial value and the jobs are too scarce. I was lucky. I stayed in Philadelphia for five years teaching at a community college and trying to see if I had any chops as a painter. I dabbled in sculpting, too, and I was equally mediocre. After a while, I decided I would rather be an unspectacular teacher than a starving artist, so I got to know the art departments at all the colleges and universities in the area. Nothing resulted from that, until I was recommended for a temporary assignment here by the head of the department of fine arts at Rutgers-Camden, of all places."

"He liked your portfolio? Obviously. He forwarded your name to a colleague."

"I was sleeping with him at the time. I believe he thought moving me to New England might remove a complication. No, we weren't in love. I was just as glad to be away from it."

"So, here you are, tucked away now in the city where you grew up. The city you wanted to escape, as I recall."

"Here I am and have been for the past twelve years. That temporary appointment turned into a tenure-track position. I'll never get tenure, though. I do absolutely no research, and my portfolio is barely adequate. But I don't care. I love the teaching part of it. I love being in the studios. I stumbled into something

I didn't know I could do, and now I don't think I'll ever leave it."

"I remember telling you that you were wasting your time in graduate school. I'm glad for you, Glynnis. It makes me wonder who was really wasting time back then."

"Here's the place," said Glynnis, and she led them through a dimly lit entryway to a long and narrow room filled with high tables and deep, plush booths. The bar was almost empty. They slid into a booth to sit side by side.

"So, Conor Finnegan, fill in the blanks from the past twentysome years. I had always thought that you would live your life on Capitol Hill and maybe run for office. You seemed born to it. When last I saw you, you were a hotshot legislative assistant with high ambitions and higher ideals."

"I grew up quickly, Glynnis, with some help from my colleagues on the senator's staff. They tired of those ideals rather quickly, so they spat me out like a watermelon seed. I went to some obscure congressional committees for a time, then to the Committee on Foreign Relations, quite by accident. That's where I became a world traveler."

"I think I'm envious."

"Don't be. The travel was hard, and what I saw was abysmal. I'd go to a country like Cambodia, and when I came back everyone would ask me if I got to Angkor Wat or the Royal Gardens. No, but I saw some really pathetic slums and naked kids that fished for surprises and played in sewage ponds. I saw children die right in front of me. I saw children that might as well have been dead for all the response they showed. Every trip, I saw kids that had almost no chance, and I realized that there wasn't a damn thing my work with the committee could do about it. I could report back on how project dollars were being spent and evaluate the groups that were doing the work, but it all seemed so pointless. We accomplished nothing except to make ourselves feel better in the effort."

"My romantic Irishman," Glynnis said softly. Her eyes captured the light from the candle on their table and glimmered with a depth Conor knew well and would forever recall. Her beauty was still spiritual and echoed within him in ways that transcended the loveliness of any other woman he had ever known. Her face carried the small lines and fissures that age commands, but Conor did not see them. Instead, he saw a face at once insightful and remote, one that had seen him in his best days, the days where they soared together in defiance of all demands, of all expectations and pressures, in defiance of time itself. They had loved each other in the purest form, and now she sat before him again, a presence as unlikely and mysterious as the goddess Brighid or Arthur's Guinevere.

Sweet Lorelei, Singing on the Rocks of Time.

Their wine came, and Glynnis raised her glass. "To old friends," she said, and Conor replied as they clinked their glasses, "To youth and the coming of wisdom."

Through the first glass they spoke of common friends and where they were now, of Tom McIlweath and Dan Rosselli, people who had witnessed their time before. They spoke of family and lost parents, and Conor recounted his journey to see his grandfather as a salve to his confusions after everything had fallen apart.

Their second glasses brought them deeper. Conor felt his limbs relax with the alcohol, and his thoughts calmed to reflection. He took careful note of each moment and tried to catalogue in his memory the dimensions of this place, each glimpse of Glynnis next to him, the tremor and tone of her voice.

"So then, to the awkward but essential questions," he said. "Married? I don't see a ring."

"No, Conor. I came close once or twice."

"But something always held you back."

"Yes. I've lived with a number of men. That's much easier,

don't you think? When the inevitable separation comes about, the complications are few."

She paused to sip her wine. "No, that's not entirely true," she resumed. "I suppose I've never found anyone that made me think about eternity. No one since you." She smiled slyly. "You set a pretty high standard."

Conor looked down at his glass. He traced his forefinger around its rim and said nothing.

"And you, Conor Finnegan," Glynnis said, "tell me about your women."

Conor took a deep sip and let the red wine travel in warmth through his entire length. He continued to look downward as he replied, "I was married once. An act of insanity. I knew at the reception that I had made a colossal mistake, that I had entered a permanent contract based on a temporary insecurity. She was a timid, dull, lifeless girl who wanted a father more than a husband. The whole thing lasted longer than it deserved. I'm still not sure I've recovered emotionally or intellectually. But after you, I needed something stable, something predictable. Maggie was all that and nothing more."

"And since then?" Glynnis whispered.

"Nothing that had any chance of lasting. A few encounters, that's all. I don't know whether I've been unlucky or if it's something else. I'm a bit gun-shy, I suppose. I've felt the hurt when things go wrong, and I don't think I can go through that devastation again."

He took hold of Glynnis's hand and looked into her eyes. "You damn near killed me, Glyn. And I know there'll never be anyone else like you."

Glynnis nestled into his shoulder then leaned up to kiss his cheek. "We were kids, Conor. We didn't know anything."

"I know that, Glyn. No one's fault. It was just that the time was wrong. It was never a matter of character or intent. If we had met ten years later, it might all have come out differently."

Conor paused and held her hand tightly. He spoke again in barely a whisper.

"You were my first love, Glynnis. First loves never die."

They sat that way within each other for an indeterminate time. Neither spoke. Glynnis listened to Conor's heartbeat, felt the rising and falling of his chest with each breath. Conor smelled the floral luxury of her still-long hair and breathed in deeply her constant, lingering scent of lilacs.

After a time, Glynnis squeezed his hand, sat back away from him, and said, "I have an early studio tomorrow, Conor. I should be going."

Conor squeezed her hand again in response. "I know. I fly back to Washington early tomorrow, then into the office. I'll get this." He grabbed the check to place with his card at the edge of the table.

They rose together and walked back to the street. Conor turned to head back to the campus garage where his car was parked. "I go this way," said Glynnis, gesturing in the other direction. "That's where I catch the T."

"Can I give you a ride? I haven't taken you home in years."

"Thanks, Conor, but no. We both have places to go now." Then Conor found himself once again in her arms, her head buried in his chest. He held her as tightly as he dared.

"I'm so sorry for how it all ended, Conor." Glynnis's tears wet his coat. Conor felt his own tears build quickly.

"I know, Glyn. Losing you was the hardest thing I've ever had to do." He pulled back enough to kiss her hair. "But it's okay now, you know? It's okay. I love you, girl, and I always will. That's enough, don't you think? We don't need anything more."

Glynnis looked up at him, kissed his lips deeply, then stepped back holding his hands. Conor saw the glint of wetness at the corner of her lovely eyes. "Love is a drug, my sweet Irishman. Maybe the most dangerous kind."

"And we're both addicted, Glyn. I see no chance of recovery for either of us."

They hugged again. When they broke, Conor said, "Will I see you again?"

"You know where I am. Call me the next time you're in Boston. I never get to Washington."

He kissed her forehead once more, held her close a last time, then turned up the street. "Take good care of yourself, my darling friend."

Into the night, her slender form grew smaller, fainter and turned a far corner.

* * *

The next morning, Conor boarded the shuttle from Logan to Reagan National. He crammed himself into a coach seat against the window, closed his eyes, and tried to sleep the flight away. For the most part, he succeeded. The plane landed without concern. Conor pulled his computer case from under the seat in front of him and stretched into the aisle to deplane.

The clear light of a new day had calmed him. The images of the night before remained, but with those images had come an unexpected peace, and he chose not to fight it. There would be time enough later for interpretations. He did not expect to see Glynnis again.

Conor claimed his bag and headed for the taxi line. Breakfast had been a hotel bagel with tepid, flat coffee, so he stopped to grab a Starbucks latte. Rather than wrestle with a computer case and a travel bag, he took his coffee to a small iron table in the pavilion. He had time enough, just this once, not to rush. The office and its assorted challenges could wait.

"Do you mind if I sit here?"

The question came from behind him, and as he turned to the voice, his blood jumped. The woman asking it was fair. She had blue eyes that whispered sharp and clear Scandinavian mornings and a swatch of blond hair pulled behind her ears that cradled a heart-shaped face. She balanced a cup in one hand and a travel bag in the other. She had no place else to go.

"Please," Conor said, then stood to take her cup and place it next to the other chair across the table. As he glanced around, he saw that there were no other free tables, although most had free chairs.

The woman's name was Adrienne, and she had just taken a position in Washington with a public relations firm. She had been in town no more than a month and knew no one aside from her colleagues. That morning, she had flown in from Minneapolis after closing on the sale of her condominium. Conor learned this as they drank their lattes. Adrienne did most of the talking.

"Forgive me for going on," she said. "I still don't know anyone here other than my colleagues, so I guess I don't have the chance to talk to anyone very much. Thank you for indulging me."

When they finished their drinks, both rose to take their empty cups to the recycling container. "Do you want to share a cab?" she asked. "I'm heading in the same direction." Together they joined the taxi line.

On the short ride, Conor regarded again her pure beauty, the unsullied smooth brightness of her face, the gentle lilt of her soft voice, and, more than anything, the wide crystalline clarity of her wondrous eyes that went on forever.

Conor's office was several blocks from Adrienne's, but when the taxi stopped to drop her off, he got out, too. Conor paid the fare while she waited on the sidewalk. When the fare was settled, she turned to walk into her building.

Conor hesitated. He watched the sway of her narrow hips, her small, almost delicate steps, taking her away.

And indeed there will be time to wonder, Do I dare?

In a few bounding steps of his own, Conor caught up with

her. "Adrienne," he said, and she turned to face him. "Do you think we could carry on this conversation over dinner tonight?"

* * *

Later, after meeting Adrienne outside her building that night and walking two blocks to one of the city's best Spanish restaurants, after eating and drinking and talking for nearly three hours, after exchanging numbers and clearing schedules for the next time together, after a softly hesitant kiss at evening's end, Conor took his own cab back to his apartment across the river.

He woke the next morning from a deep and dreamless sleep. He showered, ate a quick breakfast, and put his papers in order for that day's work.

Where shall I go now? What shall I do?

Ready, then, and down the stairs, where Conor Finnegan stepped once more into the gently turning world.

ACKNOWLEDGEMENTS

Here is what I want from a book, what I demand, what I pray for when I take up a novel and begin to read the first sentence: I want everything, and nothing less, the full measure of a writer's heart. I want a novel so poetic that I do not have to turn to the standby anthologies of poetry to satisfy that itch for music. . . . I want a book so filled with story and character that I read page after page without thinking of food or drink, because a writer has possessed me . . .

—Pat Conroy, *My Reading Life*

This book, like all books, is not the product of a single writer. No matter what we do, what task we chase or which profession we pursue, we need community. We need each other to accomplish anything of value. I wake each morning in profound gratitude for the lives that have touched my own, for the wise and gentle souls that make each morning, each day, worthwhile.

To my everlasting gratitude, I have in fact been possessed by writers whose worst efforts far surpass my best. Their works instruct me, humble me and, most of all, inspire me to do better, to find an airy lyricism that can capture thought and ideas and make them soar. Those who know me best know my reverence for Pat Conroy, quoted above, who saw something in my first novel that I did not have the courage to see for myself. Now that he is no longer with us, I have found that there is no shortage of writers whose collegiality and encouragement are freely given. First among them is Niall Williams, the great Irish novelist, who offered key advice after the publishing of my first novel and through the refinement of this one.

My new friends at the Irish Writers Centre in Dublin are an ongoing source of inspiration through their own creative, original and dynamic works, their honest evaluation of the works of others, and their constant good humor. *Go raibh maith agat.*

A number of friends read the earlier versions of *Through the Waters* and shared thoughts, ideas and reactions. Among them are three people whose friendships I have cherished since childhood and whose wisdom, compassion and grace brighten every conversation. Caroline Jam Miller, Kevin Johnson, and David Welch together occupy a corner of my heart that is theirs alone.

Steve Jam is a writer whom I expect we will hear much about in the years to come. He writes with joy, and wit, and cleverness, all of which carry a keen insight into our collective flaws. Steve was an early reader of this manuscript. His suggestions helped strip away what was unnecessary and were instrumental in shaping the book's final form.

Cheryl Ross is a brilliant editor who agreed to tackle the sprawling, disjointed original manuscript, and, in so doing, tightened it, focused it and polished it to whatever shine it now has. She was relentless and precise, painful at times, but constant in her belief in this book and how it should read. I am eternally grateful for her persistence, her professionalism, and her amazing command of the writing process. I can imagine no one better for any writer.

I have the greatest publisher any writer could have. John Koehler has a writer's heart, and he uses it to nurture the craft of the authors who are fortunate enough to work with him. Every publisher would do well to emulate his integrity, his honesty, his courage, his good humor, and his genuine love of the written word.

There would be no reason for this book—or its author—to exist without the constant strength, encouragement, beauty, and comfort of Lynn, who gave a drifting life purpose so many years ago, and Michael, grown now into a young man whose own future promises excellence and engagement in all the right things. This book, this life, is for them.

CPSIA information can be obtained
at www.ICGtesting.com
Printed in the USA
FSHW010624081220
76555FS